UNBALANCED

BOOK 3 IN THE

BY THE NUMBERS SERIES

Featuring Carly Turnquist

by Leeann Betts

Second Edition 2016

ISBN13: 978-1-943688-15-9

Published by PLS Bookworks, Denver, CO

Where Publishing Dreams Become Reality

≠≠ Unbalanced ≠≠

≠≠ Unbalanced ≠≠

≠≠ Unbalanced ≠≠

Dedicated first and foremost

To the Glory of God the Father.

Without Him, no story is worth telling.

To my husband Patrick.

Patient. Good. Faithful. Man of God.

≠≠ Unbalanced ≠≠

Other Books By Leeann Betts:
Counting the Days: a 31-day devotional for accountants, Bookkeepers, and financial folk.
No *Accounting for Murder* (Book 1)

There was a Crooked Man (Book 2)

Future books include:

Five and Twenty Blackbirds (Book 4) –

April 2016

Books by Donna Schlachter:
Second Chances and Second Cups; A sweet collection of stories of second chances from a second-chance God.

By Leeann and Donna:
Nuggets of Writing Gold — a compilation of articles and essays on the craft of writing.

All books available at Amazon.com (print and digital)
And Smashwords.com (digital only)

Follow us:
Donna: www.HiStoryThruTheAges.wordpress.com
www.HiStoryThruTheAges.com
Leeann: www.AllBettsAreOff.wordpress.com
www.LeeannBetts.com

We are also active on Facebook and Twitter

≠≠ Unbalanced ≠≠

Most people think accountants live boring lives.

Carly Turnquist is about to
prove them wrong.

Bear Cove, Maine—population 312 at the height
of the lobster season—is caught in the 1880's, its heyday, right
where it wants to be.

Carly Turnquist is caught in 2003,
where her story continues.

Surely the nations are like a drop in a bucket;
they are regarded as dust on the scales;
He weighs the islands as though they were fine dust.
(Isaiah 40:15 NIV)

≠≠ Unbalanced ≠≠

≠≠ Unbalanced ≠≠

Chapter 1

If not for her son's wedding, this would be the happiest time of Carly Turnquist's life.

She loved her career as a forensic accountant, tracking down assets, including cash, bank accounts, and stocks, and proving legitimate ownership. For most people, working all day collating the evidence file for her last client, a brokerage firm that suspected one of its account managers of embezzling funds, would have left them tired and cranky.

But Carly Turnquist, snoop *extraordinaire*, was on the case. She'd successfully unwound the convoluted trail of fraud and deceit, confirmed that the account manager was indeed guilty of stealing over a million dollars in the past year. She made recommendations for improved internal audit practices to ensure this didn't happen again. The result was the trial was on the court docket, and Carly had been served a subpoena to testify less than a week after the wedding.

No, work was invigorating. What really got her goat was she'd been stuck preparing dinner by herself. Mike was still working in their basement office on a program for a client. Her step-son Tom and his fiancé Sarah had pulled into the driveway just minutes before she was ready to put the food on the table. The handsome couple walked toward the house, hand in hand. Sarah tossed back her hair, laughing at something Tom said to her. The peaceful and happy picture they made brought a smile to Carly's lips.

Tom burst into the house, his nose in the air as he sniffed for evidence of what was on the menu for dinner. His exuberance made the front door slam open in the same boyish manner that had driven her crazy for years.

Before she could stop herself, those all-too-familiar words flew from her lips. "Don't slam the door."

Tom laughed in the same way that melted her heart when she'd first met him over ten years before. "Sorry, Carly."

He and Sarah surrounded her in a giant bear hug, causing her to juggle the plates in one hand as she grabbed for the doorframe with the other.

"Let me go." She tucked her chin and caught a plate threatening to slip over the edge. "If you break a plate, you have to wash dishes for a year."

Mike appeared at the top of the stairs, a smile replacing the look of concern on his face as he took in the scene before him. Carly winked over Tom's shoulder at her husband.

Tom released Carly and turned to his father. "Dad, good to see you again." Awkwardly they did a little dance of reaching to hug, then changing their minds to shake hands.

Finally, Mike pulled his son to him, patting him on the back affectionately. "Good to see you, too." He looked over Tom's shoulder at Sarah, who took the dinner plates from Carly and headed to the dining table. "And you too, Sarah. Even though you are stealing my boy away from me."

Sarah lifted her elbow in a wave as she went past. "Hi, Mike. Been fitted for your tux yet?"

Mike groaned. "No. Lots of time. The wedding is a week away, and I don't want to get a tux that is too small."

"Too small?" Tom grabbed silverware from the drawer and headed for the dining room. "You're supposed to get one that fits, Dad."

"Don't you remember what happened at our wedding, Tom?" Carly stirred the pasta sauce at the stove. "He got fitted two weeks before the wedding, then gained ten pounds from nervous eating."

"I remember." Tom came back into the kitchen. "Anything else you need on the table, Carly? We're starved."

Mike patted Tom's shoulder. "You're always starved. I think you must still be a growing boy."

Carly passed Mike the pasta bowl then opened the fridge door, peering inside. "Here, Tom, take the salad, and I'll give Sarah the pasta sauce."

In just a few minutes they sat around the table, passing serving dishes around, scooping portions of spaghetti and sauce onto their plates. Once the first helping disappeared, dishes made the rounds for seconds. Carly sat back, appetite satisfied, as her two favorite men stuffed themselves. She stood to clear the table.

Sarah reached over and touched Carly's arm. "Sit down, Carly. Tom and I can clear the table. You already did all the hard work of cooking."

Tom mumbled unintelligibly, his mouth still full of food. Carly sat again. Not one to stand on ceremony, she rested her elbows comfortably on the table.

Finally swallowing, Tom spoke. "How are the wedding preparations going, Carly? Anything we can do to help?"

Mustering her best smile, Carly shook her head. "The church is set, the flowers and cake ordered, telephone invites have gone out, the caterer is booked. Wait a second, let me get my notebook." She rose and went to the small table near the telephone in the kitchen that served as her unofficial working zone. "This notebook has all the information I need to get this wedding done on time and on budget." She fumbled through some junk mail she needed to toss in the recycle container. "Hold on. I made a note this afternoon about the photographer. I put the book right here to remind me to call first thing in the morning."

But the notebook wasn't there. Frantically she pawed through the supermarket flyers and a couple of magazines that had come in today's mail.

The small wire-coil book wasn't there.

Leaning against the kitchen wall, she thought. Someone must have taken the notebook. Which was silly, of course. Why would anyone want to take it? She and Mike were the only ones in the house this afternoon, and he wouldn't dare touch the book. He'd already told her in no uncertain terms that the wedding was in her hands. He wanted the young couple to elope. In fact, he'd offered them money, figuring if they skipped the big ceremony and reception they could save money.

Belatedly, Carly realized he was probably right. Still, she didn't want to see her only son married without notice. And the fact he was her step-son, not her natural born, didn't change her feelings on the matter.

Drawing a couple of deep breaths, Carly tried to reason where she had put the notebook. Without that information, she'd have to look up names and numbers again, and the notebook contained all her notes on verbal agreements with suppliers.

This couldn't be happening.

Mike leaned against the door leading from the dining room. "Carly, what's taking you so long?"

"Just a minute." She sifted through the pile of papers. "I can't find the notebook."

Had she used the notebook somewhere else in the house? Between her panicked breathing and the rustling papers, she didn't know Sarah had come into the kitchen until the woman stood at her elbow.

"Carly?"

Carly looked up. "I need to get you a bell, you're so quiet."

Sarah chuckled. "Come back in and finish dinner. We'll help you find the book later."

"You're right. I can remember the few things we need to talk about for now."

Re-joining the men in the dining room, Carly sat down in her chair, her energy dripping away like a leaky faucet. Funny how worrying about something made her so tired.

Mike reached over and patted her hand. She smiled at him. He always managed to lift her spirits.

She drew a deep breath before reciting the preparations already seen to, checking them off on her fingers. "Church, minister, organist, music, guests, caterer, attendants—all confirmed. Oh yes, and flowers. Hall decorations, party favors, cake." She paused, furrowing her brow as she concentrated. "What's left? The photographer, who I have to call tomorrow. His number is in the book. A friend of a friend referred him, so if I can't find the book, I'll just have to make a couple of calls to get his number again. No big deal." She sat back in her chair. "I think that's it."

Sarah nodded. "Sounds like it. We're looking after rings and the honeymoon."

Tom nodded in agreement.

"And I'm looking after my tux," Mike added. "Next week."

Carly gasped.

Mike's left eyebrow lifted in question, a funny habit he had that Carly simply adored. "What is it?"

"I've been so busy worrying about your arrangements, I haven't even thought about my dress. Or my hair."

Silence enveloped the room. Tom fidgeted with his water glass. Mike studied her as if she'd grown another head.

Sarah was the first to respond. "As the mother of the groom, everyone will expect you to be well-dressed and well-coiffed."

Carly nodded. "I know. I forgot all about me."

Sarah stood and gathered the plates. "No worries. Your orders are to spend tomorrow looking after the dress and the hair dresser." She headed for the kitchen then turned around. "You spent all your time making certain everyone else was looked after, and forgot all about yourself. Can't have that happening. You are almost as big a star of this show as Tom and me."

Carly shrugged. "No worries. After all, I have a whole five-and-a-half days until Saturday afternoon." She turned to Tom. "Now, show Sarah what a good husband you're going to make her, and help with the dishes."

That night, Carly dreamed about the wedding as she slept. Everything was perfect and went exactly as planned. Except she was walking down the aisle in her camisole and slip, because she'd forgotten to get a dress.

≠≠ Unbalanced ≠≠

* * *

The next morning Carly awoke with the day's list of things to do already circling her mind like vultures over a carcass. Padding to the shower, she turned the hot water on full, hoping to wash away the cobwebs left over from her dream. She had woken several times during the night, only to pick up the dream from the beginning each time.

The shower didn't completely remove the remnants of her night. The house was quiet by the time she padded into the kitchen, rubbing her eyes. Mike sat at the table, coffee cup in hand. He raised one eyebrow in question.

Carly shook her head. "Not ready to face the day yet."

Mike patted the chair next to him, and Carly obediently sat. He filled a cup with coffee and set it on the table in front of her. Pulling on oven mitts, he opened the oven door and pulled out a cookie sheet. Carly wrapped her hands around her coffee mug, enveloped in a curious combination of anticipation and dread of the coming week. She inhaled the steam from the hot beverage, creating an oasis in what promised to be a hectic day. Savoring her first sip, her glance caught the calendar on the wall, each day packed to overflowing with notes of things to do and people to call.

She sighed as Mike placed a platter of cinnamon rolls on the table. "Those smell good."

Mike mock-bowed from the waist. "Your pleasure is my pleasure, Madame."

Carly peeled the rolls apart, placing one on each of their plates. "What did I ever do to deserve you?"

Mike frowned in thought. "I don't know. But you're stuck with me, so make the best of it."

His response brought a smile to her lips. "Funny."

He shoved an entire roll into his mouth and icing oozed from the corner of his mouth. Carly reached over and wiped off the icing with her index finger. Mike darted his tongue out and licked her finger quickly, flicking the icing on his nose.

Carly laughed, offering him a napkin. "Maybe that will teach you to eat

≠≠ Unbalanced ≠≠

more slowly."

Mike crossed his eyes. "My mother worked on me for many more years than you have. Don't count on it taking hold now at this late time of life."

Carly stood. "Can I fill your cup again?"

"Sure. Then I have to go."

She filled his cup and cracked open the oven door to let the heat into the kitchen. Nothing like a little extra warmth on a cool morning. "Working at the client's site today?"

"At least for this morning." Mike downed the last of his coffee. "Want me to help you look for your notebook?"

"No, I'll be fine. Eventually my brain will remind me where I had it last."

Carly tidied up the kitchen after Mike left, then pulled an old envelope from the trash can to use as an interim notebook. She made a quick but short list of the things she needed to do today: Dress and Hair Appointment. Surveying her list, she smiled. That wasn't a very long list. She should be able to cross everything off by the end of the morning.

Making the call to the only beauty salon in Bear Cove, a combination beauty parlor and barbershop, she asked for the owner. "HI, Margaret. It's Carly. Can I make an appointment for this coming Saturday, the fourteenth, in the morning, to get my hair done?"

The sound of pages flipping back and forth filled her ear as Margaret checked her calendar. "Sorry, Carly. I'm all booked that day. How about the next Saturday?"

Carly sighed. Sometimes she worried she'd consume all the oxygen by sighing so much. "Tom gets married on Saturday. At two in the afternoon. The next week won't do."

Margaret clicked her retractable pen several times, popping her bubble-gum in Carly's ear. "You shoulda called me earlier. You know that's my busy time of the week."

"Sorry, Margaret, I just remembered last night. Can you work me in somehow? I just want a simple cut and blow dry."

Margaret tsk-tsked. "Now, Carly, you aren't going to be satisfied with a simple blow dry for your son's wedding, are you?" More bubble popping. "No, siree, we can't have wedding pictures of you with a blow dry."

Carly sat at the small table, one eye on the clock. Time was ticking away. "What do you suggest, Margaret?"

Pen clicking furiously, pages flipped some more. "I'll rearrange my clients, and I'll set you up for a full job. Maybe a perm."

Carly's heart skipped a beat and she stared at the receiver. "No, Margaret. I don't want a perm."

"Sure, sure, I know. You don't like to fuss with your hair. You don't have to fuss with a perm. Trust me."

Carly rolled her eyes, mimicking the kids. She knew Margaret's perms. Half the women in town had fallen victim to them. Tight little curls on top, shaved short up the back. If Margaret weren't so pathetically stuck in the seventies, the style would be funny.

"Please, Margaret, I know you're busy, so if you could just put me down for a wash, cut, and styling, that would be great."

"Well..."

"Please."

"Will you promise to come back another time and let me see how I can transform you? I just went to a conference and learned some great highlighting techniques."

"Fine. We can talk when I see you on the fourteenth." Carly hung up, hoping by the time her appointment rolled around, Margaret would have forgotten her offer. The last thing Carly wanted was a transformation. She'd seen those strange little toys the kids collected—hands and feet turning into wings and fins. While some days she might wish for three hands, she'd at least like to keep the two she had. "Now on to the dress."

The only dress shop in town other than the Wal-Mart up on the highway, which no one in their right mind would realistically call a dress shop, was the "Well Dressed". When she didn't get an answer at the shop, she called Penny's home number.

Penny answered on the first ring. "Hello, Carly. I hoped I'd hear from you eventually. How are the wedding plans going?"

"Fine, except for one small detail. I forgot I needed a dress."

"No wonder, given the number of times I've actually seen you wear a dress."

Carly flinched at the bite in that response. "Well, you know how it is. Working from home doesn't give me much opportunity to wear dresses."

"I personally think most women, especially women our age, shouldn't wear pants. It's unbecoming."

Carly frowned. Penny Holcomb was over fifty if she was a day, several years older than Carly. She didn't include herself in Penny's age bracket. And she resented being included involuntarily. "Well, anyway, I know you're closed today, but the wedding is on Saturday. Could you meet me at the shop this morning so I can buy an outfit?"

"I don't know, Carly. As much as I'd like to help you, I had plans for today."

"What about tomorrow? If I need alterations, will that give you time to have them done for Saturday?"

"Won't be enough time. My seamstress is already backed up." Penny sighed. "I declare, Carly, you seem to find ways to get into the biggest jams of anyone I know."

Carly bit her tongue to hold back her retort. Penny's words hit too close to home sometimes. That was one of the drawbacks of living in a small town. Not only did people know every detail of everyone else's life, they felt the need to comment on any behavior not deemed to conform to town standards.

And as much as Carly loved Bear Cove, she didn't like the feeling of constantly living under a microscope.

Take her last situation—she preferred to refer to them as situations, not jams as Penny called them, or messes, Mike's favorite term. Not even escapades, which Tom loved to toss around to describe her curious nature and unique ability to ferret out a mystery. The last situation she'd been involved in included cattle rustling, murder, and a twenty-year old mystery. And before that, the mayor died and money went missing. Not to mention the time before that when she found her friend locked inside a furnace.

Carly hadn't realized mysteries would drop into her lap when she moved to Bear Cove after marrying Mike. Not like she went looking for them. But somehow she did get involved. And being an outsider who meddled in what everyone said was none of her business didn't exactly endear her to the residents. Bear Cove folks didn't condone criminal activity. They just didn't like to upset the status quo. And jailing one of the pillars of society in the coastal town did not endear her to anyone.

Penny had never hidden her opinion regarding Carly's penchant for justice. The fact Penny was even talking to her at all was an improvement in their strained relationship. And the fact Penny was best friends with a murderer didn't give her any special status, at least as far as Carly was concerned.

And really, forgetting to buy a dress until nearly the last minute couldn't be her fault. "You're right. I guess I'll just go up the highway to the Wal-Mart and see what they have."

Penny gasped. "You will do no such thing. Imagine have pictures taken of yourself standing next to your son and his beautiful bride with a dress off the rack like that. I can meet you at ten o'clock. For one hour."

"I appreciate that, Penny. See you at ten."

"And Carly?"

"Yes."

"No buying off the sale rack. Only off the regular racks. And not something that's going to take hours of alterations, either."

Carly drew a deep breath, letting the air out slowly before replying. "Fine. See you at ten. Got to go."

Piqued because Penny read her mind about the mark-down rack, Carly dug her check book out of her purse to confirm she had enough money to buy a dress at full price. Her thrifty nature normally limited her to the mark-downs, so for her to promise to buy at full price was a landmark day for Bear Cove. Carly could almost hear the wagging tongues around town when word got out.

She checked the clock on the stove. She had about twenty minutes before she needed to leave for the dress shop. Hoping to find her notebook, she

≠≠ Unbalanced ≠≠

went through the flyers and unopened mail again, sorting several piles on the table. She tossed unwanted flyers in the purple recycling bin and wrote a couple of business checks to pay bills.

Despite her best efforts, the missing notebook was still—well, missing. When she glanced at the clock in her office, she saw she'd spent more time than planned looking for the notebook. Somehow this book had taken over her life, the very thing she'd tried to avoid. Keeping all the information in one handy-dandy place was supposed to make her life easier not more complicated.

Carly hurried to get ready to meet Penny. Already she had visions in her mind of the perfect dress. Sarah's gown was ivory and lace, and her flowers were pink coral. Carly thought a deep coral suit would be perfect, and, in accordance with her thrifty nature, would also serve as the perfect outfit for a special night out with Mike.

She grabbed her keys from counter near the phone. "See you later, Doc. I'm off to buy a dress."

Movement near the stove caught her eye, and she paused on her way out the back door. Doc the cat nosed around near the stove. Looking at his food dish, which was empty as usual, she sighed. She wasn't meant to be on time. Penny would be furious. Quickly she dumped a scoop of food in his bowl, topped up the water dish, and absentmindedly stroked his back. Completely ignoring her, Doc continued his investigation near the stove.

"Cats," Carly muttered to herself, since there was no one else to hear her, except Doc, and he certainly didn't seem interested in her. Feeling a little peeved at his apparent lack of gratitude over having his bowl re-filled, she nudged at him with her toe. "Doc, what are you looking for?"

As soon as the words were out of her mouth, she regretted them. Visions of mice popped into her head. She couldn't have mice, not four days before the wedding. She was hosting some of the out of town visitors, not to mention the rehearsal dinner.

She couldn't have mice.

Carly tried to think, panic rising in her, threatening to overtake her best intentions of peace and calm. Mike was out of the house. Tom and Sarah were at work. She had to get to the dress shop before Penny gave up on her.

She didn't have time for mice.

Now she was more angry at the mice than afraid of them. Pushing Doc impatiently to one side, she got down on hands and knees, intent on spying out their hiding place and scaring them out of her house. Peering under the stove, all she could see was some uncooked elbow macaroni spilled last week. Angling her head to one side, she stuck her nose in the small crevice between the counter top and the side of the range. Nothing—wait, there was something in there.

Getting to her feet from that awkward position reminded her of her resolution to lose that last five pounds. Working from home was hard on the willpower. She didn't have to walk very far to get to work, and the fridge was always within easy reach. Not to mention that the only kind of exercise she engaged in involved jumping to conclusions or passing the buck. At least, that's what Mike said.

The guy was a comedian. Not a good comedian, but that was another story for another time.

She grabbed the sides of the stove, and with a mighty heave, managed to loosen the appliance from its tight spot. A couple of more nudges, and she could get her hand between the side and the cupboard. Reaching in, she half-expected to bring out an old piece of toast or an expired flyer.

Nope, her prize was more substantial than that.

Her notebook.

Waving her trophy in the air, she let out a rush of breath at the relief. Not only were there no mice or moldy Melba toast in evidence, this book was crucial to her mental well-being. She looked around for Doc, intending to gather him up and give him a big hug. But Doc, in that inscrutable way of cats, was sitting in the middle of the kitchen floor, his back leg up in the air, licking an unreachable spot.

Carly sighed. The day was looking up. No pun intended.

* * *

Carly's walk to the dress shop was quick and uninterrupted. Most of

≠≠ Unbalanced ≠≠

Bear Cove was at work. Nestled on the Atlantic Ocean, the town had that settled-in look of many small towns on the coast. The only thing setting Bear Cove apart from the rest was its unwritten code about minimum development. No tourist trap pricey downtown area for Bear Cove. Most of the residents still shopped for their groceries in the small grocery store next to the combination barber shop/beauty salon. Everyone knew everyone in Bear Cove, and the residents wanted life to stay that way.

When Carly had moved here just over ten years ago, she felt like an outsider, and many of the townsfolk treated her like one. "If you weren't born here, you don't belong here" was one of the town's unwritten but often implied mottos. The other one was "We like it the way it is." Several tough years passed before she began to feel at home, and the town finally accepted she was there to stay after she saved her former boss's life.

She'd earned the right, apparently, by rescuing one of their own.

The only person Carly saw on the way was Maria Beckwith. Her friend must have had a tougher row to how than Carly did herself. Three strikes against the young newlywed—she wasn't born here, she was Hispanic, and she was the town's only female police officer. A thing not done by a gentlewoman, apparently. At least, judging by sniffs, raised noses, and averted glances in the past. The town tolerated Maria only because she was married to the town's pharmacist. Carly continued to encourage Maria to put in her time until the town loosened up and let her into their inner circle.

Given her own experience, no telling how long that might take.

As Maria cruised by in the town's police car, Carly raised a hand to wave, but Maria wasn't looking in her direction. Carly let her hand drop, feeling a little foolish. What was it about waving at someone who didn't see her that always made her feel silly?

As Carly rounded the corner from Jamaica Street to Main Street, the wind blowing in off the water made her eyes tear up. Salt mixed with humidity stung her face, and she stopped for a moment, brushing tears from her face. Her vision thus clouded, she blinked several times before continuing.

Finally able to see again, although her eyes weren't completely clear, she paused in front of Penny's dress shop to survey the window display. This was her kind of shopping. Window shopping. Working from home had definite advantages, besides being near the fridge. She also saved a lot of money on her wardrobe. She owned a couple of dresses and a suit or two for client meetings, but other than that, her primary outfits were jeans or sweats.

Penny worked on the window display for the coming spring selection by adding a couple of wicker chairs in the center of the platform and setting out pots of artificial tulips and daffodils. Carly watched, glad for a reason to stay outdoors for a few more minutes to enjoy the sun on her head and to delay the dress-buying experience.

Drawing a deep breath, she tasted a trace of salt on the air as she braced herself for what she knew was not going to be a pleasant experience. She just wanted a simple suit, but Penny would make sure it was an Outfit. With a capital O. Carly just wanted not to embarrass Sarah at the wedding, but Penny would want to make a fashion statement.

Savoring the smell of the nearby ocean, Carly turned to pull open the door and step over the threshold into the Fashion Queen's sanctum, feeling somewhat like a fly lured into the web by a spider. From behind her, she heard a shout. She turned around. A man with a kit bag ran down the steps of the bank and jumped into an older car idling by the sidewalk. He slammed the car door and gestured to the driver. The car sped away with a squealing of tires, heading down the street toward her.

Curious as to the cause of such a hurried departure, Carly was even more surprised when old Mr. McMasters, the bank security guard, hobbled down the steps, shouting at the top of his lungs and firing his gun several times in the general direction of the speeding car.

Between the gunfire and the screaming of the tires, Carly couldn't make out what he was shouting, but he was obviously upset.

As if that wasn't enough to convince Carly to postpone her shopping trip today, maybe permanently, the driver of the car, in his haste to elude the scattering of bullets, jumped the curb.

The car headed directly towards Carly as she stood, mouth agape, on

≠≠ Unbalanced ≠≠

her way into the dress shop.

Chapter 2

The action unfolded around Carly in slow motion: the gun firing, the car driving recklessly down the sidewalk. The older model vehicle crashed into a large concrete flower container, sending shards of the pot and clumps of dirt flying into the air. And still she couldn't move. Fear knotted her stomach, and her feet froze in place.

At the last instant, the driver veered back onto the street through an empty parking space. The rear fender of his old car nicked the front fender of the pickup truck in the next spot, and pieces of red plastic flew off from a tail light. All Carly knew as the getaway vehicle sped past her was that she wasn't dead.

And the driver looked vaguely familiar.

But she didn't know any bank robbers.

Did she?

Her mouth still open, her knees trembling at the enormity of what she'd just witnessed, she managed to pull open the door and walk in. Loud classical music assailed her eardrums, and for a moment, she stood, disoriented and confused, willing herself to breathe.

Penny came from the rear of the store, several scarves in her hands. Carly closed the door and leaned against its solid surface. She willed her knees to stop shaking, and drew several deep breaths.

"Carly, you are late. I thought you were going to stand me up again. You really need to be more punctual. If you can't be on time, then you should be early. Come this way. I have just the dress. . ." She peered at Carly over her half-glasses, her brow drawn down into a straight line. "Is something wrong? You look a little pale."

Carly motioned to her ears, then pointed at a speaker hanging near the door. Penny nodded and reached past the cash register to turn down the stereo system. Strains of a Vivaldi concerto dropped to normal levels.

"Carly, what is the matter?"

She lifted a hand to stop Penny from talking. Everything had happened too quickly. She needed time for her brain to figure out what she had just seen.

* * *

Penny bustled forward, taking Carly by the arm and leading her to a bentwood chair strategically placed near the front door. Many years before, Penny figured out that if the husband wasn't comfortable, the wife was unlikely to stay in her store long enough to buy something. She'd installed a chair or two near the door, placing a small table with fishing magazines within reach.

While times were changing and women tended to shop without their husbands, the chairs remained. Her clientele was getting older, and the chair provided a convenient spot to position their purchases from other stores, leaving their hands free for shopping.

And today the chair proved to come in handy once again. The last thing she needed to do was try to pick Carly up off the floor. She leaned over and looked into Carly's pale face. No question, she'd had some kind of a shock. Perspiration gave her pasty skin a sickly-green sheen, and Carly shook when she touched her arm.

"Sit there, and I'll get you some hot coffee." She glanced over her shoulder several times as she hurried back to the small alcove, which housed her supplies and a small kitchenette. The hot plate held a carafe of hot water, and Penny deftly prepared a china cup of Earl Grey tea. Hands on hips, she considered her next move. Dropping several cubes of sugar in the hot liquid, she stirred until they dissolved. "You take cream and sugar, don't you?"

Not waiting for a reply, she added a generous dose of fresh half-and-half. She was concerned about Carly. Her white face and shaken demeanor were not what she expected. Surely the prospect of buying a dress hadn't caused this extreme reaction. Was Carly sick? Contagious? Before leaving the staff area, Penny slipped a couple of zinc tablets into her mouth from a bottle on a shelf. That should fight off any nasty bug Carly was spreading around. Couldn't take too many precautions working with the public.

Penny carried the cup to Carly, pleased to see some color back in her cheeks. Carly sat back in the delicate chair, eyes closed, taking deep breaths.. She stood beside Carly and touched her shoulder.

Carly's eyes flew open and she jumped slightly.

"Are you feeling all right, Carly?"

Carly shook her head slightly. "No. I just saw the bank being robbed, and then the getaway car almost ran me over on the sidewalk outside your door."

"Oh Carly, your imagination gets the best of you sometimes."

Again Carly shook her head. "I know what I saw. I don't know why you didn't hear the gunshots and the screeching tires. We've got to call the police."

Penny patted Carly's shoulder. "I didn't hear anything. Of course, I had the music up pretty loud, and I was in the back room."

"Please, Penny, call the police."

Penny nodded. "Sure, Carly. If you say you saw the bank being robbed, I guess you did." She smiled her best calming, reassuring smile, and offered the beverage. "Drink some tea first."

Carly reached for the cup, a lopsided smile bringing a little more life to her face. Tentatively, Carly sipped at the hot brew, blowing delicately. Steam wafted away, and Carly leaned back in the chair again, balancing the cup on one knee.

"Drink it all up. You'll feel better." Penny made little motions with her hands, encouraging Carly to do as she said. "And I'll call the police." She strode around the end of the counter, searching. "Now, where did I leave that phone? I know I was using it earlier."

Penny tapped the counter with her fingernails as she thought. She'd used the phone to call a supplier. "Right. I remember. It's in the supply room." Quickly she retrieved the handset and returned to stand beside Carly. "Should I call the non-emergency number?"

Carly reached for the phone but Penny pulled the handset out of reach. "Fine. The emergency line." Pressing the "on" button, she dialed 9-1-1, keeping one eye on Carly. The last thing she needed was for Carly to faint or something in the store.

Before the cup connected with Carly's lips, the hot liquid sloshed over the rim and onto her blouse. The resulting stain spread quickly across the light-colored fabric.

Penny sighed and disconnected the phone. Maybe fainting wasn't the worst thing that could happen today. If Carly burned herself, and then sued—not to mention how difficult getting that stain out was going to be.

Penny grabbed a nearby tissue box. "Here. Dab that. I'll get some vinegar for that stain."

Carly set her china cup on the nearby table and took the proffered tissues. Penny retreated to the alcove, returning a moment later with a white cotton rag and a bowl with vinegar.

Carly sat with the tissues in one hand, the other hand holding her blouse away from her skin, staring into space.

Penny scooted down beside Carly and looked up into her face. Tears glistened in Carly's eyes, and her face held a faraway look. Penny laid her hand on Carly's arm. "Carly." Getting no response, she tried again. "They put me on hold."

Slowly Carly's eyes refocused on Penny's face, her bottom lip trembling. "I'm sorry I'm so clumsy." Her gaze dropped to the stain on her chest. "Did I ruin my blouse?"

Penny stood and smiled. "I don't think so." She passed the rag dipped in vinegar to Carly. "Here. Blot your blouse with that. When you get home, soak it in some detergent, and then launder as usual. The stain should come right out."

Carly raised her eyes, meeting Penny's full-on. "I am such a klutz."

"You are not." Penny patted Carly's shoulder. "I am always spilling things on me."

"Really?"

Not really, but she needed to set this woman's mind at rest. "Really." A tone sounded in the handset. "Got another call coming in." Penny pressed the FLASH button. "Hello, Best Dressed, this is Penny." Her eyes met Carly's as she listened to the voice on the other end of the line. Turning her shoulder slightly, she lowered her voice. "I understand. Sure thing. I understand. Yes. No problem. Good-bye." Hanging up, she turned around slowly to face Carly. Extending her hand, she held the phone to Carly. "Why don't you call the police? You know what you saw."

Carly nodded and took the phone. She pressed the numbers and waited for an answer. "Yes. I'd like to report a bank robbery." She pursed her lips as she listened. "Yes, Velda. This is Carly. I'm at Penny's dress shop. I just saw someone rob the bank." More listening. "I don't care if no one else has called in. Please just send someone to investigate." She disconnected the call then passed the phone back to Penny. "I guess she doesn't believe me, either. Still, she said she would send the Chief. He won't get here for about fifteen minutes. Seems he's out on another matter. And he's the only one on duty right now."

Penny took a deep breath before walking to the front door. She peered up and down the street. "There's no one out there. I would think if there was a bank robbery, the police would be there by now."

"I know what I saw."

"Sometimes what you think you know and what is real are two different things. Leave well enough alone, Carly. Your life is just beginning to get back to normal since the fiasco a few months ago."

"It wasn't a fiasco, Penny. It was murder and embezzlement."

"That's according to you."

Carly sighed. "That's according to a court of law. My daughter was—"

Penny didn't want to get into this today. She had other things to do than stand here and argue with Carly Turnquist—the most opinionated woman she knew—about a dear friend of hers who'd made one or two bad choices. "Somehow we never had any trouble with the law before you came here."

"You make it sound like I brought trouble with me. I didn't." Carly stomped her foot. "Trouble found me."

Penny whirled from the door, arms folded across her chest. "It could have been handled without involving the police." She looked out again. Still no movement. "Poking your nose where it didn't belong made this town look bad."

"We aren't talking about someone stealing milk money."

When she turned from the window, Carly stood close, almost touching. Penny moved a step away then turned to face her. "I'm sorry, Carly. I shouldn't blame you."

Carly smiled. "We can't control what other people do. We can only control ourselves. And sometimes we aren't very good at that."

Penny nodded. The best thing she could do was get Carly out of the store. But not before selling her the most expensive outfit she could. Small consolation, to be sure, but she took what she could get. "Shall we look for your dress, now? We can't do much else until Chief Blom gets here anyway."

She breathed a sigh of relief when Carly nodded. She didn't want to start something she couldn't finish right now. As a good businesswoman in a small town, she didn't want to have disgruntled customers. And she had Carly's promise to buy off the regular-priced racks.

She had plenty of time later to put things right. She smiled to herself as Carly headed for the first rack of dresses. Being nice to people was second-nature to her. After all, she was a salesperson. But setting her personal feelings aside was more of a struggle than usual.

How did Carly manage to raise her ire so easily?

She turned her attention back to the task. If things went well, everyone—including Carly Turnquist—would get what was coming to them. Some people needed taking down a peg. Or two. In the meantime, there was nothing wrong with making a little profit.

* * *

Carly flipped through the dresses on the first rack. None of the colors grabbed her. She had a picture in her mind and nothing else would do. "Penny, do you have anything in a deep coral pink?"

Penny shook her head. "No. That's last year's color, and I only carry current styles. This year the colors are softer, more understated."

Carly sighed. Softer and understated she wanted, but these greens and golds were too much like camouflage for her liking. She moved to another rack, spying a dress that didn't even come close to her vision for an outfit. Still, the color was pretty. Understated. Pale buttery-yellow silk, full skirt, beaded around the collar. Almost perfect.

Her jaw dropped when she surreptitiously checked the price tag. Three hundred and forty-nine dollars! She'd have to work—she did a quick calculation—almost two days to pay for that one. Casting a glance over her shoulder to see where Penny was, she was glad the older woman was unpacking a box on the opposite side of the store. No point in lingering over this outfit, or Penny would notice and hustle over, and next thing she'd know, she'd be walking out with an outfit she'd be afraid to wear.

Carly had no doubt she'd buy the dress once she tried it on. Literally. But this wedding was already costing her way more than she planned for. Still, Tom was her only son, and Sarah her only daughter-in-law, and she wanted everything to be perfect. And Sarah had no close family, so Carly felt free in taking over a mother's role.

She continued moving through the rack, searching for another outfit. Choosing by color seemed the wise way to go, but now that she saw just how pricey the outfits were, she decided to take a quick look at the tag first before she fell in love with the dress and lost her head.

By the time she reached the end of the rack, frustration mounted inside her, knotting her stomach. She swiped sweaty palms against her jeans. Turning around, she jumped slightly, her hand going to her heart. Penny stood directly behind her.

"My goodness. You snuck up on me, Penny."

"Sorry. I was just coming over to see if you needed some help." Penny glanced over Carly's shoulder. "Find anything you like?"

"Not yet." Watching Penny's smile fade, Carly's stomach lurched. Did salespeople take personally when a shopper didn't find something they liked? Carly wasn't sure of all the intricacies of shopping etiquette, if there even were such things. "What I mean is, you have so many lovely things, I can't decide."

Penny's smile returned, albeit half-hearted. "Well, I did open especially for you today. Let's see what we can find, shall we?" Penny pushed past Carly, forcing her to step aside. The first dress she selected was the yellow silk creation Carly had fallen in love with at first sight. "How about trying on this one?"

Carly forced a smile she didn't feel. Maybe Penny had been watching her more carefully than she'd realized. She quickly scrutinized a nearby rack of suits. Well, a suit had been her first choice. Perhaps she could find one more in her price range. Ignoring the question, Carly fingered the sleeve of the first suit on the rack. Although not as pretty as the pale yellow silk, the outfit had an attractive sheen.

"What is this one made of?" Running her hand down the sleeve, she flipped the tag over to read the price. She smiled. A hundred dollars less than the first one. Getting closer.

"Raw silk. Very in this year." Penny held the outfit in front of Carly. "The color would look great on you."

Carly turned slightly to view her reflection in a full-length mirror placed strategically for that very reason. The fabric hung nicely from the hanger, and the pale grey silk was cool to the touch. She nodded. "I like it. I'll try that one on."

Inside the small changing room, Carly slipped off her loafers before peeling off her stained blouse. Hanging the garment on a hook on the back of the door, she wondered if the stain would come out. She shook her head as she unbuttoned the waist of her pants. Standing on one leg to pull off the slacks, she thought of the blouses and shirts she ruined every year with stains. Seemed like no matter how careful she was or how much stain remover she bought, she still threw away good money because of spots and splashes.

Carly stepped into the skirt, snugging the waistband closed. If she held

≠≠ Unbalanced ≠≠

her stomach in a little, the skirt looked flattering. And she'd read somewhere that tucking in the tummy was good exercise and good for posture at the same time. She turned from side to side, getting the full benefit of the three-way mirror in the small cubicle.

"How does it fit?" Penny's voice thundered through the thin partition. "Remember, no time for alterations."

Carly flinched. Penny was right outside the door, and she was only half-dressed. Penny would expect to see the complete outfit, so she carefully removed the top from the hanger and put her arm through the sleeves.

The raw silk tickled her arms and back, and the front of the jacket buttoned effortlessly over her bosom. Once again, Carly surveyed her reflection, imagining the finished product of hairdo, makeup, and shoes. She wouldn't win any beauty contests, but she definitely looked fine as a woman approaching middle age. Carly snorted softly at the thought. The truth was if she really was only approaching middle age, she could expect to live to be a nonagenarian.

Carly opened the dressing room door with a flourish. "Ta da!"

Penny stepped back, her eyes squinted and her lips pursed like she was sucking on a sour dill pickle. Her gaze started at Carly's head and roamed down to the floor, then back up. Pointing to the floor and making a small circular motion with her hand, she waited.

Carly dutifully rotated slowly, holding one arm out slightly.

When she faced Penny again, she was pleased to see a small smile beginning on Penny's mouth. The older woman nodded.

Carly returned the smile. "You think it will do?"

"I think you are going to look the best you can, Carly." Penny tucked the hem up on one sleeve, then straightened Carly's arm to hang at her side. "We'll need to turn up these sleeves." She turned on her heel and headed toward the front of the store where the register was located.

The best she could? What did she mean? Carly's mouth turned down as she retreated into the changing room. Seemed like some people were never happy unless they were stealing someone else's thunder. She unbuttoned the jacket top, being careful not to pull on the buttons. Next came the skirt,

≠≠ Unbalanced ≠≠

cautiously reattached to the clothespin-like thingies on the hanger. Satisfied the jacket was secure, she pulled on her clothes, then tucked her feet into her shoes.

She handed her new outfit over to Penny, who hung the suit on a short rack behind the register.

Pulling an order pad from under the counter, Penny made some notes before peering over her half-glasses once again. "So, are you ready to tell me what happened out there?"

Carly thought for a moment before answering. "I'm not sure. It looked like the bank was being robbed."

Penny cocked her head to one side before answering. "Surely you are joking."

"I know it sounds strange. After all, we're just a small town. Why would anyone want to rob a bank here?"

The telephone chirruped in its cradle at the end of the counter.

"What makes you think it was a robbery?" Penny asked, moving to answer the phone.

Carly idly glanced into the display case next to the counter while she waited for the phone call to end and the conversation—and purchase—to continue.

Penny picked up the receiver and greeted her caller in a perky tone, "Good morning, Well Dressed, Penny speaking. How may I assist you?" She listened for a moment, then glanced at Carly before replying. Lowering her voice and turning her back to Carly, she spoke a few words, then hung up the phone. "Now, where were we?"

Carly's interest peaked. What secrets could a person be talking about in a dress shop? On two separate calls?

Penny returned to the register and picked up her pen. A strained smile hid something else—fear? Concern? Carly watched her from the corner of her eye. Penny looked at the order pad, then glanced quickly back to the telephone.

Turning to face Carly, she tilted her head to one side. "Now, where were we? Oh yes, you need those sleeves let down slightly, don't you?"

≠≠ Unbalanced ≠≠

Carly shook her head. What was going on here? Just minutes ago Penny said there was no time for alterations, and now she wasn't making any fuss about the extra work. "You said I needed them shortened."

Penny's brows knit together for a moment in thought, then her forehead smoothed. "Yes, of course. I was testing you." She gave a hollow laugh. "You passed." Scribbling furiously on the paper, she paused to ask, "When did you need this again?"

Carly sighed. She'd need to keep an eye on this if she wanted to wear the new outfit at the wedding. Daymares of losing the outfit flitted across her mind. No, she wouldn't go there. "Saturday. I'd like to pick it up on Friday."

"Right. Right. I remembered that." With a flourish, Penny tore the paper from its pad, then tucked the instructions into a jacket pocket. "All done. Come in Friday around noon, and you can try it on again. Bring the shoes you're going to wear to the wedding, and we'll make sure the length is good, too."

Not only taking up the sleeves, but now last minute hemming didn't faze Penny. Curiosity built in her like steam in a locomotive. "What about the bank robbery?"

Penny turned to face her. "What bank robbery?"

"The one I was going to tell you about. The one that happened right before I walked into your store."

Penny forced a laugh. "Oh, Carly. You have such an imagination! You read too many of those mystery books. What do you call them? Cuddly mysteries?"

Carly did not consider this a laughing matter. "Cozy mysteries. Cozy. Not cuddly." This was serious. The bank may have been burglarized, Mr. McMasters was shooting off his gun, and she had nearly been run over. "And that's beside the point. I know what I saw."

Penny reached over awkwardly and patted Carly's hand. "Surely someone would have come here before now, don't you think, if that had really happened?"

"I would have thought so."

"Just so. I mean, even if the police didn't come asking questions, one of our town's fair ladies would have found a reason to drop in, don't you think?"

Carly nodded slowly, trying to understand. "At the very least, someone would have come in to make sure I was okay. I mean, old McMasters saw me. He was shouting and had his gun pointed right in my direction. Do you think it might have been a practice or something?"

"That makes sense." Penny stood and put her hand on Carly's shoulder. "I'll make sure I bring it up at the next Women's League meeting. How do you want to pay for your suit?"

"Can I set up an account, and pay it off next month?"

"That would be fine." Penny reached under the counter for her ledger book. "Anything else?"

Stranger and stranger. Penny didn't extend credit to just anybody. "Actually, the cameo in this case caught my eye while you were on the phone."

Penny glanced again at the phone sitting on the end of the counter. She pulled a small key ring from her pocket and unlocked the cabinet then set the piece on the glass counter. Carly held the brooch in the palm of her hand.

Silver filigree encircled the colored center, and the translucent traditional profile of a woman with curly hair piled on top of her head glowed. Carly smiled and passed the piece to Penny. "Hold that next to the neckline of the suit, please."

Penny took the cameo and moved to where the suit still hung on the rack. The pale blue agate brightened the suit, and Carly was startled to see the same color reflected in the mother of pearl buttons on the jacket. She pointed. "Oh, look, the cameo has the same color as the buttons."

Penny nodded. "You're right. I hadn't noticed them before. They're so understated, and the rich silk makes the buttons almost invisible."

"I'll take it." Carly squinted at Penny. "I won't go to this wedding and see every woman there wearing this same design, will I?"

Penny sniffed and shook her head. "No. These are all original designs. One of a kind."

Carly smiled. "Just kidding, of course. Can you keep it here for me?"

Penny put the brooch into a small gift box, and tucked it into the jacket pocket opposite the alteration instructions. Patting the pocket, she turned to Carly. "Will that be all?"

Carly smiled lopsidedly. "That has to be all, Penny. If I spend any more time here, I'll have to live in my car."

"You will be the belle of the ball, Carly." Penny showed her to the door, her hand pressed into Carly's back. "You look fabulous in that outfit."

That was the nicest thing Carly had ever heard Penny say about anybody other than herself. Something strange happened here today. Brushing aside her concerns, Carly basked in the compliment, even if Penny was rushing her to make a decision.

And if there was one thing Carly didn't like it was being rushed.

Sunlight caused Carly to squint as she left the store, headed for the bank. She wanted to make sure of what she witnessed earlier. If she hadn't seen a robbery, while she would feel foolish, she would get over it.

If there had been a robbery, she could be a material witness.

At the very least, she wanted to know for sure what was going on.

Walking the block from the dress shop to the bank, Carly noted the street seemed very quiet. Still, early April in Maine wasn't always ideal for strolling along the downtown area, and temperatures had been cooler than usual. Still, she had expected to see a few familiar faces.

When she climbed the steps to the bank's front door, McMasters was nowhere in sight, which was odd. He always stood just inside the door. She should have been able to see him through the glass.

She grasped the brass door handle and pulled. The door remained closed. Thinking she had to push the door, she was even more surprised when the door still didn't open.

She cupped her hands around her eyes and pressed her face to the glass, trying to see the time on the clock. Ten-thirty. The bank didn't close until—she spied the business hours on the glass to her right—five o'clock. The bank should be open.

Banging the heel of her hand on the bank door in frustration, Carly turned to leave, and ran smack dab into Victor Blom, the town police chief, who grabbed her by the arm as she staggered backwards.

"Good heavens, Carly." He held her steady until she regained her balance. "Watch where you're going."

"I'm glad you got here, Victor." She drew a steadying breath. "I wasn't expecting to see you here. Well, actually I was, but I thought you'd be inside the bank. Investigating."

"Investigating? What would I be investigating?" Chief Blom looked at her as a scientist would look at a new life form on a microscope slide. "What have you dreamed up today?"

Carly didn't like the tone of his voice. Or his insinuation. Choosing her words carefully, Carly ventured into what was fast becoming dangerous territory. After all, would the police chief waste time bandying with her if there really had been a bank robbery? This wasn't looking good at all. "The commotion at the bank earlier this morning? About half an hour ago?" Not seeing any sign of understanding on his face, she continued. "I called and talked to Velda. I told her I'd seen the bank robbery. I can be a witness, maybe even identify the man who ran from the bank. And I saw McMasters chasing the guy who ran out of the bank with a kit bag in his hand. But he jumped into a car and sped away from the bank, Chief. He nearly ran me over."

"McMasters nearly ran you over?" Chief Blom ran his fingers through his hair, then set his cap back in place. "Carly, there's been no bank robbery in Bear Cove today."

Chapter 3

Carly sighed loudly, her bangs fluffing with the effort like a certain Miss Universe contestant of some years before. "No, McMasters didn't run me over. The bank robber nearly ran me over. He lost control of his car when McMasters was shooting at him. He drove up on the sidewalk and nearly ran me over."

Chief Blom eyed her, skepticism obvious on his face.

He didn't believe a word she was saying.

She grabbed the chief by the arm and directed him down the sidewalk, back towards Penny's dress shop. "The bank robber hit a flowerpot here in front of—"

She stopped dead in her tracks. The flowerpot was in its usual place. She hurried over, examining the clay pot carefully for damage. There was none.

Pulling on his arm, she led him to the empty parking space the car had careened through. "He hit the truck parked here."

The truck was gone.

Of course.

"And he broke a tail light."

Chief Blom shook his head. "I don't see any evidence of that, Carly. Have you been watching too much television?"

"This has nothing to do with how much time I spend in front of the TV,

≠≠ Unbalanced ≠≠

Victor. This is about the bank being robbed."

Chief Blom nodded. "That's what everyone says who has a problem with something." He patted her shoulder. "You know, I hear people who drink too much say the same thing. And people who hit their dogs and people who drive too fast. Doesn't change the outcome, though."

Carly bit the tip of her tongue to quiet an unkind retort ready to explode forth. "I don't drink. I don't beat my dog because I don't own a dog. And I rarely speed."

"Just trying to be neighborly. I can see you're struggling."

"The only struggle I'm having is with you understanding the bank was robbed earlier and no one seems to know anything about it." Carly clenched her fists. "Or maybe you don't want to know anything about it."

"And what does that mean?"

"I know how you feel about what happened before when money went missing."

Chief Blom glanced at a car driving slowly past before answering. "As you recall, that money wasn't missing from Bear Cove."

Carly rolled her eyes. "It doesn't matter where it was missing from. I also know you don't like the reporters that descended on Bear Cove like locusts on a wheat field."

Chief Blom held up one hand, palm facing Carly. "Now, Carly, I'm not one of those people who hold grudges."

"Grudges? Why should anyone be upset at me? I was nearly killed."

"But you weren't, were you? So it wasn't all that serious."

Carly drew a deep breath. "No, but the mayor is still dead."

Chief Blom pursed his lips, his brow furrowed. "This is not about the mayor or the past. This is about a serious allegation you're making about something that happened—or didn't happen—today."

Carly looked around, trying to remember who else was on the street that day. She couldn't think of anyone. Then she remembered Penny.

Grabbing the chief's arm again, she pulled him along behind her. "Penny saw it all, too. She'll tell you."

"Hey, guys, is there something I should know?"

Carly turned at the sound of the new voice and smiled at the sight of a young man patting his pockets in search of something. "What are you looking for, Matthew?"

"My notebook. I never seem to put it in the same place twice." He pulled a tattered pad of paper from his shirt pocket. "Now, if I can just find my pen." Reaching behind his ear, he held a well-chewed pencil aloft. "This will do." He eyed Carly and Chief Blom. "So, what were you two arguing about?"

Chief Blom puffed up his chest and took a small step toward Matthew. "We weren't arguing."

Matthew took a step backwards, nearly falling off the sidewalk. Arms flailing, he caught himself. He grinned at the chief. "Sure you were. I heard you from across the street." He turned to face Carly. "Come on, Carly. Give. I'm always looking for news stories for the paper. And we go to press tonight."

Carly frowned. "Matthew, you are the most persistent intern I have ever known."

"I'm the only intern you've ever known at the Register. I'm the first." He gazed off into the distance. "I'm opening doors of opportunity for thousands of journalism majors for years to come."

Carly rolled her eyes. "Matthew, you know the Register is hardly likely to bring in thousands of journalism majors. If they bring in one a year, that's more than they've ever done."

Chief Blom cleared his throat. "Right. So don't go around looking for stories that aren't there, young man. You're as bad as she is."

Matthew's teeth shone white against his dark skin as he grinned. "Sounds to me like the man doth protest too much."

Carly wrinkled her nose. "He's got you there, Chief."

Chief Blom scowled at Carly. "Don't start on me, Carly. There was no bank robbery, there was no car careening down the sidewalk. You've been watching too much police TV again."

Carly's jaw dropped. Feeling foolish in front of Chief Blom was one thing, but another entirely to be ridiculed in front of someone else. Especially a reporter. She turned to Matthew, who was scribbling furiously in his notebook. "Matthew, don't listen to him."

Matthew paused, pencil in mid-air. "So, there was a bank robbery and a car hurtled down the sidewalk and crashed into storefronts?"

Carly frowned. "I never said the car was hurtling or it crashed into stores. That's how rumors get started."

Chief Blom grabbed for the notebook. "No, rumors get started when someone hears half the story and makes a full story out of it."

Matthew tapped his temple with his forefinger. "Too late, Chief. It's all in here. And who needs the facts anyway? People will just love to hear all about the town super sleuth who was fooled into believing something happened that didn't?"

Carly gasped. "Matthew, you wouldn't."

Matthew smiled. "No, Carly, I wouldn't. I have too much respect for you. But I think the town should know if a dangerous bank robber is lurking around town."

Chief Blom grunted. "If there was a dangerous bank robber—which there isn't—I would know about it. And I don't know anything about it."

Matthew reached for his notebook, which the chief passed over to him. "Can I follow up on this, talk to people, ask questions?"

Carly nodded. "I think it's a great idea. Chief, why not let him go with me, back to Penny's, and ask her?"

"Well, if it will set the matter straight." Chief Blom faced Matthew. "But you must promise that if we don't find anything, you won't report anything." His brows furrowed. "Promise?"

Matthew's eyes squinted for a moment. "Fair enough. But if there is more to the story, I'm the one who gets the exclusive, okay?"

Carly clapped the cub reporter on the shoulder. "Fine."

The chief nodded. "But there won't be anything else to find out. Just an over-active imagination."

Carly led the way back to "Well Dressed", relieved when she saw lights on inside and movement behind the counter. Now she could get to the bottom of

≠≠ Unbalanced ≠≠

this. She hated looking foolish in front of others.

Pushing in through the dress shop door, which banged against the wall, Carly was surprised to see Penny's part-time assistant Amanda behind the counter, arranging silk scarves. "Where's Penny?"

"Nice to see you, too, Carly." Amanda's sarcastic tone exaggerated her southern drawl. Somewhere in Tennessee, maybe. Or Georgia. "How can I help you?"

"Sorry. Where is Penny?"

Behind her, the police chief grunted. "Watch where you're going, young man."

Matthew took a step back. "Sorry. You stopped so suddenly."

Chief Blom stood in the doorway, shuffling his feet. The open door let in a cold draft.

Turning around, Carly snapped at the older man. "What's wrong? Never been in a dress shop before?"

A slow smile spread across his face. "As a matter of fact, I haven't. My wife buys all the dresses our family needs."

Chagrined and properly chastened, Carly apologized. "Sorry, you guys. I just don't understand what's been going on here today." Turning to Amanda once more, she raised an eyebrow in question. "Penny?"

"Penny's not here."

"That's not true," Carly blurted. "I was here less than a half hour ago and bought a dress to wear to Tom's wedding."

Amanda ran her hand down one of the scarves, patting the material flat. "I don't know where you were thirty minutes ago, Carly. All I know is I haven't seen Penny. And there hasn't been anyone else in this store since I got in."

"Can you describe this alleged dress?" Chief Blom asked, pulling his official notebook from his jacket pocket. "Color, style?"

Behind him, Matthew retrieved his notepad again.

"I see where this is going. And I don't want to take that trip." Carly glanced at the rack behind the register. Empty. She looked in the display case. The cameo was there. "Stop playing games."

Amanda shrugged. "I don't know what you're talking about."

Why would Amanda and Penny lie about her dress? Why was the police chief denying there had been a bank robbery? Who was this unknown person who had nearly run her down?

And most important of all, if she wasn't here this morning buying a dress, what had she been doing?

Carly grasped at one last straw and turned to face the chief. "If there wasn't a bank robbery, why is the bank closed?"

The chief took a long time to answer, and Carly stared at him in triumph. She had him. There had been a robbery, and for some reason they didn't want anyone to know. Why? Had someone been shot? Were they withholding information 'pending notification of next of kin' as they always said on TV? Was something taken besides money? Was someone taken hostage? A kidnaping? Carly's mind raced with the possibilities as the chief chose his words carefully.

"The bank is closed because there was a power outage there. The security system doesn't work without power."

Carly wasn't going to give up. "But what about the bank robbery?"

Chief Blom sighed. "Look, I know you love a good mystery. I know you've been helpful a time or two in the past."

She raised an eyebrow, questioning his statement. Helpful? If not for her, her former boss would have suffocated in a furnace.

"Okay, you've been instrumental in solving some crimes, Carly. But really, I don't know anything about any bank robbery."

"How could you not know about it? Where were you when I called it in?"

"I was called out to the other end of town about a domestic disturbance. We have those once in a while, even though the town is small." Chief Blom set his notebook on the counter and hitched up his belt before turning to Amanda. "Have you heard anything about a bank robbery, Amanda?"

She shook her head. "I haven't talked to anyone since I got here."

Carly persisted. "When was that?"

"I usually come in around nine-thirty, so I would say it was within a few minutes of that, one way or the other. I've been plugging away in here ever since."

Carly began to splutter. "That's not true. I was in here with Penny at ten, and you weren't here then."

Amanda smiled indulgently at Carly. "I don't know where you were, Carly. I only know I didn't see you."

Carly shuffled her feet. Crow was never one of her favorite dishes.

The chief smiled at her, shaking his head as he would at a school kid caught with his hand in the candy jar at the corner store. "I know you fancy yourself good at solving mysteries. Fact of the matter is, there isn't any mystery to solve here. Why don't you go ahead and pick out your dress for the wedding, and let me get back to my job?"

Matthew sighed and shoved his pencil behind his ear. "This was a waste of time. A story that didn't happen. Maybe the most exciting story since the Widow Fletcher caught those kids stealing her sheets off the clothesline to use for costumes for the Mardi Gras party at the school."

Amanda moved to straighten a scarf on a mannequin. "The only thing that made it so exciting was she wrapped them in the sheets and delivered them to the police station herself."

Carly hated when people made fun of her. "This is no laughing matter."

Chief Blom's face turned red. "You're right, Carly. That was a real crime. In this case, there isn't. Do you know there's a penalty for making false police reports?"

"Are you threatening me? I'm only trying to understand what I saw."

"What you think you saw."

As the chief turned to leave, Carly remembered something he'd said. "If the bank is closed like you say because of the power being off, how come the wall clock is still showing the right time?"

The chief turned slowly to face her. For a brief moment, his expression convinced Carly she was right about a cover-up. Then the look was gone, replaced by a self-satisfied smirk. "Because it's a battery-operated clock."

The door whooshed shut behind him, effectively closing the subject.

Carly stared at her shoes, at the floor, out the window. Minutes passed, and still she couldn't bring herself to admit she'd been wrong. How could she have made such a mistake? Had she been hallucinating? What about the car going by so fast? Was she losing her mind?

Amanda came around the counter and touched her shoulder, making her jump.

Smiling through her embarrassment, Carly said, "Let's forget about this, okay? I need to find a dress for the wedding."

Matthew cleared his throat. "I think I'll take off."

Carly nodded. "Good idea."

The young reported pulled open the door. "No point wasting my time here since there's no story." He looked up the sidewalk towards the bank. "At least, I don't think there's any story. I might poke around a little bit, though."

"Fair enough, Matthew. But before you print anything about me, will you check with me first?"

He raised a hand in acknowledgment. "See you later."

Amanda sighed. "Seems like there's more people in here today than on a day when we're open." She looked at Carly. "Ready?"

Carly nodded, and together they went through the sale racks, where Carly found the perfect suit. It wasn't the grey silk she originally purchased, but cost a lot less. Her one consolation was if Penny was somehow playing a trick on her, Carly was getting her back—in spades—by purchasing this less-expensive outfit. Plus, her thrifty mind working even through this stressful situation, she could wear the pale blue suit at other functions, just as she had planned with the original outfit.

Deciding to try the suit to make sure alterations weren't needed, she went into the cramped changing room next to the kitchenette at the rear of the store. Remembering with a pang of regret the delicious cup of tea she hadn't had earlier with Penny, she unbuttoned her blouse.

There, on the front, was a stain.

≠≠ Unbalanced ≠≠

Chapter 4

Without a doubt, she had been there earlier that day. But since no one else seemed to know what was going on, Carly buttoned her blouse and grabbed the suit. She would take the outfit as is and deal with alterations later.

Right now, she had more important things to do.

Paying for the suit, she glanced around the store, willing her memory to conjure up evidence of her presence there earlier. In the small display case under the counter, she spied the cameo brooch she had bought on her first trip here today.

Or hadn't bought, depending on who she believed.

Casually, she leaned over to get a better look. "Amanda, see that cameo there?" She pointed. "I'm sure I've seen one like that on a lady at church. Do you sell many of them?"

Amanda shook her head. "No. It's a one of a kind. The artist lives in Small Harbor, and makes them one at a time. No two are the same. We've only had one cameo from her."

"Are you sure? It looks exactly like the one the lady at church wears."

"Positive. Are you done, Carly? We aren't usually open on Mondays, and I have to pick up my son."

Carly's hopes picked up again. "I know you're closed today. Just exactly why are you here, then?"

Maybe now Amanda would admit Penny put her up to this.

Amanda turned around slowly. "I came in to put out stock. Penny pays me to work overtime on Mondays, and as a single mom, I need to take advantage of every opportunity to make extra money. Will there be anything else?"

No use pushing the woman any further. She wouldn't get any more information now. She had aroused suspicion about the cameo. Why was everyone lying?

* * *

Carefully hanging her dress in a closet at home, Carly considered her predicament. She saw a bank robbery everyone else was denying. Why would her friends lie to her? If they weren't lying, how could she have made such a huge mistake?

She went back over the morning's events. Finding the notebook, walking to the dress shop, waving to Maria.

Except Maria hadn't seen her.

Then the squealing tires, the careening vehicle on the sidewalk, McMasters firing his gun. The flowerpot in the air. And less than thirty minutes later, no evidence any of that had happened.

Could she have dreamt the whole thing?

Maybe the stress of the wedding had her hallucinating?

Carly shook her head. She refused to believe that. There had to be another explanation, but coming up with a plausible one eluded her.

She went back to the kitchen, retrieved her notebook, and picked up the cordless phone to call the photographer. While waiting for him to answer, the doorbell rang, a cheery tune that always reminded her of the ice cream truck.

Going to the front door, she peered through the curtain. The lanky stranger at her door smiled lopsidedly, and the young boy with him clenched a handful of cloth from the man's pant leg. Carly looked past the man, spotting an old car parked in front of her house. She slipped the security chain in place before opening the door.

≠≠ Unbalanced ≠≠

"Yes?" She scanned the street, hoping to see a neighbor out and about. The street was empty. Her mouth went dry. She should have had the presence of mind to bring the cordless phone with her. "Can I help you?"

The man smiled and held out his hand. "Hi. You must be Carly. I'm Jerry."

Carly felt strange talking to the man through the small opening permitted by the chain, but after the morning she'd had, she wasn't about to open the door to someone she didn't recognize. Even someone with a small child at his side. "I'm sorry, I—"

"I'm Mike's younger brother. And this—" He indicated the boy. "This is Bradley, my son."

Carly smiled at the young child. She vaguely remembered Mike mentioning a black sheep brother who hadn't been heard from in many years. "Hello, Bradley."

The child clung to his father's pant leg, not making eye contact with Carly.

"He's shy." Jerry tousled his son's hair. "At that age, I guess."

Carly nodded, stepping back from the door. "Give me a second to unlatch this chain." She closed the door and slid the chain free. Had Mike forgotten to tell her Jerry was coming for a visit? Worse yet, had he told her and she'd forgotten? If so, another sign the stress was getting to her. Opening the door, she gestured to the living room.

Jerry scuffed his shoes on the welcome mat, then stepped in, leading his son by the hand. Still Bradley wouldn't look at Carly. She perched on the arm of the easy chair, indicating they sit on the sofa. Jerry sat, but Bradley stood next to him, looking like he was ready to bolt.

Carly studied the man. He bore a vague resemblance to Mike, except he looked harder, more weather-worn. She tapped a toe, nervous energy building from the inside. She had a lot to do today and hadn't anticipated houseguests. Still, she wanted to do the right thing. "Can I get you anything?"

Jerry shook his head. "No thanks. We ate a big breakfast."

She hadn't been thinking about food. Maybe a glass of water. Carly sat in the easy chair, scooting forward to sit on the edge. "So, did Mike get in touch with you to invite you to the wedding?"

Jerry tilted his head to one side. "Wedding?"

Carly folded her hands in her lap. "Our son—Mike's son Tom is getting married on Saturday."

Jerry pursed his lips. "I haven't talked to Mike in a while."

So, they weren't here for the wedding. Carly tried again. "Just here for a visit?"

Jerry gazed up at a corner of the room. Carly followed his glance. Had something attracted his attention? Nothing, at least from her vantage point. This conversation was like pulling teeth. She waited for Jerry to explain what he was doing here, now. The last time Mike mentioned his brother had been just before their wedding. Carly asked Mike if he wanted to invite family, and Mike replied he had a brother he hadn't seen for years. Somehow, his coming into town five days before Tom's wedding had to be more than a coincidence.

There I go again, looking for a mystery when there's probably a perfectly good explanation.

Jerry rose to his feet, an imposing figure of a man, slightly taller than Mike's six-foot two. He filled Carly's line of vision, and she felt a little uncomfortable alone with him. After all, she didn't know him, and from what he said, Mike didn't know he was in town.

Jerry pulled his wallet from his back pocket and thumbed through its contents. He handed her a square of paper. "Here's a picture of Mike and me when we were in high school. It's his graduation."

Carly studied the picture. Although the picture was almost twenty-five years old, there was no mistaking Mike. His boyish grin was ageless, and Carly recognized the cleft in his chin. Studying the photo, she noted Jerry didn't have the same cleft. She looked from the photo to Jerry. "Well, you've both definitely aged some, but this is you and Mike."

"Sure it is." He made a motion with his hands indicating she should turn the photo over. "And if you look at the back, you'll see the inscription."

She read out loud the blurred words. "To my baby brother Jerry.

≠≠ Unbalanced ≠≠

Someday you'll get to wear one of these ridiculous hats. Love, Mike." Although not exactly the same, the handwriting was similar enough that she recognized Mike's signature. She looked at Jerry. "And did you?"

His eyes widened slightly at her question. "Did I what?"

"Did you get to wear one of those crazy board hats?"

"Eventually."

She moved to the kitchen doorway. Somehow she felt more in control when she was standing. "Are you sure I can't get you something to eat?"

Jerry touched the boy's shoulder, and Bradley stood beside his father. "You know, this might not have been such a good idea." He turned toward the front door. "Next time, we'll call and let you know we're coming."

Carly's heart fell. The last thing she wanted to do was offend Mike's only living relative. "Please stay. Mike will be sorry he missed you."

Jerry rose and followed her. "Well, that's probably not completely true. We seem to get along better when there's a few miles between us. We don't want to be any trouble. . ."

Carly moved to the telephone receiver on the kitchen table. "How about if I call Mike and let him know you're here?"

Jerry leaned against the kitchen door jamb. "The last time I saw Mike, we didn't exactly leave on good terms. I'd rather tell him I'm here myself, make sure things are right between us. How about if I do that right now?"

Carly passed him the receiver. "His cell phone is on speed dial one. I'll get you something light to eat. It's lunch time, and breakfast was probably hours ago." She opened the fridge door, looking for leftover pasta from last night's supper. "We're pretty informal here for lunch. Mike happens to be out at a client's, and Tom and Sarah are at work. I'm on my own for lunch today." She pulled the covered dishes out and set them on the counter. "I hope you like spaghetti?"

For a moment, a glimmer of a smile flitted across Bradley's face. Then it was gone.

The boy needed some TLC.

"We love spaghetti, don't we, Bradley?" Jerry walked towards the living room. "I'll call Mike from in here."

She busied herself, one eye on Bradley, one ear on Jerry's phone conversation. "Okay. I'll just put this in the microwave to heat up."

A few moments later Jerry returned the phone to its cradle. "That Mike is one swell guy. He said he didn't even remember what our disagreement was about. What can we do to help?"

"Silverware is in that drawer over there." She pointed with her elbow as she put the dishes in the microwave to heat. "Plates are in the cupboard next to the sink. Glasses to the right of that."

For a few minutes, the only sounds were the clinking of silverware and the humming of the microwave. Jerry quickly and efficiently set the table, while Bradley stood silently to one side. Several times Carly smiled at the child but didn't get any response.

As they ate, Jerry regaled her with stories of jobs he'd held, places he'd lived. Carly asked questions about family, and Jerry seemed happy to tell her of their growing-up years. Carly told Jerry how she and Mike had met, and described life in a small town on the east coast. They talked about the job he said had brought him to Bear Cove, and finished with commiserations about old cars and the price of gas.

While they cleaned up the dishes, Bradley yawned politely behind his hand, and she noticed for the first time that his eyelids were drooping.

"You look like you have been on the road for a while. How about a little rest?" She pointed toward the staircase in the foyer. "Bradley, up in the spare room you'll find a perfect sized bed for you. And a teddy bear that belongs to your cousin, Margie. I know she'd love if you would borrow him and keep him company for a while."

Bradley gave his father a questioning look. Jerry nodded, and Bradley quietly murmured, "Excuse me, please."

"It's the first door on your left," Carly called out.

Without responding, he closed the door behind him.

Jerry put the dirty dishes into the dishwasher. "I'll go check on him in a few minutes."

≠≠ Unbalanced ≠≠

Carly wiped down the counter, checked the microwave for splatters, and then tossed her sponge into the sink. Just then, the phone rang.

Carly picked up the receiver, pleased to hear Mike on the other end. "Hi, Mike. I'm so glad you—"

Jerry shook his head and waved his hands at her. She turned to see what his problem was. He pointed at the phone, then to himself and shook his head 'no'.

Even without words, Carly knew exactly what he was saying—don't talk about me with Mike. If things were fine between them, and Jerry had just spoken with Mike, why couldn't she say something about him to her husband?

* * *

Mike sighed. "Carly, are you there? What have you gotten into now?" Sometimes she infuriated him with her riddles to solve and getting involved in mysteries. "Is everything all right?"

"Um—nothing. I mean, everything is fine. I was just going to tell you about the outfit I bought at Penny's this morning. It's a real nice pale blue color, with a little lace, and. . ."

Mike leaned back in his chair and hooked one foot over the edge of the desk. "Sounds nice. I called to see if you ever found your notebook."

"Oh, yeah, actually Doc found it. It had fallen down between the counter and the stove."

"That's great. Leave it up to that crazy cat to find it."

"Well, I was very relieved. Not only did it have my whole life, or at least this wedding, in it, but I thought it was a mouse."

"Well, as long as you found it and. . ."

"That's not all, Mike. I also had a very weird experience at the dress shop today."

Mike chuckled. "How weird an experience could you have at Penny's? Other than not being able to find shoes in the exact color you need?"

"Michael Turnquist, are you laughing at me?"

Mike struggled to keep a straight face, grateful for the telephone line and the miles separating them right now. "You know I wouldn't do that. I know how angry it makes you."

"I'll have you know, it wasn't about shoes."

Mike couldn't hold back his next chuckle.

"You are teasing me!"

"Yes, Love, I am. Now, I didn't call for a blow by blow description of your dress-buying spree, as much as I'm sure it was a blast."

"Then what did you call for?"

"I told you, I wanted to know if you found your notebook. And to let you know I won't be back for supper. I'm on a drop-dead deadline for this project. You and Tom and Sarah are on your own."

"I'll see you later, then."

Mike noted the exasperation in her voice. "Looking forward to it. We can catch up on all your exciting news then, okay?"

"Okay. Drive safely, Love."

Mike hung up the receiver, a thoughtful frown on his face.

What was Carly up to?

She never gave in without a fight.

* * *

Carly turned to face Jerry. "Do you want to tell me what's really going on here?" She held the telephone in her hand. "Or do I call the police?"

He met her question with the same innocent look Mike tried on her when he didn't want to answer a question. "I'm not sure I understand your question. Why do we need the police?" Jerry stood and stacked the plates. "I'll wash, since you cooked."

Carly's fists dug into her hips. Just once she'd like to feel bone through there. Just once. "Don't pull that answer a question with a question act with me. Mike does it all the time, and it doesn't work."

Jerry leaned against the counter top, plates still in his hands. "How is my big brother?"

Carly glared at him. "If you'd actually talked to him when you said you did, you'd know how he was. Why did you lie to me?"

He turned to the sink and turned on the hot water. "Did you think that?

Oh, I'm sorry if you got the wrong idea."

"I didn't misunderstand." She lifted the receiver to her ear. "What is going on here?"

"I'm sorry I didn't tell you the exact truth before."

"Exact truth? You said you talked to him and everything was fine. Which part of 'exact truth' wasn't the truth?" Carly thought of the child sleeping upstairs in her granddaughter's bed. "Who are you really?"

Jerry held his hands in front of him, palms facing Carly. "I'm sorry. I did call, but the line was busy. I kind of lost my nerve after that."

"Lost your nerve?"

"I guess I was hoping I could show you what a nice guy I am, and you could put in a good word with Mike for me." Jerry backed away from her, stopping when he reached the countertop. He leaned against the counter, his hands resting on the edge. He hung his head. "Like I said, we didn't exactly part on good terms."

"Why would I need to put in a good word for my husband's brother?"

"He might not be so happy to know I'm here."

Carly recalled a self-defense course she'd taken before her marriage. The instructor said to make slow moves, maintain eye contact, and never turn your back. Up until now, she'd never had to use much of that information. "So how did you know Mike wasn't here?"

Jerry pushed away from the counter. "I didn't. I figured if he was home, I'd get a chance to explain myself. When I found out he wasn't, I thought this would work, too. Let you get to know the new me, and you could vouch for me with Mike."

"The new you?" Carly's hand felt wet against the receiver. Her heart pounded in her chest and her mouth felt like a jar of cotton balls. This was the second time today she'd had the daylights scared out of her.

Jerry nodded. "Yeah. I've changed. I mean, I got the kid now. Figure me and Mike finally have something in common."

"I think it would be best for everyone if you left now and came back later when Mike is here."

"That will work. Can I leave Bradley here with you for a couple of hours?"

"Leave him here?" Carl gripped the phone tighter. One part of her wanted to help Jerry and Mike reconcile, but the other ninety-nine parts of her were afraid for her life. Still, what harm could a child do? "Where are you going?"

"I have a chance at a job, but I don't want to get Mike's hopes up before I know for sure." He tapped his fingers on the counter. "I haven't had the best of luck with employers. I just need a break for a change."

Carly mulled that over in her mind for a moment. Something still didn't seem quite right with his explanation, but she couldn't put her finger on it.

Jerry shrugged. "If you don't want me to leave him, I could take him with me. I just thought he'd be more comfortable sleeping in a real bed."

Carly dropped her hands to her sides and smiled. "I'm sorry, Jerry. I am under a lot of stress right now. Tom's wedding has my nerves on edge because somehow I ended up being in charge of all the arrangements."

Jerry stepped forward and faced her. "I'm sorry I came at a bad time."

Carly stepped back, running into the counter. Nowhere to go. She swallowed back the fear rising in her throat. "Mike will be thrilled you are here." She glanced at the clock on the stove. "Will you be back in time for supper? Mike won't be here, but Tom and his fiancée Sarah will be."

Jerry zipped up his light windbreaker and turned to the back door. "If I'm not, let Bradley know I'll be home in time to tuck him in tonight."

"Okay. I'll save you a plate of dinner. You can always warm it up later."

Jerry nodded and lifted his hand in a wave, then was gone through the door, letting in a blast of cool air and a couple of dead leaves.

Carly sighed as she bent to pick them up to toss in the trash. Jerry sauntered down the back walkway toward the alley as if he didn't have a care in the world.

As if he wasn't leaving his son in the hands of a perfect stranger.

She wished she could get rid of her problems and her worries as easily as those dead leaves.

Because she definitely had some worries.

About how Bradley would react when he woke up and found his father gone.

About how Mike would react to his brother dropping in from out of nowhere just days before the wedding.

About the wedding.

Oh, yes, and about the bank robbery no one else knew about.

* * *

Sarah strode down the sidewalk toward the parking lot, her heels clicking a soothing rhythm on the concrete. A glance at her watch confirmed she was on time to meet the client. Five more minutes to her car, twenty minutes to the client's office, and she'd still have five minutes to spare.

Five minutes meant she could stop and look once more at the pumps in the window of the shoe store next to the car park. She'd been eyeing them for a couple of weeks now, torn between justifying their purchase and convincing herself she didn't need another pair of shoes. She stopped and checked the display. Still not on sale. She pushed her bangs out of her eyes, glad she had an appointment on Saturday to get her hair done before the wedding. A fancy up-do of some kind. She'd leave the details to her stylist.

She allowed her thoughts to travel to her upcoming nuptials to the man of her dreams. Tom was everything she wanted in a husband. And if he was anything like his father—which she sincerely hoped—she'd made a good choice. Visions of her walking down the aisle of the church in Bear Cove filled her vision, and she lost herself in the daydream for a minute or so.

Movement out of the corner of her eye caught her attention. Across the street, a man lounged against the building as though trying to look as though he wasn't staring at her.

Which he was.

She'd noticed him when she exited her office building. Plaid hooded shirt, faded jeans, scuffed boots. Staring at the door—and her—his stance straightening as she pushed through the revolving doors.

And here he was.

≠≠ Unbalanced ≠≠

Still.

A shiver passed over her, reminding her of one of her grandmother's favorite expressions: feels like a goose walked over my grave.

She turned and headed for her car, suddenly aware of the dimly-lit basement level she generally chose because of its lower rates.

No more.

From now on, she'd park on the first level where there were plenty of light and lots of people around.

She rounded the corner, heading for the elevator, then decided to duck into a stairwell and see what happened.

Footsteps neared and she held her breath as she pressed against the cold concrete wall.

The same man sauntered past her, his hands shoved into his pockets, the profile of his face hidden by the hood, his build disguised by the bulky jacket and sloppy jeans.

No doubt in her mind, this guy was following her.

≠≠ Unbalanced ≠≠

Chapter 5

Carly opened one eye, glad to see the readout on the digital clock radio next to the bed. She still had more than three hours of snooze time. Next to her, Mike snored softly. She prodded him gently in the ribs, and he turned over, pulling the blanket and sheet with him. Tugging on the edge, she managed to retrieve enough of the covers to ward off the early morning chill.

Dinner had been a strange time without her husband. Jerry hadn't turned up to eat, and trying to explain to Bradley where his father was, when she didn't know either, only added to the disconnected feeling that had followed her ever since her trip downtown.

Still, the evening had gone better than she expected, especially when Mike came home to learn that his brother had shown up out of the blue. While he wasn't thrilled about Jerry's arrival, Mike made an effort to set Bradley at ease.

Carly rolled over and sat up, sticking her feet into her novelty cat slippers. She padded toward the bathroom to get a glass of water. On the way, she stuck her head in the spare bedroom to check on Bradley. Curled up in bed, the small child formed a tiny ball pressed against the wall, still clutching her granddaughter's teddy bear in his arms.

Carly smiled. There was nothing like a teddy bear to make a child feel safe and at home.

≠≠ Unbalanced ≠≠

Except maybe a parent's hug.

As she reached the bathroom door, a click from the direction of the back door echoed like a gunshot. Freezing in her steps, she waited. The door squeaked slightly, then another click. Her throat constricted, forming a lump as though she'd swallowed something the wrong way, and her heart pounded.

Someone was in the kitchen.

Glad the hall light was off, she shrank against the wall, uncertain whether to run to her bedroom, and Mike and the telephone, or to barricade herself into Bradley's room to protect the child. She held her breath at the telltale squeak where someone had walked on the bottom step coming upstairs.

Feeling along the wall for a weapon, a place to hide, anything, her hand hit the light switch, and instantly light bathed the hallway and stairway.

And so was Jerry, caught in the harsh glare, blinking. "Oh my gosh, Carly. You nearly drove me out of my skin!"

"I scared you? You're the one sneaking into my house at four o'clock in the morning, for crying out loud."

"Sorry. I didn't know you'd be out wandering the halls in your nightgown." He glanced at her feet. "And where did you get those slippers?"

She looked down. "I'll have you know Mike bought these for me on our last vacation."

Jerry smiled. "My brother, ever the romantic. Buys his wife furry tiger slippers."

"They're not tigers, they are cats. And they look just like our cat, Doc."

Jerry shoved his hands in his pants pockets. "Anyway. Sorry I scared you. Is Bradley all right?"

Carly gestured over her shoulder towards the spare room. "He's in there. You can crawl in with him, or sleep on the sofa. I guess we never got to the point of discussing the sleeping arrangements."

Jerry opened the door and peeked in. Closing the door, he turned to her. "I'll sleep on the sofa. Don't want to risk waking him."

Carly moved to the linen closet and took down bedding. "I'll get you a blanket and pillow."

"Don't worry about it. I'll use the afghan I saw there. I'll be fine."

"It might get chilly. Take the blanket." Carly yawned. "We can set up something more permanent later on."

"Okay. And thanks, Carly." He turned and walked down the stairs, flopping on the sofa. "Good night."

Carly returned to the bedroom. That Jerry was a strange fellow. Staying out until all hours. Leaving his child with someone he'd just met.

Because truth be told, even though they were related through marriage, Carly still felt like Jerry was a stranger.

And a strange stranger at that.

* * *

Despite feeling as if she'd only had three hours of sleep, Carly rose on the second snooze alarm. When Mike turned over to face her, she said she wanted to get to the grocery store early. He nodded and closed his eyes. Soft snoring told her he was already in his second sleep.

She showered quickly, dressed, and headed to her car. With two more mouths to feed, along with Tom and Sarah popping in at all times, there wasn't enough food in the pantry to sustain them all.

Moving quickly through the aisles of the small grocery store, she paused to check her list, then her watch. Everything she needed was in her cart, along with about ten items she'd forgotten to put on the list. Her watch said she had about twenty minutes to get home before Mike headed off for the day. She checked out quickly and drove home, stopping just short of driving over the morning paper in the driveway.

Before taking the grocery bags into the house, she picked up the paper and scanned the front page. Her gaze froze in horror on a headline: Local sleuth seeing things. She read on.

"One of Bear Cove's fine citizens has apparently been bored by the lack of crime in our fair town, and decided to make up some of her own where there is none to be found. Carly Turnquist told this reporter yesterday she witnessed a bank robbery, and that the robbers attempted to silence her by chasing her down Main Street with their car. The Bear Cove Police Department spokesperson has denied the incident occurred, and suggested Ms. Turnquist refrain from watching too much COPS TV. To date, no official report has been filed. The bank manager failed to return this reporter's telephone call up to press time. Ms. Turnquist, who has been active in several police investigations in the area, operates an accounting business that tracks down missing money. Perhaps her skills could be put to good use to track down this missing robbery."

Carly released a huge breath and leaned against the fender of the car. Great, just what she needed right now. An over-zealous intern reporter trying to make a name for himself.

What would Mike think?

* * *

Carly dropped her grocery sacks on the kitchen floor. Upstairs, Mike whistled softly. Carly smiled. The house was peaceful, the day was lovely, and Doc was curling around her ankles. On the surface, everything was fine.

But underneath, Carly's emotions swirled like a milkshake in a blender.

Except in this case, she felt like the one being chewed to pieces.

She put the groceries away, keeping the eggs, juice, milk, and other breakfast fixings on the counter. Deep in contemplation, she thought she was alone until Jerry cleared his throat softly.

Carly slapped a hand to her chest. "Goodness, you startled me." She looked past Jerry into the living room. He had folded the blanket neatly on top of the pillow. "Did you sleep okay?"

He rubbed a hand over his bristly jaw. "Sure did. Best night's sleep I've had in a week."

Carly smiled. "Good. Tonight we'll come up with something better for you."

Jerry dropped his gaze and shuffled his feet. "That would be great."

"Want some breakfast? Mike should be down shortly, and I can do eggs, pancakes, and cold cereal. You choose."

"Just coffee would be good."

Carly shoved the last of the cans into the cupboard. "Okay. Give me a minute to get the coffee started. Why don't you wake Bradley and you guys can get done in the bathroom before you come down?"

Jerry nodded and bounded up the stairs two at a time. Carly smiled. Considering how late he'd gotten in last night, he sure seemed to have a lot of energy. She turned to the near-antique coffee maker and set to filling the coffee and water reservoirs. Soon the percolator gurgled and bubbled, filling the kitchen with the heavenly smell of fresh-brewed java.

Carly closed her eyes and inhaled deeply. One of her favorite smells, guaranteed to relax and refresh her almost without having to drink a single drop. She shook her head. What was she thinking? Of course, she was going to have a cup of coffee. Maybe several cups. She had a busy day ahead of her, and already she was starting on a shaky foot.

On the counter lay the Bear Cove Register, the derogatory news article screaming at her from the front page. How was she going to break this to Mike?

* * *

Mike finished dressing and sat on the bed to put on his shoes. The clock radio had just shut off, telling him he needed to head downstairs to grab something to eat before heading out to his client's site for the day.

At the sound of voices in the hallway, he moved soundlessly to the door and peeked out. Jerry and Bradley walked to the bathroom, towels and toiletries in hand. Jerry casually looped his arm around Bradley's neck and pulled him close. The child squirmed away, and Jerry laughed softly.

Mike smiled at the picture before him. He remembered when he had felt too old for his father to hug. He'd been just about Bradley's age. His smile dropped. What he wouldn't give to have his father's arms around him now.

Mike checked his reflection one more time in the mirror. Long sleeve shirt open at the neck, grey chinos, grey loafers. Business casual. Not bad for a man in his fifties.

Early fifties.

Leaving the bedroom, Mike went down the stairs and into the kitchen. Carly was busy at the stove, her back to him. Walking softly, he slipped in behind her and put his arms around her, burying his face in the back of her neck. He breathed in deeply. "Hmm-mm, you smell good. Or wait, it's not you."

≠≠ Unbalanced ≠≠

He spun her around to face him. "It's the coffee and the pancakes that smell so good."

Carly flung her head back and laughed. "Nice thing to say to your wife. Pancakes smell better than I do."

"I didn't say that. I just said they smell good." He planted a kiss on her lips. "And don't forget, I mentioned coffee, too."

Carly mock-punched him in the arm. "Right, so you did. So I come in second-best if coffee is involved?"

Mike pulled one eyebrow down as he considered her statement.

She swatted him lightly on the chest. "Too long thinking. You lose."

He pulled her close, inhaling her shower-fresh scent mixed with the smells from the kitchen. "Oh, lady, I'd love you even if you didn't smell like breakfast."

Carly pushed him away. "Make yourself useful and set the table." She turned back to the stove. "For four. I don't think Tom and Sarah will be here this morning."

Mike took silverware from the drawer and plates from the cabinet, setting them on the small kitchen table. He paused to pet Doc, and watched as a squirrel ran up the tree outside the kitchen window then turned to Carly for more instructions.

"Milk and juice are on the counter. Syrup is in the cupboard next to the stove. And glasses."

"Boy, she sure has you trained well."

Mike jumped at the voice that sounded so nearly like his own. Their mother had often complained because she got them mixed up on the phone. A bittersweet longing to hear his mother's voice again welled up inside him. He pushed it away reluctantly. Maybe another time he could wax nostalgic. "Hello, little brother."

"Hello, big brother." Jerry gestured to the small boy standing beside him. "Bradley, this is your Uncle Mike. Mike, Bradley."

Bradley pulled back, and Mike squatted in front of him, holding out his hand. "Good morning, Bradley. Nice to meet you."

≠≠ Unbalanced ≠≠

Tentatively, Bradley put his hand in Mike's. For an instant. Then he gripped his father's leg again.

Mike stood. "I hope you brought an appetite. Carly has made enough pancakes to feed an army." He indicated the table. "Have a seat. We'll have the food on the table in a minute."

Jerry directed Bradley to the table, pulled out a chair and sat next to his son. Bradley sat quietly and watched his father pour a glass of juice. Jerry spoke quietly to the child, and a tiny smile flitted across the boy's face. Nodding, he lifted the glass and drained the juice.

Mike carried the platter of pancakes to the table and Carly followed with the sausage and hash browns. Jerry served some for himself and his son, then passed the dishes to Carly. Bradley picked up his fork and began shoveling hash browns in. Jerry touched the boy's arm. The child flushed and set his fork down. He chewed his mouthful of food, took a small sip of juice from the glass his father refilled, and swallowed.

Jerry smiled at Carly. "Sorry if our manners seem a little rough. It's been a while since we've been in a home with a lady."

Carly smiled. "I understand. I know how Mike and Tom can be after just a few days away from home."

Noting Jerry's plate was nearly empty, Mike offered him the pancake platter. Jerry slid four more pancakes on to his plate and doused them with syrup.

Carly stood and went to the counter for the coffee carafe.

Mike nodded and she refilled his cup. "So, what do you have planned for today, Jerry?"

Jerry swallowed the mouthful he was chewing before answering. "I have a couple of things I need to do. Can I leave the kid with you?"

Mike glanced at Carly, instantly recognizing the crestfallen look that passed over her face. He knew that look. Her I-want-to-say-no-but-I'm-too-polite look. He touched the hand that clutched her coffee cup. Her eyes searched his face.

He turned to his brother. "Jerry, we'd love to help, and if you'd given us some notice you were coming, we probably could have rearranged our schedules."

Jerry held his hand in front of him. "No problem, bro. I can take him with me. He can wait in the car." He tousled his son's hair. "Right, kid? You're used to that."

Mike's stomach flip-flopped. He disliked leaving children unattended in cars. The weather was cold out there right now and not likely to get a whole lot warmer. Early spring in Bear Cove was usually harsh. "Can you rearrange your schedule to run your errands tomorrow, Jerry? Then either Carly or I could watch Bradley, or maybe Tom—"

"Don't trouble yourself, Mike. I know it's my fault for just dropping in on you like this. Next time I'll remember that maybe my brother will be too busy to just stop his life and help me out." Jerry stood suddenly, pushing his chair back. He grabbed Bradley's arm. "Come on, kid. Let's get out of their way."

Mike looked at Carly.

She sat still, her hand holding her coffee cup, her mouth hanging slack.

"Jerry, please wait. Let's discuss this first." He stood and followed Jerry. "Carly, can you rearrange your day? Maybe I can call my client—"

Jerry pushed Bradley ahead of him towards the front door. "Don't worry about us, Mike. We'll be fine." He reached the front door. With one hand on the knob, he turned to look at Mike and Carly. His face contorted into a sneer. "Just like old times, hey, brother? You and me could never agree on anything."

* * *

Carly's mouth went dry, and the pancakes in her stomach felt like they had turned to lead.

Do something. Stop him.

Her heart cried out to her husband, but no words worked their way over her tongue.

Bradley seemed to have shrunk into himself. In fact, the louder his father got, the smaller he became. Carly understood his reaction. Her father had been a loud and boisterous man. While never mean, he'd still frightened her when he spoke too loudly. "Jerry, we can make plans for the next few days to help you out. Just give us a chance."

Jerry's face relaxed slightly as he looked at her. "Sure, Carly. We can work something out."

Carly smiled. "Great. Will you be home for dinner? We usually eat around six."

"Maybe, maybe not. I'll call and let you know."

Carly knelt in front of Bradley. "Here, let me help you with your jacket. It's cold out there." The child allowed her to finish fastening the button, even offering a tiny smile. Carly's heart melted at the sight. "Would you like to come back again?"

Jerry pulled Bradley closer to him. "Like I said. I'll let you know."

Carly tugged the boy's cap over his ears. "See you later."

Jerry opened the door and pushed his son through. "Right."

"Call if you aren't coming back for dinner. Otherwise, we'll expect you at six. Tom and Sarah will be here, too, so you'll get a chance to meet them."

Jerry followed his son out the door and down the sidewalk, opening the car door for him. Carly kept her eyes pinned to the small child in the passenger seat as Jerry struggled to get the old jalopy started. When the engine finally caught, a huge plume of black smoke belched out. Squealing tires and several backfires later, and the car was gone down the street.

Carly's heart sank as they left. She still wasn't sure how she felt about Jerry, but she knew Bradley desperately needed someone to love him. Somehow their departure seemed very final.

* * *

Jerry checked the rear view mirror several times as they headed down Main Street. Mike had landed in a pretty town. A bit small for his liking, but pretty. In the distance, the sun reflected off the ocean, making it appear as if there were giant diamonds floating in the harbor.

Giant diamonds. If only he could a big haul of diamonds, to just pick them out of the water. Like his last job. Play a joke on someone, Chad said. No risk. No cops.

Seemed too easy.

≠≠ Unbalanced ≠≠

But everything went according to plan.

Too easy, almost.

Until he nearly ran over the woman on the sidewalk. And not just any woman.

His brother's wife.

When she'd opened the door that first time, he'd prayed for the walkway to open up and swallow him, certain she'd recognize him.

But if she had, she didn't say.

Of course, her being in the wrong place at the wrong time wasn't his fault. And if Chad hadn't insisted on creating a scene by squealing the tires out of there, he wouldn't have fishtailed the car and hit the planter.

Not. His. Fault.

It never was.

And if he told himself that often enough, he'd eventually believe it. And maybe, someday, it would even be true.

He glanced across the seat at his son. Take the kid for example. Cute, but he could be a pain in the neck. Who would have thought his mother would just take off and leave her kid? Weren't mothers supposed to look after their kids, even if the marriage went south?

South. Jerry smiled to himself. South is where he should be right now. He should have taken the money from his last job and gone to Mexico or Venezuela or somewhere warm. But no, what does he do? He uses it to buy this piece of crap car instead. He should settle down and make a home for the kid. Get him in school. Be like a real family.

Jerry snorted. Real family. Right. A loser like him and a kid who is afraid of his own shadow.

Making the turn from Main Street on to the highway access, Jerry reached over and turned on the radio. "See if you can find a station."

Bradley obediently fiddled with the knob, drawing in static and gobbledygook. After several minutes, Jerry sighed. Kid couldn't even find a radio station.

"Never mind. I'll find one." Turning the knob slightly, the static lessened and a male voice spoke. Sounded like the news or community bulletin board or something like that. "That's how you do it, kid." Jerry leaned back in the seat and adjusted the side view mirror slightly. Adjusting the seat back, he settled his head on the headrest. "Relax, kid, we've got a long drive ahead of us."

The voice on the radio droned on about bake sales and card games and 4-H shows, mesmerizing Jerry. He was only half-listening until a familiar name was mentioned "... son of Mike and Carly Turnquist of our very own Bear Cove is getting married this Saturday. The ceremony will be at the Bear Cove Bible Chapel, and everyone is welcome to attend. That's at three o'clock in the afternoon, so mark your calendar to come celebrate with them."

Jerry puckered his lips slightly. Mike's son getting married. Right. Carly mentioned that. How time flew when you were having fun. Maybe he should plan to stick around for the wedding. Been a long time since he'd gone to a wedding. Somehow, Mike forgot to invite his little brother to his wedding.

He snorted. More likely Mike didn't want him around. Still, he just might show up at this one. See what kind of hobnobbing Mike was doing these days. Never know what business opportunities might arise from such a happy occasion.

Yes indeed. You just never knew.

Jerry swung the car around and headed back to Bear Cove. Maybe he could scare up a job or two to keep him busy for the next few days. He'd need some help, but he knew just who to call.

≠≠ Unbalanced ≠≠

≠≠ Unbalanced ≠≠

Chapter 6

Carly scanned the list of chores she needed to accomplish today. Tackle the breakfast mess in the kitchen first, she decided, then move on to other housecleaning.

Mike was gone for the day, but he promised to be home on time for dinner. No way she wanted to be alone if Jerry and Bradley showed up. She put the dirty dishes in the dishwasher and set the appliance to heavy-duty clean since she wasn't taking the time to scrape plates today. Wiping down the counters and the stove took just a few minutes.

Taking a quick appraisal of her work, she smiled as she remembered one of her grandmother's favorite sayings: There, you'd never say we had a party here.

And while breakfast and the ensuing uncomfortable moment with Jerry hadn't exactly been a party, she had managed to feed four people in short order. For a woman who hadn't learned to cook until she left home as an adult, not too bad.

Next on her list was to fix up a proper place for Jerry to sleep. She pushed open the door to the room her granddaughter Margie slept in when she stayed over and spotted the cat on the bed.

"Doc, you lazy thing. Who said you're allowed to sleep in here?" Sitting on the edge of the bed, Carly stroked his orange marmalade fur. "Well, if you're going to stay, you can help me get this room ready for Jerry and Bradley." She stood, hands on hips. "I think the room is big enough for me to bring in the roll-away cot, and Jerry can have the bed while Bradley camps out on the cot. What do you think?" Doc yawned widely. "You're not really very interested, are you?"

Carly squinted as she considered the space in the room. "If I add a sleeping bag, Bradley would think it was like camping. Kids like to camp out, don't they?" Doc stood and did his best Halloween cat stretch in response. "Right. Like your opinion really counts."

Getting the room ready consumed her for the next half hour as she made sure both Jerry and his son would feel welcome and comfortable. As she worked, her mind wandered back to the bank robbery no one else seemed to know anything about. How could she have been so wrong? Had she been working too hard?

One quick last-minute inspection of the room before she pulled the door shut and carried Doc into the hallway brought a smile to her face. But one slight discrepancy caught her eye. She moved the teddy bear from the bed to the cot. Bradley seemed to appreciate the toy last night, and teddy bears like hugs.

Next on the list was the list itself. She poured herself another cup of coffee and sat at the table, the cordless phone beside her. A glance at her notes reminded her to make confirmation calls to the photographer, florist, and cake shop. She penciled in her hair appointment for Saturday, shivering once again at the offer of a perm.

Calls made, coffee cup empty, she chewed on the end of her pencil. As she did, her stomach growled. The small cuckoo clock in the kitchen sounded. Wow. Almost lunch time. Where had the morning gone? She microwaved a cheese sandwich—her version of grilled cheese, and sat to eat. She switched the radio on to keep her company, just in time to catch the noon news.

Sitting at the table, ready to take her first bite of sandwich, the local news came on. Instantly her ears perked up.

"... of the Bear Cove Police Department would not confirm the report of a robbery at the Aroostook National Bank here in Bear Cove yesterday. One person, our very own Carly Turnquist, has told our reporter she witnessed a bank robbery. However, there has been no other evidence of this robbery. In another story ..."

Carly set her uneaten lunch down and tuned out the rest of the news. A rookie reporter making sarcastic remarks in his first byline was one thing. But having the story broadcast over the airwaves was something altogether different. Much more serious. Her heart raced as she considered her options. Matthew Richie she could deal with, but she didn't know anyone personally at the radio station.

Grabbing the phone book, she scanned the listings for the station and dialed, asked for the News Room, and waited while the call transferred. An automated message thanked her for calling and invited her to leave a message. Carly responded by hanging up.

She needed to deal with this in person.

* * *

A brisk walk to the small radio station housed upstairs over the flower shop did little to dispel Carly's frustration. She took several deep breaths intended to calm her spirit and slow her racing heart, but instead was rewarded with a short coughing fit from the cold air. She turned the old brass doorknob and strode into the office. One thing she had learned over the years was to appear confident and in control. People understood confidence and control.

She just hoped she could pull off confident and in control dressed in jeans and a sweatshirt.

The small inner office smelled of popcorn, and Carly's stomach growled again. She'd rushed off before she'd actually eaten her now cold and congealed cheese sandwich. Sighing against the irony, she stepped to the only desk in the room.

A short woman sat with her back to the door, typing on an old Remington typewriter. Carly stood for a minute.

The woman kept typing.

Carly waited.

No response.

Carly cleared her throat softly.

Still no response.

Finally, Carly spoke. "Excuse me?"

When there was still no reaction, Carly reached across the desk and tapped the woman on the shoulder.

Whirling around, the older lady caught herself on the edge of the desk with one hand, the other one clasped to her chest. "My goodness, you scared the bejumpins out of me."

Carly stepped back in alarm, holding her hands in front of her, palms facing the woman. "Sorry. I guess you didn't hear me come in."

The woman muttered something about people barging in and not announcing themselves, even as she reached to her right ear and fiddled with something. To Carly it looked like the woman was getting ready to clean out her ears, which, given the circumstances, would have been advisable.

The woman fixed beady eyes set slightly too close together on Carly. "What can I do for you?"

"I need to speak to whoever is in the News Room."

Picking up her coffee cup, the woman peered at Carly over the rim. "What for?"

The abrupt question caught Carly off guard. Just what was she hoping to accomplish by her visit here? Set someone straight? Get them to retract their story? Get more information?

"I wanted to get some information on a news story I just heard on your station."

The woman set her coffee cup down before reaching a gnarled hand across the desk. "I'm Molly. I guess I am the News Room. Truman Quick is my son, and he does the announcing and engineering stuff. What did you want to know?"

Carly pulled a vinyl chair sitting near the door closer to the desk, then sat down. "It's about the bank robbery."

Molly laughed, a low rumble starting in her chest and ending in a phlegmy cough. She pulled a tissue from a box on her desk and turned away from Carly.

Carly averted her eyes to the ceiling, noting the dust and stained tiles. Must have had a leak at some point. Could use a good cleaning.

Molly tossed the tissue into a nearby trashcan and turned back to face Carly. "Now, where were we?"

"I was asking about the bank robbery."

"Right. That's why I laughed. Because there wasn't a bank robbery."

Carly placed her hands on the desk. "Oh, but I was—"

She stopped. She didn't know this woman. This woman didn't know her. Maybe she should keep the details under her hat. At least for now.

Molly squinted. "You were what?"

Carly smiled her most appealing smile. "I was hoping you could help me with some research I'm doing."

Molly leaned back in her chair. "Like for an article or something?"

"Something like that." She certainly didn't want to lie, but what Molly thought she needed the information for was entirely up to Molly. She couldn't control what conclusions people jumped to. She had a hard enough time controlling her own conclusions. "Do you have some time?"

Molly rolled her chair to a two-drawer file cabinet and pulled out the bottom drawer. Her fingers did the walking for a half-dozen files or so, until they came to the one she was looking for. "Here it is. I filed it under 'bank robbery', although there wasn't a robbery." Her chesty cough once again necessitated the tissue. "Excuse me. Getting over something."

Right. Like a two-pack-a-day habit.

Carly's stomach did a quick flip-flop. She swallowed hard, willing the bile in her gut to stay down. She forced her mouth to turn up at the corners. "How do you know for sure there wasn't a robbery?"

Molly leaned back in her chair and counted on her fingers. "Let's see. The police said it didn't happen, the bank manager said it didn't happen, there were no witnesses except this one crazy woman." She squinted in thought. "Oh, yeah, and the guard."

"The guard?"

"Right. This woman said she saw the guard shooting at the getaway vehicle?" Molly leaned forward, elbows on the desk. "He didn't go in to work that day. He called in sick."

* * *

Mike stared at the computer screen, willing the debugging routine to hurry up and finish.

The great thing about computers is they only hurry when you delete the wrong thing.

He leaned back in his chair and smiled, his eye catching sight of the telephone. He needed to hear Carly's voice. To know that at least some part of his life was normal. He picked up the handset and dialed, listening to the rings. Four, five, answering machine. "Hi, Carly. Just had a few minutes. Wanted to check in. Give me a call when you get home."

The numbers and characters streamed across the computer screen, his program running like a top. There was a certain pleasure in watching his work do its job. But still, there was some little thing wrong, as evidenced by the incomplete results on a report he was testing.

Kind of like Jerry, he thought. He remembered the day Jerry had stunned his parents by announcing he had no intention of going to college, and instead was going to head out 'on the road', to 'find himself'. Find himself? Mike's father asked Jerry where he'd gotten lost that he needed to find himself. In reality, Jerry wasn't looking, except for a reason to run.

And run he did. Mike hadn't heard word one from him for nearly four years. And even then, the only reason Jerry called was to borrow bail money.

Mike sent the small amount, hoping this was the wakeup call Jerry needed. Turned out, he was wrong. The pattern continued for years, with Jerry showing up like a bad penny every three or four years.

Until about eleven years ago. When Mike refused to give him money.

And that was the last time he'd heard from Jerry until now. In fact, he hadn't even been sure Jerry was still alive.

Mike brought his focus back to the screen. Lines of programming language filled the screen, a diverse mixture of commands and directions, all pointing toward the final goal.

≠≠ Unbalanced ≠≠

Not much like life, but at least predictable.

Unlike Jerry. Or maybe just like Jerry. He was predictable in his own way. Certain to mess up, sure to come asking for money at some point. Guaranteed to get angry and leave.

He will always hurt you and break your heart.

Yet he was family. And in the end, sometimes family is all a person has.

Maybe there was hope for Jerry after all. He had a son now. Could this be his attempt at settling down, providing a home for the boy, making up for lost time?

Mike shook his head. Unlikely. But he'd give Jerry a chance to redeem himself.

Everyone was worth saving.

Everyone was redeemable.

Even a screw-up like Jerry.

* * *

Jerry cruised around Bear Cove looking for a pay phone. He sighed in frustration. So many cell phones, so few pay phones anymore. Spying one in the parking lot of a convenience store, he pulled a sharp right turn without signaling, earning a blare on the horn from the car behind him. He gave the driver the one-finger salute before pulling to a stop next to the phone booth. Leaving the car running, he fished in the ashtray for some coins. Beside him, Bradley held on to the door handle to keep from sliding off the slick vinyl car seat.

Jerry reached outside the car to press the door release. The piece of junk door on this piece of junk car wouldn't open from the inside. "I'll be right back." Peripherally he took in the boy's silent nod of acknowledgment. Inside himself, Jerry smiled. If he had done only one thing right, at least the kid was obedient. "Stay here."

Jerry dropped some coins in the phone slot and listened for dial tone before dialing the number he knew by heart. As he waited for the person on the other end to answer, he shivered against a sudden cool wind off the harbor. Blowing out a breath, he watched the cloud float away on the brisk sou'wester.

Not wanting to stand outside any longer than necessary, he concluded his business quickly and was back in the car within three minutes.

Bradley huddled against the passenger door. Kid was scared of his own shadow. He needed some toughening up.

Jerry reached over and pulled the child closer to him. "Want to go shoot some hoops? I bet there's a park near here."

At Bradley's silent nod, Jerry tousled his hair then jammed the car into drive, squealing the tires as he left the parking lot. He'd seen a park just down the road from the bank.

As he drove, he thought about the news on the radio. For whatever reason, the cops were denying the first robbery had even happened. He figured this bank deserved a second chance to make the headlines.

And he was just the guy to help.

* * *

The afternoon went by in a blur as Carly tried to come up with a logical explanation for what was going on. While the wedding planning had been stressful, she was sure she wasn't losing her mind.

Yet everyone else seemed to think she was.

Knowing if she tried to work, she was likely to mess something else up, instead she concentrated on cooking and cleaning. Homemade soups were easy to make, no-brainers really, and always a welcome lunch substitute. And as her mother used to say, a house could never be too clean.

While a couple of pots simmered on the stove, she occupied her energies on scrubbing tiles and cleaning toilets while her mind focused on the conundrum at hand. Had she really seen McMasters, or had she merely expected to see him? And what about the broken flower planter and tail light? If this was a cover-up, someone must have gotten rid of the evidence.

And if she really hadn't seen those things, then what? She wasn't on any medication. She hadn't been drinking alcohol. Her eyesight was fine, and she didn't sleepwalk.

Carly rinsed out her cleaning rag and looked around the bathroom. Spying a fleck of dust up in the corner, she stood on the toilet lid to reach. She stretched on her tiptoes, straining to snag the errant bit of fluff when she felt something wrap itself around her ankles.

Startled, she lost her balance. Realizing in that split second she was going to fall, she grabbed at the nearest thing she could lay hands on.

Unfortunately, the vinyl shower curtain and tension rod had not been designed to hold her weight.

Her ribs hit the side of the tub, her shoulder connected with the ceramic tile floor, and stars flashed in front of her eyes before everything went dark.

* * *

Jerry pulled his jalopy into the driveway behind Mike's car. He glanced at the clock on the AM radio, noting he was just a couple of minutes past six. No point in letting them think he was anxious to spend time with them—better to let them think he wasn't coming at all.

Rather than having to move his car later, he put the car into reverse and backed down the driveway. Pulling into an empty parking space in front of the house, he nudged Bradley. "Come on, buddy. Let's see if their offer for supper was real or not."

Bradley's eyebrows shot up and a huge smile filled his face. "We get to eat with them again?"

Somewhere deep in Jerry's heart he felt a twist at the boy's words. "Well, that's what they said last time I talked to them."

His gruff manner and rough handling of the boy were for the kid's own good—toughen him up to be a man. That's how his father raised him, and look how he turned out.

Right, look how you turned out, Jerry old boy. Living in a car, single dad, son afraid to look you in the eye. No job, no way out.

Jerry eyed his son. "What did you say?"

Bradley dropped his gaze and his smile. "Nothing, Dad. I didn't say nothing."

Jerry grabbed the boy's arm and squeezed, perversely pleased at the grimace of pain the gesture provoked. "You're not making fun of me, are you?"

"No, sir, I wouldn't do that."

≠≠ Unbalanced ≠≠

Jerry mock-punched Bradley's arm. "Good. Let's see if they left us some scraps."

Bradley scooted over on the seat toward his father, and Jerry leaned out to unlatch the door. Today the passenger door handle had let go inside the door, and while Jerry had lambasted the boy, blaming him, he knew the kid hadn't broken the latch. He struggled enough to keep this wreck running, let alone keep the hundreds of other parts fixed. When he thought about the work needed, being able to get in and drive seemed more important than a door handle.

Or a seat belt.

Jerry slammed the door, smiling at the satisfying thud as the door latch connected. Yes, siree, Chrysler made the best two-door cars in the country. No need to slam them, really. He just liked to hear the solid sound of metal on metal, a mark of good workmanship.

The two walked up to the front door without speaking. Having spent the entire day together, there wasn't much else to talk about. Jerry snorted. Fact was, he didn't know what to talk about with the kid ever. They acted like strangers around each other most of the time.

He rang the doorbell and waited, running his fingers through his curly hair, checking out his reflection in the glass. Sideburns tinged with grey. A lot more than Mike had, even though he was four years younger. Well, why not? Mike had life easy, while he always had to work extra hard to get what he had.

He turned to glance at the child and his gaze passed over the car parked on the street. Oh, yes, he had a lot to show for his hard work, didn't he?

* * *

Mike groaned inwardly when the doorbell rang. He didn't need visitors right now. Carly sat on the toilet lid, a damp washcloth wrapped around ice cubes she held to her right shoulder, wincing every time she moved.

"Honey, I've got to go answer the door. Keep the ice on that bruise. Luckily you didn't hit your head, or I'd have you carried out of here no matter what you said." He stood, stiff from sitting on the floor for the past thirty minutes. "I'll be right back."

≠≠ Unbalanced ≠≠

She nodded, adjusting slightly. He pushed her hand back to where the ice needed to be, and she smiled at him. Striding to the door, he noted the time on the clock in the kitchen as he went past: five minutes after six.

The kids weren't at the door, because he'd already called them and asked them not to come over tonight. When they heard of Carly's fall, they argued but he was adamant. She didn't need people hovering over her. She was going to be all right and refused to go to the walk-in clinic or the hospital. Finally, Tom and Sarah had agreed to let her rest that evening, but made Mike promise to call them if anything changed.

He pulled open the front door with more force than was necessary, but his worry about Carly had turned his normal laid-back attitude into impatience and frustration. He opened his mouth to ask whoever was there to come back another time.

The words caught in his throat. His brother and his nephew stood in front of him. Like invited guests. Like family.

Which of course they were.

He snapped his mouth shut against his disappointment. They were the last people he wanted to see right now.

And the last people he would turn away.

Instead, he pulled the door open wider. "Come on in." He glanced back the hall at the bathroom. A shadow moved through the doorway and disappeared down the hallway. Looked like Carly was going back to their bedroom. "Don't stand out there all night. You'll let the flies out." He smiled his best loving-uncle smile at Bradley. "Hi, big guy."

The boy stepped into the living room, his father close behind. Mike noted the child's glances toward the kitchen. "Sorry, we invited you for dinner, but there isn't anything ready to eat."

Bradley's smile fell away, and he moved closer to his father.

Mike squatted down to look the child in the eye. "Carly fell and hurt her shoulder, so she didn't get dinner cooked. How does pizza sound?"

The boy smiled shyly, not looking directly at Mike. Mike clapped him on the shoulder. "Great. I'll call and order up a couple of extra-large extra specials.

≠≠ Unbalanced ≠≠

And soda. And maybe some cinnamon sticks for dessert."

Jerry stepped forward. "Look, Mike, if this is a bad time, we can go."

Mike shook his head. "No way. Carly told me to make sure you both got something to eat, and she made up your room so you could both sleep in there tonight." He looked at Bradley again. "She even made it like you're going camping, with a sleeping bag, and a cot, and a lantern, and everything. Why don't you guys get cleaned up while I order the pizza, then check out your room?"

Jerry nodded. "Sounds like a plan. Come on, camping buddy."

Mike checked the fridge door for the number of their favorite pizza parlor. Having ordered their dinner, he headed back upstairs to check on his wife.

He wasn't sure how, but somehow drama followed Carly wherever she went.

Even when she didn't go anywhere at all.

* * *

Carly's shoulder and ribs hurt, but she was thankful she hadn't landed on her face. She didn't need to worry about a black eye or a broken nose just days before her son's wedding. She lay on her bed, grateful the room was cool and dark, and listened to the drone of voices downstairs. She dozed off for a few minutes, waking when Mike sat next to her.

Opening her eyes, she smiled. "Everything under control?"

The smile on his face didn't quite make it to his eyes. "As always. Pizza is on its way. Jerry and Bradley are cleaning up for dinner. And the color is coming back in your face, which is a good sign."

She laid her hand on his forearm. "I'm sorry if I gave you a scare."

"Scare? Me?" He pointed his index finger at his chest. "Not me. I'm coming to expect you to turn an otherwise quiet, uneventful day into a soap opera."

Carly lowered one eyebrow and squinted. "Are you saying I do this on purpose?"

He gathered her into his arms and held her as tenderly as a newborn.

≠≠ Unbalanced ≠≠

"No. It just seems to happen."

Carly cuddled into his chest for a few moments, savoring the strong feel of his arms around her. She felt so safe there, cradled from the world.

And then she remembered—three hungry men—well, two-and-a-half—expecting dinner on the table.

Carly pushed herself upright, nearly upending Mike from the edge of the bed. "I need to get up. Get dinner on the table."

Mike shook his head. "You are not lifting a finger around this house tonight. We can manage to slice a pizza and get it on plates."

She swung her legs over the side of the bed. "Don't be ridiculous. I'm fine. See?" She stood, swaying a little at first as the room spun around, but feeling more secure as her head cleared. "I'm fine."

"You are not fine. You fell and hit your shoulder hard on the floor. You've got bruises, and you're lucky nothing was broken."

Carly took a couple of steps. "I feel fine. Nothing a few slices of pizza and a soda wouldn't cure." She smiled at Mike. "And I can't stay in this room all night. I'll go stir-crazy."

"I don't know about this."

"I'll make a deal with you. I'll help with dinner, and I promise if I feel woozy or anything, I'll let you know, and you can take me to the clinic." She held out her hand. "Deal?"

Various emotions moved across her husband's face—worry, frustration, a desire to take care of her, and even love.

He should never play poker.

Then he nodded, grasping her hand in his, and laying his other hand on top of hers. "Deal."

He pulled her into his arms, and they held each other close. Carly was glad of his solid presence next to her as the room spun for a moment.

The doorbell rang, jolting them from their embrace. Mike reached for his wallet and pulled out some cash. "Pizza delivery."

Carly followed him down the hallway, taking the stairs carefully and holding the handrail tightly. She had a couple of dizzy waves, but each one seemed to pass more quickly than the last, and she made her way downstairs without further incident.

Coming into the brightly lit kitchen, she blinked several times, the ache in her head intensifying with the light. She glanced at Doc's dishes, which needed refilling. Bradley sat at the table quietly, his father next to him. Carly smiled at the child when he looked at her, worry evident on his face.

"Would you like to help me feed our cat, Doc?"

Bradley looked to his father, who nodded.

The child jumped down off his chair. "I sure would."

Carly pointed to the bag of cat food in the corner of the kitchen. "You can put a scoop of food into his dish, and fill up his water dish with the bottle in the fridge."

At the sound of the chunky bits falling into his dish, Doc materialized as if out of nowhere. Bradley proudly completed his tasks, then stroked Doc's back as the cat ate. Doc arched his back against the boy's touch, and he pulled his hand back.

Carly sat in her chair. "Don't worry. That means he likes you petting him."

Bradley reached out again and touched the cat's back, and Doc stopped eating. Winding his way around the boy's legs, the old cat meowed softly. Bradley held out his hand, and Doc sidled up to him, lifting his chin.

Mike came in the kitchen carrying two large pizza boxes and several bags. "Go ahead, scratch him under his chin. He really likes that."

Jerry took the pizza boxes while Mike set the bags on the table, opening each one in turn. "Soda. Dessert. Napkins. Dipping sauces." He looked around the room. "I think we're all set. Let's eat."

Soon they were chattering away like they'd been eating together for years. Carly was especially pleased when Bradley opened up and joined the conversation.

At the end of the meal, as they munched on cinnamon bread, Jerry tossed his napkin on his plate. "I have a favor to ask. I have a job offer in Riverton tomorrow, and I was wondering if you could look after the kid for me?

≠≠ Unbalanced ≠≠

There's a guy has as good as given me the job, and I might be gone for two or three days. Can you do it?"

Carly's head pounded anew. Two or three days would take her to Friday, and the wedding was on Saturday. There was still a lot to do to get ready. Plus there was this whole thing about the bank robbery that wasn't to get to the bottom of.

Yet, Jerry needed their help. They'd already put him off today. And if he got the job, he would be able to settle down and take care of his son properly.

She felt Mike's hand on hers. She didn't need to look at him; she already knew the answer.

She smiled at her brother-in-law. "We'd be happy to look after him for you."

The smile on Bradley's face was all the reward she needed.

≠≠ Unbalanced ≠≠

≠≠ Unbalanced ≠≠

≠≠ Unbalanced ≠≠

Chapter 7

The chill spring air of the next morning seeped in through the bedroom window, and Carly enjoyed the sight of the sunrise, its rays kissing the harbor lightly as a promise.

She stretched under the covers, thinking over the previous evening. Her life seemed to be taking on a mind of its own. If she wasn't busy enough before, now she had the added responsibility of caring for a young boy.

Yesterday looking after the child seemed like a good idea.

In the harsh reality of a new day, however, she wasn't so sure.

She pushed back the bedding, exposing one foot to the chill morning air like a swimmer testing the waters before taking the plunge. Grimacing, she pulled her foot back into the warmth of the covers.

I'm not getting up yet. No way.

She burrowed under the blankets, only dimly aware the other side of the bed was empty.

"Carly? You awake?"

Carly peeked from a fold in the bedding at her husband. "Go away. I'm not ready to face the world yet."

Mike sat on the edge of the bed, the springs creaking under his weight. "Want some coffee?"

Pulling back the bedding, she sniffed the air, her eyes closed. "You made coffee?"

Mike smiled, warming her heart like no blanket could. "I thought you might like to have your first cup in bed."

Carly sat up, squinting at him through eyes longing for more sleep. She ran her fingers through her hair before reaching for the mug he held out to her. Sipping the hot brew, she relished the bold flavor. "Good stuff. What's up?"

"Besides Bradley and me and Jerry, no one."

Carly sipped again. "The boys are up? What's going on?"

Mike shrugged. "I don't know about Jerry. He was already gone when I got up. I guess he left to drive to his interview." He folded his arms across his chest and smiled. "As for us, we're going fishing."

"Fishing?"

"Yeah, that sport where you tie a worm on a string and hope to catch a slimy water dweller."

Carly turned to prop her pillows behind her back before leaning back. "Right. Without falling in."

Mike's brows furrowed. "That only happened one time."

Carly laughed. "Our second date."

"You married me anyway, didn't you?"

Carly warmed her hands with the mug. "I figured you needed someone to look after you."

"Right. Anyway, we boys are going fishing. Bradley says he's never been, and I thought it might give us a chance to get to know each other."

"What about your client?"

Mike stood. "Because I stayed later yesterday, I got done what he needs for a couple of days. He already knew about the wedding on Saturday, so he was pushing to get as much done as we could for that. He doesn't think one more day off is going to make much difference."

"You told him about Bradley?"

Mike opened the closet door and reached inside. "Yeah, and he knows about young boys. He has four of his own."

"I'm glad you can spend the day with him. Gives me a chance to juggle my schedule a little so I can spend more time with him over the next couple of days." She pulled her foot back under the blanket, thankful for the extra warmth. "Do you need me to pack a lunch for you? Something to drink? A change of clothes?"

Mike shrugged into a down-filled vest. "Very funny. I'm not going to fall in."

Carly set her coffee cup on the night table then swung her legs over the side of the bed. She snugged her feet into her cat slippers before standing. A second or two of dizziness passed. "Says you."

"Says me." Mike pulled her close to him, planting a quick kiss on her cheek. "I made a lunch already, got lots of drinks, and Bradley is waiting downstairs for me. I showed him where Doc's food is, and he was going to take charge of the cat's needs, including litter box duty."

"How sweet of him to offer." Carly peered at her husband. "He did offer, didn't he?"

"Sort of. I said we all have chores around the house. I said he could do either trash duty or cat duty. He said he knew how to do the trash, and would like to learn how to take care of a cat. So I showed him."

"Bradley is a guest in our home, Mike. Guests don't do chores." Carly took a deep breath. She'd straighten this out later. "And he's a child."

"He isn't a guest, he's family. And if Jerry was here, he'd do chores, too." Mike released her and headed to the bedroom door. "We probably won't be home until late afternoon, but we'll be home for sure by supper."

"Should we plan on having fish for supper?"

Mike blew her a kiss. "Why don't we save the fish for breakfast tomorrow? Maybe you could cook up one of your world famous casseroles?"

"Right. And that covers you in case you don't catch anything except a cold when you fall in."

Mike waved off her suggestion as he headed down the hallway. "I'm not going to fall in. See you later."

Carly laughed again. "Sure. Got your cell phone?"

"Got it."

Carly listened to the sounds from the main floor as the two gathered their things and headed to the car. Within minutes, the house was quiet again, and Carly headed into the shower, determined to wash away the last vestiges of sleep and get on with her day. She had a lot to accomplish today.

Not to mention creating a world famous casserole.

* * *

The drive to the lake just outside town was never long enough for Mike. The early sun filtered through the trees, peppering the road with shadows that always reminded him of soldiers standing on guard. Small pockets of mist dotted the narrow strip of land between the asphalt and the forest. In the distance, a loon called out, its eerie wail raising the hair on Mike's arms. He loved this drive. He could almost hear the fish jumping. Licking his lips with relish, a sly grin pulled one corner of his mouth.

Take a change of clothes, indeed.

As they drove, Mike watched Bradley from the corner of his eye. The child seemed to have blossomed overnight. Where before the boy had been quiet and reticent, now he literally bounced in his seat.

At a stop sign, Mike turned to look at him. "Excited?"

Bradley nodded, not taking his eyes off the surrounding countryside. He'd asked questions about the various buildings as they drove through Bear Cove. He pointed to one in particular. "That's the bank my dad went into."

"Really? When did he go in the bank?"

"The day we came to your house."

"The bank wasn't closed?"

"Not when my dad went in."

"Did you see anyone else go in the bank with him?"

Bradley looked out the side window. "I'm not supposed to talk about it. My dad said it's a secret and a surprise." He pointed to one of the long wooden buildings built over the beach. "What's that?"

"That's called a chandler. They provide supplies for the fishing boats, like ropes, nets, lobster traps, and stuff like that."

Bradley nodded. "Cool."

"Maybe we could go and see it tomorrow. It kind of looks like a huge store full of all kinds of strange stuff."

Bradley nodded again, bouncing slightly on the seat. "Okay."

"What are you most excited about?"

"Catching a fish."

Mike smiled. "You know, even though we're going fishing, we might not bring home any fish."

He stopped bouncing. "We won't?"

"Well, I don't always catch fish when I go fishing."

His nephew chewed on his bottom lip. "My dad says if you don't come out ahead you shouldn't bother."

Mike heard his brother in the child's words. Jerry always had been about getting ahead. Looking both ways before pulling onto the highway, Mike waited until a motorcycle sped past before answering. "I guess it depends on what you consider 'coming out ahead' means. I think sometimes I use fishing as an excuse to just spend some time alone outdoors."

"I don't like to be alone."

Mike checked his odometer. A short rise almost hid the turnoff to the lake, and the county snowplows just about always knocked over the small sign in the winter. Having learned he couldn't depend on the sign, he watched for the turnoff by mileage.

Coming over a small rise, he slacked off on his speed, glancing in the rear view mirror. "Here's our road." He made a quick right turn, and the car bounced on to a gravel road that was barely visible from the highway.

Bradley grabbed the door handle as they slowed down. "Where did the road go?"

"This is just a small county park. People can't camp here. They mostly come to fish and have a picnic."

The winter had been hard on this little-used pathway through the brush, and the highways department hadn't been out to give the road its annual grading. Behind them, dust stirred up by the tires swirled in billows, drifting on the slight breeze. As they rounded a turn, the cloud of dust caught up with them, engulfing the car and momentarily blinding Mike. He braked gently to a stop, and the dust rolled over the car before settling back to the ground.

Bradley laughed. "That was like a snowstorm, Uncle Mike."

Mike started the car forward. "Yes, it was, and almost as hard to see through."

"The good thing about that storm is it wasn't cold."

Mike nodded. "Right. But the bad thing is you can't make snowballs from it."

"Is it much further?"

"Only a little bit." Mike smiled. "We'll stop at the parking area, use the facilities, and then walk on down to the lake."

Bradley pointed through the windshield, his eyes wide. Mike followed with his eyes. A couple of rabbits sat by the edge of the road. He gave them wide berth, passing them on the right.

Bradley peered out his window as the creatures ran off into the grass. "Wow. I never seen rabbits before. Except when they were in a cage, I mean, or on TV."

"Lots of rabbits out here. We'll probably see more today."

They drove around a curve in the road that opened into a parking lot. Scattered around the lot were several picnic tables and grills, as well as information boards, a small ranger station that was closed for the season, and a building housing the restrooms. Mike parked near one of the picnic tables and turned off the engine. Bradley had the door open almost before the engine stopped.

Mike reached over to touch the boy's arm. "Hold on there. We have to go over some rules, okay?"

Bradley sat back on the seat, arms folded across his chest. His bottom lip pouted out. "There's always rules."

Mike leaned back in his seat. Like father, like son. Jerry didn't much like rules, either. "We have rules to keep everyone safe. These are rules for me, too."

≠≠ Unbalanced ≠≠

Bradley looked at him. "You mean, like rules you got to obey, too?"

"Yes. Rules aren't rules if everyone doesn't have to follow them. And these are pretty simple. No going off alone. No going in the lake. No making loud noises."

Bradley smiled. "And no falling in the lake."

Mike laughed. They were going to have good day. "Right. No falling in the lake. For either of us."

* * *

Carly checked the clock on the stove as she poured her second cup of coffee. She still had a few minutes to relax, even given the extra time she'd spent in the shower. Pulling her notebook toward her, she flipped to yesterday's page, crossing off hair appointment and dress. Done. Call to photographer. Done. Florist, done. All in all, given the previous day's happenings, she'd still managed to get accomplish a lot.

Today's list included office work, calls to a potential client, and checking in with Sarah about the final guest list. That should still leave her time to check into what really happened at the bank yesterday and plan dinner.

Carly called the potential client and got voice mail. She left a short message, her phone number and email address, then hung up.

She checked "call client" off her list and slid the point of her pencil down to the next item. "Call Sarah", where once again she had to leave a message. "Hi, Sarah. Just checking in. Have you made calls to guests to see if they can make it? We're getting down to the wire with the caterer. I need to let them know tomorrow how many to prepare for. Give me a call."

Carly made a note in her book to follow up the next day with both the client and Sarah if she didn't get a return call. Picking up her coffee mug, she resolved to finish everything on her desk so she wouldn't have to think about office work until after the wedding. She loved the research and investigation portion of her work, but she hated the filing and routine paperwork needed in case she testified in court, which often happened. Being a forensics accountant could be exciting work but could also be mind-numbing boredom.

Sifting through her in-basket, Carly moved efficiently through the process. She created file folders and packed documents in boxes, greatly diminishing the pile of work. The phone rang as she stuck the last pieces of paper into its file.

Retrieving the cordless handset, she sank gratefully into her office chair. "Hello?"

"Hi, Carly. This is Pastor James. How are you?"

"Hi, Pastor. I'm ankle deep in wedding plans." Carly's stomach rose in her throat. "You aren't calling to tell me there's a problem with the wedding or the church for Saturday, are you?"

"No, not at all. I'm calling about you."

"Me? Whatever for?"

"Have you read the Aroostook Herald?"

"No-o-o. Should I?" Carly subscribed to the small daily newspaper that served the whole county, but she rarely read it. Bear Cove seldom managed to warrant publishing space, and life in the other towns and cities in the county didn't really interest her. The last time she'd done anything more with the paper than line the trashcan was when her granddaughter's picture was in the paper for winning the Riverdale spelling bee.

"I think you need to read the story on the bottom of the front page, Carly. And if there's anything I can do to help, let me know. I'll let you go now."

Carly stared at the receiver for a moment before pressing the off key. What could possibly be in the paper that she needed to read?

Heart pounding, she hurried to the front door. Grabbing the bundle of pages, she closed the door and returned to her office. Spreading the paper on her desk, she flattened the front page with her hand.

The headline read "The Robbery That Wasn't". Underneath was a file photo of Carly, taken at a fundraising function for the county children's hospital. Carly's mouth went dry as she read the account that made her sound like she was an eccentric headline grabber.

And to make matters worse, she read the byline. Bear Cove's own Matthew Richie.

With an AP attribution.

≠≠ Unbalanced ≠≠

The story was going national.

* * *

Mike drew a deep breath, relishing the cool wind on his face. The fog over the lake was just beginning to burn off, exposing sections of the near-still water. With the light breeze, the flies were out in full force on the water, and the plops and ripples indicated the fish were biting. If he could just get them to bite what he was offering, he'd be a happy man.

Actually, just being here, with Bradley, made him happy. He had spent some time showing the boy how to cast his line, reel the fly in, make the bait dance on the water. And most importantly, not to snag the small trees ringing the lake. The child had taken to fly-casting like a natural. Within a few minutes, he'd snagged his first bite.

Mike moved over to stand beside him, ready to offer assistance, net in hand to bring the catch to shore, if he ever got that far. "That's it. Hold your rod up. Keep the tip up. Okay, let the fish take some of the line and run with it. That's it. Not too much." Mike's heart pounded as the boy experienced the thrill of the catch. "Okay. Now, lay your hand against the reel, slow it down a little. Not too much. Wear him down some, but you don't want him to stop because he might try to dive to the bottom."

Bradley smiled up at Mike, his eyes dancing with joy. "Like this?"

Mike nodded. "Perfect. Okay, now start to wind the reel back. Make him come back towards you. Slow. Slow. You don't want to pull the hook out of his mouth. Good. You've got it."

The fish leaped from the water, the early sun glistening off its wet scales, reflecting back in rainbow colored hues.

Mike gasped. "Wow! That's the biggest trout I've seen in this lake. You've got yourself a keeper there."

Bradley pursed his lips as he concentrated on reeling in the fish. "I think he's getting tired. Do I go faster now?"

Mike shook his head. "He might be trying to trick you. Keep reeling steady. If you go too fast, he might pull back and the hook will pop out."

He acknowledged Mike's instructions with a nod and kept reeling. Once again, the fish breached the surface, tail flapping wildly from side to side, before plopping into the water, sending up a small spray. Mike stepped carefully into the water, extending the landing net. When the fish was within reach, Mike neatly scooped it up, holding the prize high over his head.

Bradley let out a whoop, and Mike held the net out for him to see his catch. "Golly, that's the biggest fish I ever saw."

Mike pushed two fingers into the gills and held the fish out for Bradley to see close up. "Want to hold it? I've got a camera in my backpack to take a picture."

At his nod, Mike demonstrated how to hold the fish by the gills. When he had a secure hold, Mike reached into his pack and retrieved his camera. With the lake and fog as the background, Mike snapped a picture of his nephew holding his first catch. The fish flapped its tail in an attempt to escape, and Bradley's smile fell away.

"I think I know why you don't always bring home fish."

"You do?"

The answer was so soft Mike wasn't sure he'd heard correctly. "Say that again?"

Bradley looked at the fish. "I'd like to let him go." The fish jumped in his arms, and the boy nearly lost his grip. "Can I?"

Mike nodded. "I'll show you how. But it has to be his decision whether he lives or not."

"What do you mean?"

Mike took the fish from the child. "He has to want to live. If he doesn't, and we let him go, he'll just die anyway. Let's see what he wants."

Mike knelt near the water and held the fish in both hands in the shallow water, one under its head, and the other near its tail. He rocked the fish back and forth. After a moment, the trout flipped its tail and swam out of Mike's hands, disappearing below the surface.

Mike stood. "I guess he wanted to live."

Bradley nodded. "It did. Still, we don't have any fish to take home."

Mike dried his hands on his pants. "We still have some time. Want to try

≠≠ Unbalanced ≠≠

again?"

"I'd like that."

* * *

Penny Holcomb reached the sidewalk level from the train station and paused, looking around to get her bearings. She loved her twice-yearly visits to New York City. The Big Apple. The City So Nice They Named It Twice. Strangers streamed up the stairway behind her, bumping her slightly, encouraging her to move or get out of the way.

She loved it when people knew what they wanted.

Checking the slip of paper in her hand once more, she strode confidently toward the Garment District, so named because of the high concentration of upscale designers of fine clothing in the area. Approximately one square mile of the most famous names in apparel, the Garment District provided the foundation of inventory for her shop. Just because she did business in a small town didn't mean she couldn't have designer goods.

Penny strode confidently toward her destination, a small hole-in-the-wall shop owned and operated by an up-and-coming designer Penny had been cultivating and patronizing for several years. Suzy Quinton, "Suzy Q" to her friends, had an eye for color and texture that still amazed Penny. And she was a good deal less expensive than Donna Karin or Calvin Klein.

Pausing at an intersection, Penny turned to check her reflection in the plate glass window behind her. Focusing on her hair and smoothing the travel wrinkles in her skirt, her eye caught movement inside the shop. Familiarity caused her to take a closer look. She moved closer to the window, squinting against the noonday sun reflecting off the glass and steel around her.

She smiled. Sarah Chapman, future daughter-in-law to that nosy Carly Turnquist, in the arms of a man.

She pulled a small camera she'd brought with her from her purse, intending to take pictures of the outfits she saw today for future reference.

No point in missing the perfect opportunity.

To put Carly Turnquist in her place.

What would she think about her son's betrothed kissing a man in an intimate wear shop in New York City?

And that man wasn't her fiancé.

* * *

Sarah pushed the stranger away, heat rushing to her cheeks. "I don't know who you are, but you'd better let go of me before I call the police."

The man stepped back, his hands at shoulder height as though in surrender. "Sorry. I thought you were my sister."

Sarah drew a deep breath. "I've heard a lot of pickup lines in my life, but that one beats them all."

He offered a crooked smile. "Really. She has red hair, about your height and build. From behind you looked just like her."

She stood with hands on hips. "And were you supposed to meet her in this store?"

"Actually, yes."

Sarah glanced around at the racks of women's intimate wear. After her meeting with client, she'd popped in to buy something for her wedding night. Something sexy without being too much. "In a women's store?"

He shrugged. "It's her birthday. I wanted to buy her a new bathrobe. She said to meet here on her lunch hour." He backed away. "Like I said, I'm sorry."

The well-dressed man seemed to offer no immediate threat. She'd overreacted. The strange fellow following her earlier today had likely heightened her sensitivity to potential danger.

Not that she had any reason to think this man—or the other one—had any reason to harm her.

She had no enemies. Nobody who'd want to see harm come to her.

She offered a quick smile. "Sorry that I almost slugged you."

He nodded and grinned. "Next time I'll be more careful about who I hug."

Sarah kept her eyes on him until he left the store before breathing a sigh of relief. A sales clerk scurried over to her, asking if she was okay. Where had the woman been for the past five minutes while the man accosted her?

≠≠ Unbalanced ≠≠

No, not accosted. Simply a case of mistaken identity.

Could happen to anybody.

Romantic thoughts driven from her mind, she left the store. She didn't need another negligee. Her best friend had given her one at her bridal shower. She had other things to focus on.

Like getting married in three days.

* * *

Mike hitched his shoulders, working out the kinks. He'd stood too long in one position, setting his fly in just the right spot to catch the big one.

Apparently, though, not quite the right spot, since his fishing basket sat empty nearby. He glanced over at Bradley, the young boy intent on casting his fly once more.

"Hey, want some lunch?" Mike's voice carried across the water, echoing back from the low hills surrounding the lake.

Bradley frowned. "Ssshh, you'll scare the fish." He reeled in his line. "I sure would like to eat, though. Fishing makes me hungry."

Mike set his rod against a large boulder. Reaching into the small cooler he'd packed that morning, he pulled out a couple of cans of soda and some sandwiches. Tossing a can to his fishing partner, he indicated the rock. "Let's sit here instead of walking back to the car. Unless you need to go to the latrine?"

Bradley popped open his soda and took a long swig. Wiping the back of his hand across his mouth, he shook his head. "I'm fine for now. I'll go after I eat."

"We'll go after we eat. No getting separated, remember?"

Bradley snapped to attention and threw a salute, grinning. "Yes, sir."

Mike laughed. "You are more fun than a concert." He set a sandwich on the rock for the boy then took a large bite of his own. Washing the bread and sliced ham down with a swallow of soda, he faced the water. "Tell me about your dad."

"What do you want to know?"

"How have you two been doing since your mom left?"

"I dunno. All right, I guess. I mean, we travel around a lot."

≠≠ Unbalanced ≠≠

"You go to school?"

"Some." Bradley chewed his sandwich slowly. "Sometimes we move around too much. My dad bought some books and he does what he can."

Mike set his can on the rock and faced the child. "Is your dad looking for a job?"

"Sure. He gets lots of work. He said he can get a job wherever he goes. He knows someone everywhere." Bradley popped the last bite of sandwich in his mouth. "Any more food?"

"Feel free to eat whatever you want." Mike gestured toward the cooler. "And snag me an apple while you're there, will you?"

The boy tossed the fruit to Mike. The throw was a little off, and Mike had to jump to catch before the apple landed in the lake. "You are bound and determined to see me land in the water today, aren't you?"

"Not really. The sun was in my eyes, that's all."

Mike looked around. "The sun is behind you."

Bradley tore open a bag of potato chips. "Whatever." He ate some chips. "Why all the questions about my dad and me?"

Mike chewed and swallowed before answering. "Well, I haven't seen him in a long time. You weren't even born then."

"Dad talked about you all the time." He dropped his gaze. "But you aren't like he said."

Mike paused. He needed to choose his words carefully. "How so?"

"My dad said if we stayed with you, there would be rules. I don't like rules." He took another swig of soda. "I didn't think I would like Carly."

The weight in Mike's heart lifted slightly. "And now that you know her better, what do you think?"

Bradley crossed his arms over his chest, his brow furrowed in thought. "My dad says she's uptight about the wedding."

"Maybe people change. I think if you give us a chance, you'll see we're okay."

"My dad says nobody changes. We can't trust nobody." He began to back away slowly. "So I don't want to get to know you better. If you're okay, that means what my dad says is wrong."

Mike reached for the boy. Bradley's eyes filled with tears. "It doesn't have to be a matter of choosing like that."

Bradley turned and began to run. Mike started after him, the child's sobs strange in the peace and quiet of the lake. He knew the sounds of a heart breaking, of a world crashing in, when he heard them.

"Bradley, please come back and let's talk about it."

The child darted into the brush, winding his way through the birch saplings. Being shorter, he was able to move more quickly than Mike. Soon, all Mike heard was a distant thrashing in the woods. The boy was out of sight, running from the person who wanted to help him.

Mike paused, bent over at the waist, hands on knees, to catch his breath. Sweat trickled into his eyes as he searched the brush for one small boy.

One small boy, running as fast as his legs could carry him, into who knew where?

≠≠ Unbalanced ≠≠

≠≠ Unbalanced ≠≠

Chapter 8

Sarah hung up the phone and pulled her appointment calendar toward her, making a note of a scheduled meeting with a new client after she returned from her honeymoon. She smiled at the two weeks marked off in her calendar—she hadn't taken a real vacation in a long while, and the fact this one was her honeymoon added to its importance. She glanced at the date and could hardly believe she was getting married in only three days' time.

She sighed and leaned back in her chair. The pile of folders on her desk seemed to grow bigger by the minute. Tina, her assistant, had popped in while she was on the phone and deposited another stack on the corner of her desk. She sighed again and leaned forward to retrieve them. Better to deal with them now. Paperwork was not her forte. She was a people person.

Flipping through the folders, she sorted them into stacks: deal with now, delegate, deal with later. Unfortunately, the deal-with-now pile was the majority. Opening the first folder on the pile, she pulled a notepad out of her desk drawer and began making notes. Quickly she was able to sketch out a logo for a client and jotted down four tag lines for their latest campaign. The second file needed just an email reply, which she did, then tossed the file in her out basket.

The third file was more complicated and required her full attention. As she was partway through the solution, her computer chimed, indicating she had new email.

"That was quick."

Sometimes email wasn't an advantage at all, particularly when the little envelope in the lower corner of her screen interrupted her train of thought. She clicked on the icon on her desktop, and the newest message opened.

Sarah's breath caught in her throat. Her eyes opened wide, and her mouth went dry as she stared at the screen. Finally remembering to breathe, she exhaled, feeling all her hopes and dreams escape with the air.

Uncomprehendingly, she took in the picture of her in the arms of a man, her lips caressing his cheek, her eyes closed. The man was facing away from the camera, so she couldn't identify him.

Except she knew for sure he wasn't Tom.

The ugly words printed in capital letters underneath the photo screamed at her: CANCEL THE WEDDING OR THIS GOES PUBLIC.

* * *

Carly spent most of the morning trying to track down the little snitch named Matthew Ritchie who had spread a story he promised he wouldn't, to no avail. Apparently, he was out on a story, according to the newspaper office and his mother.

Out on a story indeed. Carly read the article again, hoping against hope to learn someone was playing a joke, a very sick joke, but she would choose to be the victim of a bad practical joke any day over the reality of this story. This was no joke.

She hung up the phone after making yet another unsuccessful call to Matthew's cell phone. He was out of the area or ignoring her calls. Her mind elsewhere, she jumped when the phone rang. She grabbed at the receiver, hoping Matthew was returning her call.

"Carly, this is Maurice Knowles." The crisp voice on the other end was all business. "I'm returning your call."

Carly's hopes soared. Knowles was the potential client she'd called earlier that day. A senior partner in a law firm that specialized in divorces and estates, he'd contacted her to outsource his asset investigations. If she got the

≠≠ Unbalanced ≠≠

contract, she'd have more than enough work to keep her busy. "Yes, Mr. Knowles. Thank you for getting back to me so quickly. As we discussed earlier, I believe I am the person you need for this—"

"I won't need your services."

Carly's stomach flip-flopped. "I thought we were practically ready to start."

"We were, until I saw your name all over the local papers and news."

Carly's mouth went dry. Knowles was in Boston. To have her name in the Boston area news and papers was not good. "I can explain, Mr. Knowles."

"I don't want your explanations. I need credibility, sound judgment, honesty, and integrity when I hire a forensic expert. I don't see that in you. Good day."

The dial tone in her ear indicated the conversation was over.

And maybe her career was too, if this got out to her other clients.

* * *

After searching for Bradley for over an hour, Mike returned to the beach and packed up their fishing equipment and lunch trash. He headed back to the car, scanning both sides of the trail as he walked slowly along, calling Bradley's name repeatedly. He was sick at heart to think he managed to lose his nephew.

Every few feet he stopped to listen, hoping to hear a small boy running in the woods. Birds chirping and crickets singing indicated there were no little boys in the bushes. Reaching the car, he stowed his things in the trunk, unlocked the car, and sat in the front seat. Sweat worked its way down the middle of his back, even though the day was cool and overcast. If he were a young boy, where would he go? Bradley didn't know anyone except him. This place was fairly far off the beaten path. Unlikely he found his way to the main road.

Still considering where to look next, Mike waited as a small pickup truck pulled into the parking area. A grizzled man got out, his old beagle dog close to his heels. Mike recognized Jacob Roy, the town's mechanic. He pulled a fishing rod and tackle box from the bed of the pickup, and he and the dog headed toward the lake.

≠≠ Unbalanced ≠≠

"Hi, Jacob." Mike got out of his car and waved. "I don't suppose you've seen a boy of eight or nine on the road as you came in, did you?"

Jacob waved back and stopped. He rubbed his stubbly whiskers as he thought then nodded slowly. "Ayuh. Did."

Mike's heart leaped in his chest. "Heading toward the highway?"

"Ayuh."

"How long ago?"

"Just now. Mebbe half a mile past the curve."

Mike smiled. "Thanks, Jacob. See you around." He got back in the car and turned the key, starting the engine. Now, if he could just convince Bradley to get back in the car with him instead of running away, he would be happy.

And if he couldn't use persuasion, he'd use coercion.

He'd grab the little runaway and toss him in the car.

* * *

Jerry slammed his fist on the table. In the corner of the bar, the television set showed the faces of the happy owners of the winning horse. Patrons gathered around, clapping the man on the back. Everyone wanted to touch a winner.

No one wanted to touch a loser. Not a loser like him.

He'd just blown the fifty dollars from his last job on a sure thing in the off-track betting parlor. A sure thing. Right. For him, the only sure thing was he was a loser.

He pondered his half-empty beer glass on the bar in front of him. Sweat trickled down the glass into a puddle on the scarred wooden surface. Lately everything he touched turned to nothing. He let his eyes go slightly out of focus as he thought of his next move. Movement to his right caught his attention, and he looked blearily through the haze of cigarette smoke at the man sitting next to him.

He smiled in recognition. Chad Peabody. His old buddy from way back. A guy who was always good for a few laughs, a couple of beers, and a job or two. He straightened on his barstool and signaled the barkeep. "Whatever he wants is on me."

≠≠ Unbalanced ≠≠

The man behind the bar nodded and looked to Chad for instruction.

Chad waved him off dismissively. "Not here to drink. Heard you was looking for work."

Jerry nodded, his head bobbing on his pencil-thin neck like a car ornament. "I am, Chad, I am. I need something. Soon."

Chad sucked on a cigarette, exhaling a cloud of smoke that nearly engulfed him. "Got a job. Nearby. Not too much risk."

Jerry's head started to throb, either from the nodding or the beer, he wasn't sure. Stopping the nod was easier than stopping the drinking. "Great. Let's go somewhere private and talk."

Chad squinted through another cloud of smoke. "You clean?" His pale blue eyes took in Jerry's shabby shirt and pants, his worn shoes. "How much you have to drink?"

Jerry held his hands up, palms facing Chad. "Just one beer, I swear. Nothing else."

Chad held his gaze for a moment longer then nodded. "Okay. Let's go." He slid off the stool and turned to the door.

"Where?"

"What do I look like, an atlas? Just follow me and don't ask questions. You'll get all you need to know when you need to know it."

Jerry followed the cloud of smoke with legs outside. Chad paused on the sidewalk and nodded to someone down the street. A newer black four-door sedan pulled out of a parking space a few doors down and cruised quietly to double-park in front of the bar.

Chad hitched his head towards the car. "Get in."

Jerry cast a glance at his old clunker parked across the street. A month ago, he was riding high. New car, three new suits. Money in his pocket.

But that was before his run of bad luck in Atlantic City.

He kicked at a pebble on the sidewalk. He'd get even with that crooked dealer.

As his daddy used to say, 'success is the best revenge'.

Chad followed his gaze. "You got a problem?"

Jerry shook his head. "No."

"That your old car?"

Jerry grinned. He felt like a fool, worrying in front of Chad about that piece of junk. Still, the jalopy was all he had in the world, and contained his and Bradley's clothes. "Yeah."

Chad laughed, a deep, phlegmy laugh, full of nicotine and lung cancer. "Don't worry. After this job, you can have any car you want."

Jerry climbed into the back seat, sliding across the soft leather covering. Soft music played in the speaker near his ear, and the headrest was the perfect height to lay his head back and sleep. He was too excited to close his eyes, though. Chad had something big coming up, and he was just the man to cash in with his old buddy.

Things were looking up.

* * *

Mike maneuvered the car down the winding gravel road, keeping an eye out for Bradley. He didn't want the boy to run off into the woods again. He couldn't face telling Jerry he'd lost the child. No, there was no way he could do that.

As Mike passed the curve and came out onto the straightaway, he scanned the sides of the road and the road ahead of him. Several rabbits darted across the road, hip-hopping in zigzagging lines of panic. He stopped and waited until they disappeared into the bushes before pressing the gas pedal and picking up speed again.

Ahead a figure walked toward the highway, head down, and hands in pockets. Mike drew nearer, slowing when he recognized Bradley. Not sure what he would do if the child ran from him again, he drew even, matching the car's pace with the boy's.

Bradley glanced over, and Mike was relieved when he saw a look of recognition cross the child's face and yet he didn't run. Mike accelerated slightly and pulled ahead of him, then stopped the car near the edge of the narrow road. He turned the engine off and got out of the car.

Standing near the back bumper of the car, he waited for Bradley to decide what he wanted to do. The boy drew even with the car, and wordlessly opened the front passenger door and slipped into the seat. Fastening his seat belt, he crossed his arms across his chest.

Mike returned to the car, got in, and started the engine. He looked across to the child who stared at him in stony silence. "Where do you want to go?"

Bradley drew a deep breath and jutted his chin in the direction of the highway. "That way."

Mike exhaled. "Okay. Then what?"

"I saw a place up there where we can turn around."

"Turn around?"

"Yeah. I never did catch my fish. I'd like to do that, if you aren't too angry with me for breaking the rules."

Mike grinned. "I guess I broke one of my own rules."

"Yeah? Which one?" Bradley uncrossed his arms and rested his hands in his lap.

Good. He's not in flight mode.

"The one that says I won't scare young boys away. Some little kids can't take too much talk at once."

Bradley turned his head to face Mike and squinted. "I'm not a little kid. I can handle it. It's just that the men in our family tend to walk a lot when we're worried or mad or stuff."

Mike reached over and tousled his hair. "I know what you mean, and you're right. The men in our family do tend to walk."

Bradley smiled, his teeth a curious mixture of baby primaries and adult permanents. "I want to see if you really can catch a fish without falling in the lake."

Mike leaned his head back and laughed, enjoying the feeling.

Just a few short minutes ago, he hadn't been sure he would ever laugh again.

* * *

Carly hung up the telephone yet again. Exasperation was not a word usually found in her vocabulary before today. But that was before Matthew got stars in his eyes over a feature story snapped up by the AP at her expense. He was still hiding out somewhere, the little weasel. And her phone hadn't stopped ringing all morning and well into the afternoon. Neighbors called about the article. Reporters from other papers and news channels wanting to interview her. Clients calling to cancel or postpone her services. And the attorney from the court case she was testifying for next week had called, setting up an appointment for first thing tomorrow morning.

And he didn't sound happy.

Even Tom had called, concern evident in his voice. And Denise checked in, asking if she should come for a few days.

Carly assured everybody she had everything under control. Only she really didn't feel like she had everything under control. About the only thing she was confident of was that her research and findings for the trial were airtight and beyond reproach.

The lawyer's closing words did little to reassure Carly. "I hope so, because, between you and me, this case hinges on your evidence and your credibility. Without you, I don't think we'll get a verdict in our favor."

Everything seemed to rest on her broad capable shoulders.

Except right now, Carly didn't feel very capable. In fact, she felt very ineffective, very much out of her element, and very fragile.

And she still had a wedding to pull off in three days.

≠≠ Unbalanced ≠≠

Chapter 9

Sarah stared at the picture on the screen again, trying to identify the man. Three hours of work hadn't calmed her as she'd hoped. Not able to pick out his features clearly, she turned her attention to the background—out of focus, slightly grainy. Maybe taken through a plate glass window with a camera phone.

There was no date on the photo. She squinted in concentration at the outfit she wore in the picture—slacks and a blouse, her blue jacket. The same outfit she had on today. Was it the man in the intimate apparel store? The one who said he was waiting for his sister?

Sitting back in her chair, she pondered the situation. Why would someone be so cruel as to send her this picture? Or this threat. She'd had the feeling someone was following her. But not this guy. What were the chances two someones were involved? And if there were two, were they connected? And what was so important about her wedding that they wanted her to cancel?

Her gaze wandered to the framed engagement photo of Tom and her, which sat on the corner of her desk. Tom's smile, even in a picture, lit up her whole office. She recalled the day they'd had the photo taken. Both of them slightly nervous.

She had teased Tom about getting married. "Once this picture is taken and the announcement goes in the papers, you'd better not think about canceling this wedding, Mr. Turnquist."

Tom squinted at her. "You mean I could cancel before we get the picture done?"

She mock-punched his arm. "Don't even think about it."

He rubbed the spot. "I'm not worried about my cold feet."

Not worried about his cold feet. Did that mean he worried about hers? She shook off the thought. She didn't have cold feet.

But someone else obviously did.

Else why would they send this, now?

She glanced at the clock. Should she tell Tom about this? Maybe laugh off the whole situation?

Would he laugh with her?

She stared at the photo again. It was the man in the shop today.

Except she hadn't closed her eyes or put her arms around him. He'd caught her off guard when he'd hugged her, pinning her hands to her side.

Someone had doctored this picture.

* * *

Mike pulled the car into the driveway. He glanced at the clock on the dash. A little before two, and he already felt like he'd put in a full day. In some ways, he had. Up early, pack the gear, drive, fish, lose Bradley, find the boy, fish some more.

Amazing how much he'd accomplished already today.

He glanced over at the child. Bradley's chin was on his chest, and he snored softly. Mike smiled. There were few things as beautiful as a child at sleep. And not just because they were quiet and still. Fine lashes lined the boy's eyes, and the sun highlighted the peach fuzz on his cheeks. Mike reached over and gently touched his nephew's chin with his forefinger.

The boy's eyes flew open, his arms coming up to fend off the touch.

Mike snatched his arm back. "Sorry. Didn't mean to startle you."

"S'Okay." He stretched and yawned. "Guess I fell asleep."

Mike nodded. "Just for the last couple of miles." He opened the door and walked to the rear of the car, popping open the trunk. "Let's unload and go show Carly the fish we brought home."

Bradley joined him at the trunk and reached in to grab the small fish cooler. "Do you think my dad is here?" He looked to the street. His father's car was not in evidence. He shrugged. "Guess not." His shoulders drooped as he walked toward the front door. "Glad Carly is home."

Mike's heart ached. He remembered going fishing and wanting to show his father what he'd caught. The only difference was his father had always been there for him.

Count on Jerry to disappoint yet again.

Mike shook his head as he loaded his arms with fishing gear. It wasn't all Jerry's fault. He was out looking for a job. And he'd said he was going to be gone for a day or so. Maybe the fact he wasn't here was a good sign.

Mike's mood lifted. "We can clean the fish and keep them in the fridge for when your dad gets back, okay?"

Bradley nodded, his mouth set in a grim line.

Mike had a queasy feeling in his stomach.

Like Jerry wasn't coming back.

No, that was silly. His son was here.

He wouldn't leave his son.

Would he?

* * *

Jerry studied the three men gathered around the small table in the dingy hotel room. Two of them, Vinnie and Lonnie, didn't look like they were very successful at what they did. Threadbare collars, worn jeans, scuffed tennis shoes comprised the standard uniform amongst the petty crook class of burglars. The third, Chad, appeared to spend his ill-gotten gains on something more than booze and drugs, wearing his pressed khakis and button-down shirt like one of those mannequins in a store window.

He glanced at his own outfit and grimaced. He fit right in with this crowd. He started when he heard his name called. Looking around, he realized everyone was staring at him. "What?" His voice, louder than he intended, echoed off the walls of the fleabag hotel. He lowered the volume and sat straighter. "Sorry. What did you say?"

Chad Peabody grinned. "Pay attention, man. We've got stuff to discuss here. Plans to make."

Jerry grunted. "Then let's hear some discussing and planning."

Peabody sucked on his ever-present cigarette, holding the smoke until his eyes practically bulged. He exhaled through his nose, watching the cloud of smoke rise on the unseen currents of air. "We are ready to make a move in this area. We want to make a quick hit then disappear before the cops catch on to us."

The others nodded.

Jerry leaned his chair back on two legs. "Makes sense."

Peabody pulled a piece of paper from his jacket pocket. "We've got a list of places in this area that have small to medium hauls, with little to no security." He spread the sheet on the table, flattening the creases with one hand, while bringing his cigarette to his lips again. "Me and Jerry got the bank in Bear Cove on Tuesday."

Vinnie laughed. "You mean you *say* you got it."

Peabody frowned. "We got it."

Vinnie leaned his chair forward, his rough hands gripped into fists. No way Jerry wanted to rile that guy. "Then how come the news all says there was no bank robbery?"

Chad grinned. "We got paid five hundred bucks to pretend we robbed the place. All we had to do was walk in with a duffel bag, run out and jump in the car. The old guard fired a couple of shots into the air, and Jerry drove the getaway car."

An empty spot filled Jerry's gut. He'd only gotten fifty bucks out of the deal.

He should have asked for more.

Always the loser.

Chad smiled. "And you should have seen that woman on the street. Jerry got a little excited, and we ended up on the sidewalk. Nearly ran the old

≠≠ Unbalanced ≠≠

bird down."

Jerry's stomach flip-flopped. He'd heard the news stories. That old bird was Carly. His brother's wife. The woman who was looking after his kid.

Chad's evil chuckle reminded him of that old-time actor who always played bad guys in the movies. Vincent something-or-other. "I'd like to have been a fly on the wall for that other broad, too."

Jerry's ears perked up. "Which other woman?"

While he hadn't had much luck with women, something didn't set right about calling them names.

Maybe he needed to find a better class of business partners.

Chad smirked. "The one my aunt got the picture of." He puffed out his chest. "I played the part of a street bum and followed this chick around for a few months. Got her name. Where she lived. Even overheard her giving her cell number to someone." He drew hard on his cigarette again. "That piece of information earned me an extra Ben Franklin."

Vinnie leaned forward. "Was she good lookin'?"

"Not too hard on the eyes, even though she's not my type."

Jerry studied the man sitting across the table from him.

Was he making a mistake in partnering with these guys?

Then again, he didn't have many options.

Peabody coughed and spat on the floor then leaned forward, hands holding the paper on the table. "Now, here's the plan." He brushed away cigarette ash that dropped on the list. "Since they say the bank was never robbed, I think it's time to give them something they can really talk about."

Jerry squinted. "Something to talk about?"

Chad tapped the paper. "Sure. You'd be surprised how much money flows through that bank. Since they're the only game in town, they hold the accounts for all the businesses, the mayor's office, police department, and library. Everybody. And they all pay on the same day."

Vinnie nodded. "I'm in."

Lonnie slapped the table, the sound echoing off the walls. "Me, too."

Chad glanced at each in turn. "Friday. There should be over fifty thousand bucks in cash in the bank. And most of the town will be at the wedding rehearsal party for some guy and his woman." He leaned back in his chair. "See, I've been asking around. We'll need a car and driver. Jerry, that's where you come in. Vinnie, we'll need some guns. That's your job. And Lonnie, we'll need some explosives. That'll be your job."

Lonnie grinned. "I'm very good at my job." He studied the paper. "What's your part, Chad?"

Chad folded the sheet and tucked it into his jacket pocket. "I'm the brains. I'm the accountant. And I'm the director and producer all in one." He stuck a forefinger into Lonnie's chest. "You get the stuff, right?"

Lonnie sat back, the grin slipping from his face. "Right."

"And I'll get the heaters."

Jerry began to doubt the wisdom of this plan. Vinnie was so old school. Nobody called guns 'heaters' anymore. That went out in the fifties.

Chad fixed a stare on him. "And you drive. Better than you did the last time. No leaving behind any evidence. Got it?"

Jerry nodded.

Drive. He could do that. He'd done that before. And driving was the safest job of all. No one shoots at the driver.

Anticipation rose in his gut like a fountain, one of those fancy ones that goes up and down in time to music. The music of clanking coins. Or swishing bills.

This was his chance to make a huge score, one that would set him and the kid up for a long while. No more small time stuff. No more living in his car.

He licked dry lips.

He wished he had a beer.

Or maybe two.

* * *

Carly met Mike at the door, enveloping him in a huge hug. She needed the feel of her husband's strong arms around her. When he was around, whatever problems she faced seemed much smaller somehow.

Pulling away from his embrace, she looked into his eyes. He smiled, and her heart melted. "How was your fishing?" She looked past him and spied Bradley standing in the doorway, cooler in hand, looking at the floor. She pushed past Mike, and stooped down. "So tell me. Did he fall in?"

The child brought his eyes to meet hers, uncertainty written all over his face. He looked to Mike, then back to Carly. Finally, he smiled. "Almost."

Carly stood, laughing. "And did you catch anything, or is that cooler emptier than Santa's bag on Christmas Day?"

Bradley fought to keep a straight face, chewing the inside of his cheeks. "We have good news and we have bad news."

Putting her fists on her hips, she lifted her brows. "Oh? Tell me the bad news first."

He set the cooler on the floor and sat on the lid. "I caught the biggest fish Uncle Mike said he ever saw from that lake and then we let it go again and Uncle Mike showed me how to set it free so he would swim away and not drown."

She looked to Mike. "Really?"

"Really." Mike patted his pocket. "And we have a picture."

"So what's the good news?"

"The good news is we caught more fish, even after I—" Bradley stopped, color racing up his neck and into his face. "I mean—"

"Even after you what?"

Mike put his arm over Bradley's shoulder. "That's guy stuff, and it's just between us, okay?"

Carly looked from one to the other as Bradley's color returned to normal. Something had happened out there that morning. But it looked like Mike has everything well in hand. If he said things were okay, they were.

Carly headed to the kitchen. "You boys can clean those fish and bag them. I planned to grill some chicken for dinner today. How does that sound?"

"Sounds like a plan." Mike hugged her from behind. "When's lunch?"

"I thought you took lunch with you."

He nuzzled against her neck. "I'm hungry again."

She stepped back from the counter, pushing him away with her hip.

≠≠ Unbalanced ≠≠

"You are always hungry. Why don't you help Bradley get washed up first, and I'll put on soup and sandwiches?"

"Sounds like a plan."

Mike and Bradley chatted as they went upstairs to wash. She wondered what had happened at the lake that morning, wishing she were a fly on the wall, so to speak. Nosey, nosey, she chided herself. Always getting involved in mysteries-that-aren't.

Which reminded her. She needed to talk to Mike about the mystery-that-was, even though everyone else seemed bent on ignoring the situation.

* * *

Lunch went by fast—the boys were hungry and Carly never liked bringing up bad news on an empty stomach.

Not even on a not-quite-empty stomach.

Like her mother used to say: bad news can wait.

But when Mike jumped up from the table while he was still chewing the last mouthful and said he just remembered he needed to finish something for his client, Carly realized she'd lost her chance to talk to him. Likely for hours.

So she sent a yawning child to his room for a rest—not a nap, as Bradley insisted, because he was too old to take naps.

Well, Carly had no such qualms about calling a little lie-down a nap, and she settled herself on the sofa with an afghan slung over her and a very happy Doc on her tummy. She'd almost fallen asleep when the phone rang.

Knowing Mike was already ensconced in his office—or man-cave as she called it, since he seemed to hibernate once he got in there—Carly sighed and reached for the cordless phone on the end table near her head. "Hello?"

"Hi, Carly." Tom's voice reached across the miles as though he was a next door instead of in New York City. "Got a minute?"

"Sure." Carly struggled to sit up, not an easy task with a large marmalade cat and a heavy knitted throw weighing her down. "What's up?"

"Have you seen the paper?"

Her heart sank. Of course she'd seen the paper. Both of them. Both with the story of the non-robbery blasted all over the front page. Then again, Tom wasn't in Bear Cove or Aroostook County. Maybe he was talking about something completely unrelated. "What paper?"

"The one with a picture of Sarah kissing a man."

Sure she'd misheard him, she tapped the receiver against the arm of the sofa. "Can you repeat that, Tom? It sounded like you said there's a picture of Sarah kissing a man. In the newspaper?"

Tom sighed, the sound heavy and dripping with pain, even from a couple hundred miles away. "That's what I said."

"Not Sarah." Carly kicked off the covering. Had the room become unbearably hot all of a sudden? "Are you certain it's not one of those gag newspapers you can buy at a novelty shop? Maybe a friend wants to tease you right before your wedding?"

"I thought the same thing. So I went down to the newsstand in the building and checked out their copies." The sounds of newsprint rustling filled her ear. "Carly, I don't know what to do."

"First of all, why would anybody print such a picture? It's not like Sarah is a pop star or something."

"It's in the section that has candid photos taken around the city. It's a way for aspiring photographers to get their work noticed."

"Is the photographer's name on it?"

"That's the strange thing. It isn't. No attribution at all."

"Have you talked to Sarah?"

"No."

Carly frowned into the receiver, hoping Tom would hear her mood. "Are you afraid to call her?"

"No."

"Then what?"

He sighed. "I don't know. It seems like we just went through all that trouble in New Mexico at the ranch with Brandon and her keeping secrets. I don't want to open that can of worms again."

"You mean, you think the picture might be true? That she's seeing someone behind your back?"

"No, it's not that."

"Come on, Tom, then what is it? Either you believe the picture is true or it isn't."

"I just don't know. I don't know what to do."

"What would you want Sarah to do if the situation were reversed?"

There was such a long pause Carly wasn't certain if he'd hung up. "Tom?"

"You're right. I would hope she'd not believe it and give me a chance to explain."

"Then I guess you know what to do."

"Thanks, Carly. Sometimes you make things so sensible."

"What? Only sometimes?"

He laughed. "You're right. You always make things sensible."

"That's better. Now, go on and call her. If you know about this crazy picture, she does, too. She'll be wondering why you aren't calling and telling her you don't believe what it seems to show."

Tom said goodbye and hung up, leaving Carly with a dial tone in her ear.

She hoped her husband was as full of grace as her son.

Because she needed to take her own advice and talk to Mike.

* * *

Mike paced the length of the office, wishing he'd built a fifty-foot extension on their shared office space for times such as these.

Which, with Carly, seemed to come around more and more often.

He ran his fingers through his hair when he came up against the opposite wall. "I can't believe you're telling me this."

Carly sat in her chair, her feet propped on the open bottom drawer of her desk. "Would you rather I didn't tell you at all?"

"No, that's not what I mean. But Carly, you just got home a few months ago after nearly dying in New Mexico. And I only took you there with me because of the fiasco with the mayor and the embezzled money and all that. How can you find something else to get tied up in so quickly?"

She crossed her arms over her chest, and he instantly regretted his harsh tone.

He perched on the corner of her desk and held out his hand. She hesitated then slid her small hand into his. "I'm sorry. I didn't mean that the way it came out."

She nodded, her eyes glistening with unshed tears.

Oh, how he loved this woman. If anything ever happened to her— he'd almost lost her at least twice in the last six months. He tried again. "What I meant to say is I worry about you."

She dropped her gaze and her bottom lip jutted out. "I know. I don't do it on purpose."

He chuckled. "No, I don't suppose you do. But you don't run the other way when you see a mystery coming, do you?"

She met his eyes. "I'm like a fireman."

He drew his brows down in question. "Huh?"

"When everybody else is running away, they're running to."

A smile tickled her lips, making him want to kiss her. But he resisted. If he let her get away with this now, she'd have him wrapped around her little finger even more than she already did. He shook his head. "So let me get this straight. You saw a bank robbery that nobody else saw. You bought two outfits but only brought one home. Penny and Amanda are in cahoots to bankrupt us by denying you bought anything there and thus making you purchase yet another outfit, except one outfit is on account so you're not going to pay for that one. Chief Blom says there's been no robbery, and a local journalism student had the break of his life when the Associated Press picked up his story." He released her hand. "Am I missing anything?"

She shook her head. "Except I didn't say nobody saw the robbery. McMasters saw it. But according to the radio station, he'd called in sick that morning. But I saw him there, firing his gun into the air." She crossed her arms again. "I just don't understand it."

"I don't understand it, either. You're making all this up. Right?" Oh, he certainly hoped so. "I mean, it's part of a bad dream you've had, right?"

≠≠ Unbalanced ≠≠

"No. It's all true."

"No one person can have this much trouble, Carly. You're not Columbo or Nancy Drew."

"Trouble just seems to find me. I didn't go looking for a bank robbery. I was on my way to the store to buy a dress for your son's wedding." Her eyes flashed with a look he knew only too well. She was angry. "And I wouldn't have been there except I'd been spending too much time making sure everybody else was looked after."

He grinned. "Funny how when you get upset the kids are always mine, but when you're cool, calm, and collected, they're your kids."

"Never you mind. I'm just telling you now before you hear it on the radio or read it in the paper or on the internet news. I'm surprised nobody called to tell you about it. The phone has been ringing off the hook here all day." Her eyes welled again. "I lost a perfectly good client, and I have to go into the city tomorrow to talk to the attorneys and judge in my trial case."

"See, this is exactly the kind of thing I warned you about. Not only are you in danger but now your messing around in things that aren't your concern are affecting your business, our neighbors, and even our family."

She stood, knocking the chair into the desk. "You didn't mind me getting involved when your daughter was accused of stealing money."

"That was something entirely different. That's your area of expertise. It's what you do."

She plopped into her chair, her shoulders slumped, the picture of weariness and surrender. "Really, I didn't go looking for trouble this time."

He pulled her to her feet and gathered her into his arms. Burying his face in her neck, he held her close as she shuddered and cried. "I know. I know." He patted her back for several long minutes until she was done then he held her at arm's length. "But somehow you manage to find yourself embroiled in other people's problems. What am I going to do with you?"

Tears streaked her face and her eyes were red and puffy. "Just love me and tell me everything is going to be all right." She clung to his chest again. "Even if you don't believe it."

≠≠ Unbalanced ≠≠

He did as she asked.

But she was right.

He didn't quite believe everything would be all right.

* * *

Sarah studied Tom across the cafe table, the newspaper between them feeling as big and impenetrable as the Berlin Wall. While he hadn't told her why he wanted to meet for coffee, she knew. Although buried in the back Lifestyles section, there was no mistaking the fact that she was the woman in the picture.

The headline read "Why Women Seek a Lover".

And there was no mistaking the implication of the picture.

Knowing Tom as well as she did, she knew the struggle he was going through at this moment. The vein at his right temple pulsed, one hand clenched into a knot, and his pasted-on smile spoke volumes.

Time to diffuse the situation.

She reached across the table and laid her hand on top of his fist, rigid and unyielding. "Tom, this is not what you think."

"Really? And what do I think?"

She caressed the back of his hand, drawing lazy circles with one finger. "I hope you think this is some gross mistake."

He squinted, drawing one brow down.

"Or a joke."

He pulled his hand from beneath hers and sat back in his chair. "Is that what it is? A joke? Because if so, it isn't very funny."

She shook her head. "It's not a joke."

"Who is he?"

"I don't know. Some guy walked up to me and hugged me. Called me by another name. Said he thought I was his sister."

Tom's look told her he wasn't buying any of her story.

She tried again. "I brushed it off as a case of mistaken identity. Then later that day, at work, I got an email with the picture saying I needed to cancel the wedding or the picture would get published."

"From this guy? Sounds a lot more serious than mistaken identity."

"I don't know who sent it."

"Where is this email? Show me."

Her mouth went dry and her heart pounded. He didn't believe her. "I deleted it."

"You what?"

"I deleted it." She reached across the table, imploring him with her eyes, her hands, to trust her. "I thought it was a joke."

"But it's not." He sat forward, his elbows on the table, hands out of her reach. "We talked about this. Cold feet."

"We were joking."

"Were we?" Once again, he pulled his brow down and stared at her. "Were you?"

She sat back, folding her arms across her chest. "Of course I was. How could you say such a thing?"

"If you wanted to postpone the wedding, I was fine with that. I didn't want this big affair anyway."

Tears blurred her vision. "You sound like you don't want to get married at all."

He leaned forward and lowered his voice. "Judging from that picture, you are speaking volumes about what you want to do."

"No, that's not true." She hiccupped. "I want to marry you."

"If you think I'm going to be okay with you keeping old boyfriends on the string, I'm not."

He mumbled something she couldn't hear. "Say that again?"

He stared at her. Where once his eyes could melt her heart, now his look froze her soul. "I said, maybe Brandon was right."

She gasped. How could he bring up that despicable man at a time like this? "I can't believe you're throwing that in my face. After what he did. After what happened in New Mexico."

"Just saying, maybe we don't know each other as well as we thought."

She stood. "If this is the real Thomas Turnquist, I would agree with you. I don't know this man at all."

He pushed his chair back and stood, towering over her five-foot-eight by six inches. His finger jabbed the picture. "And if this is the real you, I'm glad I found out before we married. Let's just call the whole thing off. Carly will be happy to be done with this, I'm sure."

He turned and headed for the front door. When he turned left on the sidewalk and walked past the window, the sunlight left her world.

Sarah slumped into her chair, the newspaper staring at her like a scarlet letter tattooed into her memory.

Her life had just fallen apart, and she didn't even know why.

Or who was behind its collapse.

≠≠ Unbalanced ≠≠

≠≠ Unbalanced ≠≠

≠≠ Unbalanced ≠≠

Chapter 10

As much as Carly wanted to get this entire mess behind her, Thursday morning came much too quickly for her liking. She got up early and left the house before the sun rose, drove into New York City, parked in a lot, and took the subway downtown for her meeting with the attorneys. The press of bodies in the train always made her feel slightly claustrophobic, and she swallowed down the panic rising in her throat.

She wouldn't be quit of this city soon enough.

Expelled from the subway like smelt into a trout pond, she allowed the flow of the crowd to carry her half a block before she ducked into a coffee shop that didn't have a line out the door and around the corner. Collapsing into a chair at an empty table near the door, she paused to catch her breath and straighten her jacket, feeling as though she'd been groped by a hundred Italians in an elevator—flustered, disheveled, out of place.

Bear Cove might have its problems, but she'd sooner live there under a microscope than in a city where there wasn't room to think.

The street outside the shop lay in shadows, the skyscrapers blocking the sun she knew was out there. People moved past, a steady column four or five deep. Cars braked and honked in a constant rhythm, punctuated by shouts and calls and beeping traffic signals.

≠≠ Unbalanced ≠≠

And always, a layer of indecipherable jabber from the thousands of people and dozens of languages on the sidewalks, in the shops, in the vehicles, most of them talking to some invisible person at the other end of a cell phone or other wireless device.

Oh yes, Bear Cove was much better.

Quiet, peaceful most of the time, friendly so long as you belonged there.

She blinked back tears.

Which she hadn't, for so long.

And which she wouldn't, again, if she didn't figure out what was going on with the bank robbery.

Or the non-robbery as the newspapers claimed.

She drew a deep breath to fortify herself for the rest of her reason for being in the city today. A meeting with the attorneys about the trial she might testify in.

And judging by his tone when he'd called yesterday to summon her to the meeting today—she'd had no opportunity to say she was too busy—he was none too happy with her right now.

She couldn't really blame him. She wasn't too happy with what was going on, either.

But she wasn't in control of the situation. She wasn't the problem, even though Attorney Sherman Maxwell seemed to think she was.

She sighed and stood. No point in delaying the inevitable.

She pushed through the door and joined the column of people going west toward the office tower where Maxwell's firm occupied the twenty-third floor.

Ten minutes trotting to keep up and then navigating the oncoming stream of folks found her pushing her way through the revolving door. The man behind her pushed faster, bumping the door against her heels. She glanced over her shoulder, but he'd buried his nose in his newspaper. She was so intent on staring at him, giving him *the look*, that she missed the exit and had to go around again.

She kept her eyes forward and made sure she got out at the next opportunity, feeling like a hamster in a wheel.

Carly couldn't imagine going through this every day to go to work. Wearing sweats and her cat slippers was a much more attractive work experience for her.

Finally, she arrived at the reception area for the law offices and waiting until the young girl behind the desk finished with her telephone call before announcing herself.

Molly, identified by the name placard on the desk, a child barely out of college, smiled, her braces glinting in the overhead lighting. "Mr. Maxwell said to show you to the conference room as soon as you arrived." Her smile dropped a notch. "He's not in a very good mood today."

Carly tossed her a quick grin. "Great. That makes two of us."

Molly led the way down the wide hallway, the carpeting muffling their footfalls. A couple of people passed them going the opposite direction, each nodding to the receptionist and offering a quick greeting. Three turns later, Carly wished she'd left a trail of bread crumbs behind to find her way out.

Molly stood to one side and opened the door. She leaned close and whispered, "Everybody else is already in there. To leave, follow this corridor and you'll end up in the hallway opposite the elevators."

"Thanks, Molly."

"Sure thing, Mrs. Turnquist."

Carly entered the corner conference room feeling like a Christian in the Coliseum in Rome. And the lions already waited for her at the table, lining one side, their backs to the windows. The only friendly face in the room belonged to a woman who sat in a corner, a small table holding a stenographer's machine in front of her. While Carly wondered for a moment why they would turn away from such a spectacular view of the city, she soon understood: the sun peeked above a distant building, glinted off the polished dome of a church, directly into her eyes.

She shifted her chair to avoid the distraction and smiled at the five men sitting opposite her. "Gentlemen."

Sherman Maxwell, attorney for the Petitioner who'd hired Carly to do the forensic audit of her soon-to-be ex-husband's assets, cleared his throat then leaned forward, his perfectly manicured nails giving Carly a moment of envy.

Just a moment.

"Ms. Turnquist, I suspect you know why this meeting has been called."

Her mouth dry, Carly worked her tongue around to produce enough saliva so her voice didn't crack. She suspected why, but she wouldn't give them the easy way out. "Settlement meeting, perhaps?"

The attorney for the Respondent, Paul Thompson, laid a hand on his client's arm. "Charles. Let me handle this."

Judge Amica, imposing even without his black robes, stood and walked to the head of the table. "Ladies and gentlemen, we are here today because of allegations made by Counsel for the Respondent." His gravelly voice sounded like he'd spent too many years in smoky bars. He laid his hands flat on the table and leaned his weight forward. "Allegations that call into question the credibility of Ms. Turnquist."

While she'd known the purpose of this meeting, to hear the words spoken aloud took some of the wind out of Carly's sails.

For a moment.

Indignation rose as quickly as her blood pressure. She glanced at Mr. Maxwell, who wouldn't meet her eyes. She drew a calming breath then exhaled slowly through her nose. No point in getting upset. The judge had the authority—and perhaps even the inclination—to toss her out of this room and out of this case. She was, after all, merely an agent hired on behalf of the Petitioner. No harm in letting everybody concerned think she didn't mind eating some crow. "Judge Amica, thank you for giving me the opportunity to speak with you today." She gestured to the others around the table. "And thank you all for agreeing to be here."

The judge waved off her words like they were pesky flies at a barbecue. "So what are we dealing with?"

Mr. Thompson stood and pulled a copy of the New York City Tribune from a file. "We have more than simple allegations, Your Honor. We have proof that Ms. Turnquist's report should be called into question." He set the page on the table and slid the paper toward the judge. "She is seeing things. Believing things that aren't true."

The judge nodded. "I've read the articles. Heard the news stories. What are you alleging?"

Thompson straightened his shoulders. "That Ms. Turnquist has a vivid imagination, as the articles say. That she sees things that are not there. That as a result, her reports are flawed, overinflated, and incomplete. Apparently she takes a position and refuses to budge despite what the evidence shows."

The man's words stung her like an attack by a horde of angry wasps.

Or killer bees.

Mr. Thompson continued. "We lodge an oral motion to dismiss this woman and her report. We lodge an oral motion to award attorney's fees for the time wasted investigating her allegations."

The judge allowed the paper to remain in the center of the table. He turned to Carly. "Your response?"

"I know what I saw. And what I saw has no bearing on what I found out about the Respondent." She pointed to a folder sitting on the table in front of Mr. Maxwell. "I did a thorough investigation and found that Mr. Williams—"

The judge held up a hand, cutting off her words. "You are not under oath. You cannot give evidence."

She sat back, her protests almost strangling her. He wanted her response, yet he didn't want to hear what she had to say. How unfair was that?

Judge Amica nodded toward Mr. Thompson. "Sit." He quirked his chin toward Mr. Maxwell. "What do you have to say? Without giving evidence."

Sherman Maxwell stood. "My client believes that her husband purchased land and their mineral rights. When an appraiser was sent to value the land, Mr. Williams neglected to tell him about the mineral rights, which resulted in appraisals that grossly undervalue the land. This is the area we directed Ms Turnquist to investigate."

The judge sat and swiped a hand over his receding hairline. "Does the Petitioner have proof of this land purchase and subsequent lack of full disclosure?"

≠≠ Unbalanced ≠≠

Maxwell shook his head. "No sir. She saw emails going back and forth during the time of the initial purchases, but her husband has changed his email address and purged his old emails. He has also changed his passwords so she cannot access his inbox."

"Seems fairly typical of a divorce situation."

"Yes, Your Honor. But she did ask the appraiser about the valuations when the numbers came in so low, and he said he wasn't told about the purchase of mineral rights. He said he hadn't asked, since most often the government or original owner retains mineral rights, so he assumed—"

The judge raised a hand, and Mr. Maxwell fell silent. Judge Amica hung his head a few minutes. When he lifted his gaze to stare at each person in turn, a shiver ran through Carly.

This wasn't going to be a happy ending.

"Ladies and gentlemen, under other circumstances, I would grant the motion. I don't like it when so-called experts—" He glared at Carly a moment. "—provide less-than-credible evidence, expecting the Court to make an informed decision." He played a tune on the conference table surface with his fingers that only he could hear. "However, we are too close to the trial date. Jury notices have already gone out. Courtroom time is at a premium. If we continue the hearing, it will take a year before the matter comes before me again."

Thompson stood. "Your Honor—"

"Sit." The judge's voice thundered through the conference room, bounced off the walls, and echoed back.

Carly sank deeper into her chair as Charles Williams glared at her from across the table. She swallowed back her fear—and her anger—and turned her attention to the attorney who'd hired her.

But Mr. Maxwell kept his eyes on the file in front of him.

Coward.

The judge continued. "However, I will take under advisement the information offered today. Mr. Thompson, when Mr. Maxwell offers this woman as an expert witness, I will permit extensive *voir dire* into her CV and background. And I will instruct the jury to take that information into account

≠≠ Unbalanced ≠≠

when considering how much weight to give her testimony."

Carly bit her tongue to keep from screaming. In essence, the judge was saying he would allow the Respondent's attorney to tear her apart on the witness stand.

She'd never had her credibility called into question before. She'd testified as an expert in courtrooms all over New England.

Her business depended on her being able to present evidence in cases like these.

Without that, she'd be resigned to working as a bookkeeper—or worse.

To not working at all.

This couldn't be happening.

She sat forward. She had to make him listen. "Your Honor, I don't think—"

An expression akin to a snarl appeared on his face, his top lip lifted on one side, his eyes piercing hers. "Ms. Turnquist, first of all, I haven't asked you to speak. Be silent. Secondly, because of the allegations against you, I doubt I could believe anything you said." He smacked his lips together as though enjoying the delicate flavor of her destruction. "And thirdly, I would say you are like most members of your sex. You rarely think. That is the only point where I would agree with you."

The man was a—she couldn't come up with the words adequate to describe what he was.

The judge stood. "Meeting concluded. Trial next Monday at nine a.m. Be on time or forfeit. That's my rule. Not nine-oh-five. Not even nine-oh-one. Nine. Understand?"

Maxwell and Thompson nodded as the judge left the room, taking all the available oxygen with him. In the corner, the court stenographer packed up her gear and scurried out, leaving the parties in silence.

The Respondent Charles Williams smiled, a lazy smile as though he didn't want to expend too much effort. He leaned into his attorney and spoke in a stage whisper. "Well, I guess that put that b—"

"Charles." His attorney stopped him. "No need to get nasty."

The man straightened. "Nasty?" He nodded toward his wife. "She's the one who got nasty by bringing this woman into our affairs. I made her a generous offer—"

Maggie Williams leaned around her attorney, her cheeks red. "Generous? A thousand dollars a month and you get three million in land? You need to look up the definition of the word."

Her husband slapped the table with an open hand. "It's more than you deserve."

Tears filled his wife's eyes. "We were married for ten years, Charles. Doesn't that count for something?"

Paul Thompson stood and pulled his client to his feet. "We aren't here to discuss any settlement offers or the potential outcome of this case." He nodded to Sherman Maxwell, completely ignored Carly, and headed for the door, his client in tow. "Say nothing more, Charles. Nothing."

But apparently Charles Williams didn't understand the concept of taking the advice he paid for, because he paused at the door and pointed a finger at Carly. "And you are going to get exactly what you deserve. Remember that. What goes around comes around."

Her mouth filled with cotton, Carly couldn't formulate a response, and the man exited the room.

Carly turned her attention back to Maggie Williams, who now cried softly, tears running down her cheeks, streaking her makeup.

Sherman Maxwell looked up. "Thank you, Carly, for coming here today."

She stood. "Thanks for standing up for me, Sherm. Thanks for backing me up." She whirled toward the door, choking back her own tears. She would not cry in front of him. "I'll see you next Monday. At nine a.m. Not a minute after."

"Carly—"

She ignored him, stepped into the hallway, and leaned against the wall. Behind her, Maxwell spoke quiet words to his client.

Married to that monster for ten years, Carly would have thought she'd have a thicker skin by now.

Then again, love could blind.

Just as she'd not seen her first husband's true nature until the pressure came on him. Hurt his back at work, lost his job. Then he'd started drinking and abusing prescription drugs. Lashing out at his employer and his former co-workers with his nasty words.

And her with his fists and whatever else was handy.

Five years she'd lived with that.

Afraid to leave him.

Afraid to stay.

When he was sober and working, he was fine. Nice. Nobody believed her when she told them what he said, what he did. He never left marks that were visible. She always made sure to wear long sleeves and high-necked shirts, long pants. Made certain not to let anybody know how ashamed she was.

She pushed away from the wall and followed the corridor out of the office area and into the common area. The washrooms flanked the elevators, and she ducked into the ladies room to check her makeup. She was spending the night with Sarah, a girls' night out hastily pulled together when she knew she'd be in the city today. Of course, that was before the break-up. Maybe she could talk some sense into the young woman, get them to see they were meant to be together. That whatever wedge had come between them was small and insignificant, one they would laugh about in five years.

And if that didn't work, she'd say good-bye and probably never see her again. Which would be a shame, since she'd already begun thinking about her as a daughter-of-the-heart.

Could her life get any more mixed up? A maybe wedding to pull off in two days. An errant brother-in-law and his adorable son to deal with. A robbery-that-wasn't. And now her credibility called into question.

No, things couldn't get any worse.

* * *

Sarah climbed the steps to her tiny walk-up apartment on the third floor of a house in the artsy district, just a few blocks from the advertising agency where she worked. She liked living so close to the office. Most of the time.

≠≠ Unbalanced ≠≠

Although sometimes she felt like she never really went home.

Still, living here meant she didn't need a car, or a parking space, or a garage. Where she paid extra for convenience, she didn't pay for an automobile. The neighborhood boasted a small grocery, a deli, a couple of mom-and-pop diners, a bank, a florist, and a drug store. Everything the independent woman needed in the city.

And apparently she'd need to slip back into that single woman mode again since she wasn't getting married anytime soon. Tom had refused to answer his cell phone yesterday after their meeting. Not that she'd called repeatedly. Once around supper and once more before she went to bed. Both times to ask if he would meet her so they could talk. So she could explain. Both times she'd gotten voice mail, but she wouldn't come off sounding like she was begging him for anything. She simply hung up. He'd know she called. He'd see her name in his missed calls list.

Unless he'd already deleted her from his contact list.

She reached her apartment and shifted her shopping bags into her left hand as she unlocked the door. With Carly coming for the night, she'd stopped in at the grocer's. Even picked up a small bouquet of mixed flowers to brighten the place.

And maybe brighten her mood, too.

Although she suspected she needed more than flowers.

The air seemed stale after the warmer-than-usual day, so she flung open a window in the living room, set her bags in the kitchen, the flowers on the table, then headed for the bedroom. Slipping off her shoes, she glanced at the clock. Carly would be here in about fifteen minutes. A shower and a glass of wine would have to wait. Maybe Carly would have a glass with her.

She changed out of the pants suit that she considered her office uniform and slipped into a pair of leggings and an oversize t-shirt. A quick fluff of her hair, and the buzzer sounded, indicating her company had arrived.

No, not company. Carly was family. Right from the start, from the first time they'd met last year in New Mexico, Sarah had seen a kindred spirit in Tom's step-mom. Adventurous, unbridled, jump before she thought—that was

≠≠ Unbalanced ≠≠

Carly.

And Sarah, too.

She pressed the button to open the street-level door, unlocked her apartment door, and then hurried to the table to put the flowers in a vase. A few minutes later, Carly's footsteps on the stairway sounded, and Sarah met her hopefully-future-mother-in-love at the door, wrapping her in a hug of giant proportions. Carly enveloped her with arms loaded down with bags and a handbag, patting her back and giggling into her ear.

After several minutes, the women separated, with Carly holding her by the shoulders, eying her up and down. "Are you all right?" She brushed a finger along Saran's chin. "You look a bit peaked."

Sarah stepped back and closed the door behind Carly. "I'm okay. You know how it is."

Carly nodded. "I do. Mike and I broke up once before we were married."

"I didn't know that."

Her hopefully-future-mother-in-law shrugged. "We didn't tell many people. I'm not even sure Tom and Denise knew."

Sarah leaned against the wall. "What happened?"

"Don't even remember now. At the time, it was a deal-breaker." She set her grocery sacks on the floor. "I think it was something about my former husband's estate. I had to break a date with Mike, and he didn't like it. He thought maybe I was still tied to my old life."

"Were you?"

Carly lifted one shoulder in question. "Maybe. We all bring baggage into our next relationship. Nobody escapes that. And sometimes it can feel like we're stuck at the luggage carousel a long time as we pick up piece after piece."

"I didn't think I had any baggage. And this isn't about a previous relationship."

"But Tom doesn't know that."

Sarah clenched her hands. "It's so unfair. I told him I didn't know who the guy in the picture was." She swallowed hard. "I wasn't being completely honest."

"You know him? Oh, Sarah. You should have told the truth."

Her stomach lurched. "I know. I don't know his name. And that picture was doctored."

Carly sat on a nearby stool. "Tell me about it."

Tears blurred Sarah's vision. "A man grabbed me in a store earlier today, hugged me, and then said he thought I was his sister."

"Good pick-up line."

She forced a smile. "That's what I said, too."

"Do you think it was staged?"

Sarah shrugged. "If so, I have no idea why someone doesn't want me to get married."

Carly laid a comforting hand on her arm. "Can you see Tom's point of view in this? An intimate picture of a man you say you don't know. He knows you well enough to know you're not telling him the whole truth, so of course he's going to jump to conclusions." She put an index finger to her chin. "I know my husband well enough that if someone did that to him, he'd be clueless that the woman was trying to pick him up. And if a man did that to me, Mike would laugh it off."

"Why? What makes you different than me when it comes to trusting?"

"History. And that counts for a lot. Now let's get something to eat. I'm starved. I picked up some food."

Sarah accepted the shopping bags and peered inside. "You didn't have to do that. You're my guest."

Carly shook her head. "Family is never guests. Besides, it's a little cheese, some salad fixings. A couple of pork chops. And cake for dessert." She giggled. "I hope you brought the wine."

Carly's easy manner set Sarah's heart at ease. "I did. Two kinds. We can save the red for breakfast to have with the pasta I bought for dinner. Your pork chops sound much better."

Linking arms, Sarah led the way into the kitchen. "Now we have twice the food to put away. Good thing my cupboards and fridge are empty."

They quickly put the refrigerator items away. Sarah uncorked the wine and poured generous portions into two wineglasses. She leaned against the counter and sipped while Carly pan-fried the chops in preparation for baking them in a can of mushroom soup. "How did your meeting go?"

Carly's smile slipped away like a greased pig at a rodeo. "Not well. The opposing counsel made me sound like an idiot, and the judge doesn't like women, so he bought the story." She sipped her wine, closing her eyes as she swallowed. She gestured with the glass. "Very good. Especially after the day I've had. What is it?"

"Moscato. I like it because it's a little sweet."

"And it will go wonderfully with the chops and salad." She set the glass on the counter and turned over the chops. "What was I saying?"

"Judge doesn't like women."

"Right. Well, the good news is he didn't continue the trial. Seems the jury notices have already been sent out, and he doesn't want to delay the trial for another year." She slid the chops into a baking dish, smothered them with the soup, and popped the pan into the oven. "I'll set it low so we aren't rushed. Dinner in about an hour?"

"Sounds perfect. Let's relax in the living room."

Three glasses of wine later, the two had danced around the elephant in the corner several times. Sarah caught up with all the Bear Cove news, and Carly knew everything worth knowing about New York City—which wasn't much.

The timer sounded in the kitchen, indicating their main course was ready, so the two trooped in to prepare the salad and set the table. Sarah loved her tiny galley-style kitchen, perfect for one person. But Carly knew her way around, making their time there enjoyable. What was it about not looking into the other person's face that made talking about difficult subjects easier?

She chopped lettuce while Carly rinsed the tomatoes and peppers. "Have you talked to Tom?"

Carly shook her head. "But I didn't expect to see him until tomorrow, anyway." She popped a slice of pepper into her mouth. "How about you?"

"Nope." That single word spoke volumes about how she felt right now. One syllable. And although it rhymed with hope, she didn't hold out much for this marriage. "I tried calling but he didn't answer."

Carly set her knife on the counter and faced Sarah, her eyes warm. "He needs some time. He's like his father. There's no point in telling him what he needs to do. He must come to that conclusion on his own."

"So what do I do? Do I call the guests and tell them it's off?"

Carly shook her head. "No. I'll get his father to talk to him. And I'll put in a good word for you." She resumed chopping vegetables. "And I have an idea. Can you take some time off work tomorrow?"

Sarah nodded. "I already had the day off since we were going to drive to Bear Cove together for the rehearsal, rehearsal dinner and—" A lump filled her throat, cutting off her words. "I'm sorry."

"Don't be. Things will work out fine."

Carly smiled, the expression filling Sarah's heart with the rhyming word.

Hope.

≠≠ Unbalanced ≠≠

Chapter 11

Five o'clock Friday morning, Jerry slipped out of the bedroom, closing the door behind him quietly so he didn't wake the kid. If the little fellow saw him leaving, he'd want to come with, or he'd make a fuss and rouse the whole household.

And that was the last thing Jerry wanted.

He carried his shoes in one hand, a backpack in the other. Today was the big day. He had a car to steal and a bank to rob.

Just another day in the life of a petty criminal.

Swallowing back the reminder of how low he'd sunk, he scurried down the stairs. In the kitchen, he propped a short note for Mike on the table: Sorry to leave the kid with you again, but I got called to work. I'll be back for him later tonight. Jerry.

If everything went right, he'd be back in time to pick up the kid and leave town.

If everything went right.

On the back porch, he paused to slip on his sneakers and tie the laces before heading for his old jalopy. If everything went right, this was the last day he'd have to look at that rusty piece of junk. Tonight he and the kid would leave in whatever car he stole for the gig today, then they'd drive through the night and dump the vehicle at the first town.

Then he'd buy a new car. Brand spanking new. He'd have enough cash to buy ten of those puppies if he wanted.

Starting his old wagon took three tries, the battery growing weaker until only his curses caused the engine to catch. By that time, simply keeping the motor running required him to keep his foot all the way to the floor, the car spewing great clouds of gray smoke into the still morning air.

Certain either Mike or the kid would be at the window any minute, he didn't wait for the wagon to warm up, but backed into the street while fog still covered the inside of the windshield. He cleared a small area, enough to see through, until the defroster kicked in.

Which might not be until July at this rate.

He chug-chugged down the quiet town, turning from Jamaica toward Main Street. Chad and the guys were in a fleabag motel at the edge of town. He'd be staying there, too, except for Mike.

And the kid.

He wanted so much better for the kid.

He turned on the radio, humming along with the tail end of an old song from the seventies.

Ah, those were the times. Him and Mike were just kids. Playing cops and robbers all the time.

He switched stations. No point in thinking about that now. Because now he was playing the robber part for real.

But those were good times. Mike the big brother, him the goofy kid who always seemed to get into trouble. Who never quite measured up.

Maybe those days weren't so good.

Think about something else, Jerry boy.

But what? Not his short-lived marriage to the redhead he'd met in a bar and married the next day. Who had then walked out on him and the kid when the boy was two weeks old.

Not his failed businesses.

Or the schemes he thought for sure would pan out.

≠≠ Unbalanced ≠≠

Or the money he'd borrowed to get straight.

Or the beatings he'd taken from the loan sharks when he couldn't pay up.

He thought for a long moment. Probably the best time of his life was that weeklong run of good luck in Vegas, where everything he touched turned to gold. Yeah, that was the time. The women at his beck and call. The casino owners comp'ing him with free rooms, free meals.

Seven days of heaven.

Until he'd crashed and burned, losing everything at the craps table.

He grit his teeth at the memory, fairly certain the table was crooked.

And when he'd cried foul, they'd tossed him out on his ear.

After they'd beaten the tar out of him.

He'd never forget the look on the kid's face when he crawled back to the car and collapsed in the back seat. Face purple and red. Eyes swollen shut. A couple of teeth loose. His lips split and bleeding. Shoulder dislocated. Him and the kid had holed up for four days in a state park just outside town, which was as far as he'd been able to drive before passing out.

Jerry focused on the road ahead, pulling to a halt at the stop sign, reminding himself to keep his attention on the job at hand. No point getting a stupid ticket or drawing attention. Chad would kill him if he messed up the simple job of stealing a car.

And he was no moron. He wouldn't just grab the first thing on four wheels that he saw.

No siree.

He was a professional.

He wouldn't even spit in his own swimming pool, to paraphrase something his father used to say.

He'd go outside of Bear Cove to steal the car. Make sure nobody would miss the vehicle for hours.

Give him enough time to get on with the next part of the plan.

And then—well, then he'd be able to look himself in the mirror when he shaved.

Another one of his father's famous sayings.

Something he hadn't been able to do in a long time.

* * *

Two hours later, Jerry flipped down the visor in the late-model SUV he'd found in the park-n-ride lot near Ellsworth. The owner was likely gone to work for the day in Bangor—or Banger, as the locals pronounced it—so there'd be no police report until later this evening.

Nothing to it.

The return drive to Bear Cove was quiet. No road noise or grinding engine sounds like in his old clunker.

This was the way to go.

All the bells and whistles, including heat and air conditioning that worked. Electric windows. Electric seats. Heated, too. He punched the button for the stereo, and classical music filled the cabin.

Yuck. He pressed the search knob and the radio began the process of locating stations within range. A country music song played, the twang of the guitar and the four-four beat a sweet sound to his ears. Finally, something worth listening to. He tapped his fingers on the steering wheel in time with the familiar lyrics, singing along when he knew the words, humming when he didn't.

As he crested a hill, flashing lights behind him caught his attention. His heart clanged against his ribs as he glanced at the speedometer. He wasn't going over the limit. Well, not by much, anyway. Jerry reduced the pressure on the gas pedal, slowed his speed by five miles an hour, and pulled into the right hand lane.

Had he made a mistake and stolen the wrong vehicle?

He slammed a fist against the dash. Would nothing ever go right for him?

Would he never catch a break?

The highway patrol vehicle drew closer, the wail of the siren filling his ears.

How was he going to get out of this?

He sighed. Might as well get this over with. Hopefully Mike wouldn't mind taking care of the kid for a few years until his old man got out of jail. Stealing a car shouldn't net him more than that. He hadn't assault anyone. Not like he used a weapon or threatened anybody. And he wouldn't try to evade.

The law enforcement vehicle pulled into the left lane, its lights flashing and sirens screaming, overwhelming the music from the speakers. Jerry switched the radio off. He'd have time to listen to plenty of sad songs while he was in the clinker.

He slowed to ten under, put on his right-turn signal, and eased onto the shoulder of the highway, the rumble strips vibrating against the tires, jarring his teeth and his nerves.

Mike would never let him live this down.

He put the SUV in park and shut off the engine, then pulled his expired license from his wallet. Needless to say, no insurance and no registration. At least, not in his name.

No point trying to pretend he was the owner. And it would be just his luck that the owner would be a woman.

Nope. Better to bite the bullet. Pay the piper. All of those clichés that never made much sense to him—and still didn't—filled his mind.

He glanced in the side view mirror. The cruiser was still in the left hand lane. Still gaining rapidly.

And then it passed him.

He blinked several times at the receding image before him until a bend in the road obscured his vision.

They weren't after him.

He had caught a break.

Maybe the first one in his life.

But a break nonetheless.

Things were looking up. Surely this had to be a good omen for the job later today.

* * *

Friday morning in New York City was a little different than Friday morning in Bear Cove.

≠≠ Unbalanced ≠≠

When Carly opened her eyes, she wasn't certain where she was until she looked around Sarah's apartment. From the street below, the early-morning traffic had already begun, the tires on wet asphalt singing along with the honking horns, ringing cell phones, and the calls of the street hawkers.

Something wonderful wafted through the open window, and she rose from her nest on the sofa, a quilt wrapped around her shoulders, and followed the delicious odor like a hound dog on the hunt. Garlic. Onions. Potatoes. And something else. Rosemary? No, not Italian. Fennel? No, not Greek.

"Picante sauce."

Sarah's voice near her shoulder made her jump, and she clutched her chest and whirled. "Goodness, you startled me."

The dark circles beneath Sarah's eyes that Carly had noticed yesterday seemed to have lessened overnight, which was a good sign. She hoped the young woman had gotten some sleep. She'd always found sleep the best restorative for a broken heart.

Sarah peered down at the cart on the corner. "Juan sells breakfast burritos there every day. His wife makes them, and he supports his family on them."

Carly inhaled deeply again, enjoying the tangy combination, her mouth watering and her stomach rumbling. "Maybe we should save the breakfast fixings for another day. I could run down and get us a couple of those." She dropped the quilt on the sofa and pulled on her blue jeans and t-shirt. "Better yet, do they freeze well? I could get extra. Leave you some, take the rest back home."

Sarah chuckled, the first time Carly had heard her laugh since—well, since. She liked the sound, the way the effort lightened the younger woman's expression. "Yes, they freeze fine. But be sure to ask for the mild because otherwise the medium will burn your *gringo* tongue. And the hot will set the house afire."

Carly grabbed some money from her wallet. "Surely they can't be as bad as all that. What kind do you want?" She waved off Sarah's offer of money. "My treat. You buy the next time."

≠≠ Unbalanced ≠≠

"You are impossible." Sarah tucked the bills back into her wallet. "I'll take the medium. One for today, one to freeze. And ask for some sauce, too."

Carly waved and left the apartment, skipping down the stairs to the ground level. She paused in the doorway to the sidewalk, allowing a woman with a small hairy dog to pass before she walked to the crosswalk and waited for the light to change. No way was she going to dodge the vehicles like she saw so many others doing.

Mike would kill her if she got hurt.

She laughed at this picture, sobering when images of a figure in a white hospital coat leaning over her with a pillow, ready to smother her. She wrapped her arms around herself to ward off the chill. Maybe she should have worn her jacket.

No, she wasn't cold on the outside.

The shivers came from inside.

The light changed and she dutifully crossed when the walk signal indicated. Juan nodded as she approached.

"Good morning." Carly pointed to the building where Sarah lived. "My daughter-in-law says you have the best breakfast burritos."

He smiled and bowed his head. "She is too kind. Good customer."

"I'll take a half dozen of the mild, and she said she likes the medium. So two of them."

He nodded. "Is good choice." He wrapped her items. "Picante?"

"Yes, please."

"Did Miss Sarah's friend find her?"

Carly's senses came on high alert. "Friend?"

"*Sí*. Man came here this morning. Ask if I know her. He say he old family friend in town just for day. Want to know where she live." His brow came down. "I pretend no understand. He not seem like old family friend."

Carly glanced along the street. She didn't see anybody loitering. Everyone seemed to have somewhere to go. "How so?"

"I tell him to call her, but he no have her number. Friend might not have address, but have phone, *sí*?"

"Usually."

"And I think it strange he comes to street where she lives, but no have address."

Carly tossed the man a smile. "You are an astute judge of character, Juan."

"As-toot?" His tongue stumbled on the unfamiliar word. "What that mean?"

Carly gave him an extra-large tip. "It means you have done Sarah a big favor."

"Ah, that I understand."

"Can you tell me what he looks like?"

Juan's brow pulled down as he thought. "Yellow hair. Good dresser. About this high." He held his hand about six inches above his head. "Tall man."

Over six feet. Sounded like the man who approached Sarah in the store. And the man in the picture.

"Do you see him now?"

Juan studied the people on both sides of the street then shook his head.

She breathed a sigh of relief. And anger. Good thing he wasn't there. She would—she would—what exactly would she do?

A man taller than Mike. Maybe dangerous. Maybe mentally unstable.

At the very least, capable of trying to destroy Sarah's reputation and her relationship with Tom.

Maybe her life.

The question was: who was he?

And had someone else told him where Sarah lived?

She might not be able to live with Sarah permanently, but she could at least keep her safe this morning.

She took her purchases and hurried back to Sarah's apartment. Sarah buzzed her in and Carly took the stairs two at a time, arriving out of breath. Maybe she needed to get more exercise than jumping to conclusions and lifting a fork.

Sarah met her at the door, and Carly pushed into the apartment and flipped the deadbolt and lock in the doorknob. "Keep the door locked at all times."

"What's wrong?"

"First, we sit at the table and eat." She led the way to the kitchen and took her time setting out plates, pouring coffee Sarah had made in her absence, and refusing to answer any questions until they'd taken their first bite. Then she filled her in on her conversation with Juan.

She wiped her mouth with a napkin. "So, I think that means this guy has been around here, looking for you."

Sarah rose and strode to the window. "I've had a creepy feeling a couple of times that someone was following me." She turned from the window. "I just put it off to pre-wedding nerves."

"Has he ever tried to make contact with you?"

"No. And I don't know if there really was someone. But the day the picture was taken, I thought I saw the same guy a couple or three times in different places."

"Juan said he didn't see him when I was down there."

Sarah turned to face her, arms folded across her chest. "What am I going to do?"

Carly shook her head. "Correction. What *are we* going to do?"

* * *

Not for the first time, Sarah understood Mike's concern when Carly jumped into situations without fully thinking through the consequences. Personal danger created no barriers to Carly getting involved.

And Sarah loved her even more for that.

Still, someone needed to be the voice of reason.

And as much as she wanted answers, as much as she wanted her life back, she seemed to be the one appointed to ask the hard questions. "What do you plan to do if we find him?"

Carly sipped her coffee then set the cup down. "I hadn't really thought that far."

"He could be dangerous."

≠≠ Unbalanced ≠≠

Carly shook her head. "I don't think so. If he was, he'd have tried something by now. I have a feeling he's going to make a move soon, though."

Goosebumps ran up and down Sarah's arms. "Like what?"

"Since getting the wedding canceled seems to be his goal, we should let him think he's accomplished what he set out to do. Then maybe he'll reveal himself."

"Why do you think that?"

Carly tapped the table with her index finger. "He wants something. I think he wants you."

Sarah shivered. "Now that just gives me the creeps."

"I know. When all those accidents that weren't accidents happened to me, I felt the same way."

"How did you cope?"

"They made me angry enough that I wanted to expose them, to get them to stop. So I fought back."

Sarah considered the words. How could she fight an invisible enemy? One who might be dangerous. Stories abounded about women killed or attacked by stalkers. Maybe she should simply leave this alone. Call the police and tell them—tell them what? She thought a man was stalking her? Just because a man mistook her for someone else?

Except, there was the grungy guy. On the street. In the doorway. Lurking near the elevator in the building where she worked.

No, that was ludicrous. To have one stalker was scary enough. Without having two. What were the chances? And why would even one guy try to ruin her life and prevent her marriage? If he was simply a run-of-the-mill stalker, what had he sent the picture to the newspaper?

Of course—the newspaper.

She picked up her cell phone. "I'm going to call the paper and find out where they got the picture."

"Good idea. I'll clean up the dishes while you do that."

Ten minutes later, Sarah's kitchen was spotless, but her conundrum was as confusing as ever. Her call to the paper had led her down a winding path of transferred calls and numerous extensions and department, landing her back on the Fashion editor's desk where she'd started. No information on the photographer or the subjects. Yes, a commercial release form was expected and presumed to be in place. No, someone dropped the picture at the front desk during a call for photos of the downtown area the week before. No name or identifying information. The Fashion Editor was doing a piece on why women have adulterous affairs and thought the picture fit.

"No, I don't know the people in the picture. Thank you." Sarah disconnected the call and tossed her phone on the table. "Well, whoever is behind this doesn't want me to know who took the picture."

"Seems that way." Carly turned from the sink. "So let's go with my plan. You said you felt like someone was following you even before this photo thing. So why don't you go for a nice long walk? Do some window shopping? Maybe go back to that underwear store."

Her matter-of-fact attitude lifted Sarah's spirits. Carly always managed to make every adventure sound like a walk in the park. And while she doubted she'd find this guy in the park, walking around in broad daylight, on busy streets, sounded safe.

At least, as safe as she could be and still lure a stalker from hiding.

* * *

One hour and fourteen stores later—as an accountant, Carly had a habit of counting everything—and her feet were screaming that they wanted a rest. She pulled her cell phone from her pocket and dialed Sarah. "Let's find somewhere to have a cup of coffee. Ignore me. Find a window seat and I'll sit a few tables away. Maybe he'll approach you."

"Okay. There's a place around the corner." Sarah's voice sounded as weary as Carly felt. "Bye."

In the upscale java shop, Carly got in line ahead of Sarah and ordered a cup of regular coffee. Judging by the raised eyebrow and snooty expression on the *barista's* face, most people bought the more expensive beverages. He plopped the cup on the counter and moved on to the next customer before she could say 'thank you'.

≠≠ Unbalanced ≠≠

Carly shrugged. She didn't need his approval.

She wove between the chairs to a table for two in a corner. Sarah caught her eye, and Carly quirked her chin toward a table in the window, looking out on the steady flow of pedestrians. Sarah nodded and turned back to the order board as if intent on selecting a beverage.

Carly sipped her boiling hot coffee and focused on the men coming in the shop or already sitting at tables. There were a couple of blond-haired men, but none who matched Juan's well-dressed description or met the height requirements. Of course, judging how tall a seated person was could be difficult, but at first glance, Sarah's mystery man didn't appear to be present.

Mystery man. She chuckled and set her coffee on the table. That's how she'd come to think of the person involved in the numbered company mystery last year. At the time, she didn't think she'd ever get over that experience. Death threats, business threats, accidents. Murder.

But she had. And so would Sarah.

The younger woman walked to the table in the window and sat, shrugging off her jacket and setting her purse on the chair next to. She sipped at her coffee, just another patron without a care in the world.

Oh, how looks could deceive.

And then Carly saw him.

A man matching the description Juan had given slowed as he neared the cafe window. He looked around at the customers inside, his gaze lighting on Sarah as she sat there, apparently unconcerned. Light hair, not quite yellow as the street vendor had described, but certainly a shade of blonde. Sharply pressed casual pants, Dockers, maybe. Button-down shirt. Light overcoat. Thin lips. Pale eyes, maybe blue, maybe green that darted left and right before landing and sticking on Sarah.

He pulled a cell phone from his shirt pocket and dialed. A moment later Sarah's phone rang.

Carly stared at the man. He had some nerve to stand outside that window and call Sarah.

How had he gotten her personal number?

≠≠ Unbalanced ≠≠

She looked up.

He was gone.

* * *

Sarah disconnected the call, her mouth dry, and her palms sweating. What had she done? She checked the caller ID. Unknown. No telephone number. No way to call him. One-way communication only.

Carly slid into the chair opposite her. "What just happened?"

"He called."

"I saw that. What else?"

"I agreed to meet him."

"You agreed to what? Are you crazy?"

Sarah tucked her phone into her purse. "You're the one who said we need to confront him." She sipped her coffee, her hands shaking. She set the cup down, afraid she'd spill the super-hot beverage on herself. "Besides, he's probably a scared little boy hiding in his mother's basement. He probably won't even show."

Carly's hand covered hers. "He was standing outside this window."

Sarah snapped her attention to the people beyond the plate glass. Was he out there now? How could she not have known he was that close?

He wasn't cowering in a hidey-hole somewhere, thinking this was all a joke. Like when they were kids and they called the neighbors, asking if their fridge was running. When the neighbor said yes, they'd laugh and say, "Well, you'd better go catch it" and hang up. That had seemed like a whole lot of fun at the time.

Not so much now.

What had she done?

"I hope you said somewhere public."

She nodded. At least she'd had that much wherewithal. "At the fountain in the park around the corner. In ten minutes." Tears blurred her vision, and she chewed her bottom lip. "Oh, Carly, this is getting very scary."

Carly offered her a crooked smile. "That's why I'm here." She stood. "You stay here until it's time to go to the meeting. I'll go ahead and get in position." She patted her hand. "Don't worry. Everything is under control."

Carly headed for the door, turned left, and disappeared into the crowd.

Sarah felt very alone in the middle of a crowd. The noise level in the cafe seemed to go up at least twenty decibels. Or maybe she just hadn't heard the racket of people competing for air space with the canned music and the *baristas* calling out orders. Her head pounded. She wanted to go home, lock the doors, and bury her head beneath the covers.

Forever.

But Carly was off on a mission.

She couldn't let her down.

She'd let Tom down.

She *wouldn't* let Carly down.

* * *

When Sarah strode into the small courtyard surrounding the fountain, Carly smiled. A familiar face was always a welcome sight.

Well, maybe not.

Another familiar face was the man sitting on a bench near the old horse trough. The same man she'd viewed through the cafe window. The same man in the newspaper photo.

The same man who'd turned her darling Sarah's life upside down, who threatened her son's happiness.

Who'd thought he could infiltrate himself into Carly's family.

Well, he had another thing coming.

Sarah paused at the bottom of the steps leading to the flat deck around the fountain. Pigeons strutted and flitted around the benches circling the monstrous concrete structure. Others perched on the edge and dipped their beaks for a drink. Children ran past, sending the flock of birds into the air with a whir and whistle of wings. A couple strolled by and tossed several coins into the water before sealing their wish with a kiss.

Sometimes life could be so simple.

But more often, the complexities of relationships, the demands of family and business, the quirkiness of individuals, created blips and road blocks that seemed insurmountable.

But not this one.

Carly was ready to wipe this blip and flatten this roadblock off the face of her life.

Sarah perched like a nervous swan on the end of the bench where the man sat. He slid a few inches closer to her. She tensed. He waited. Spoke a few words, his smile never leaving his face. She glanced around, her gaze lighting on Carly for a split second before she drew a deep breath and sat back against the bench.

She was ready.

Carly nodded and stood, headed for the bench.

And across the courtyard, within earshot, another man stood and headed on an interception course.

She passed this second man and continued to a bronze statue of children sitting on a log about twenty feet beyond where Sarah and the mystery man sat. The second man paused about ten feet away and pulled a bag of popcorn from his pocket and began feeding the pigeons, who crowded around him like revelers at the Mardi Gras parade.

Carly, standing behind the couple, eavesdropped on their conversation.

"I guess you figured out that I wasn't being entirely truthful when I said I thought you were my sister."

"I did."

"Do you know how beautiful you are?" He shifted closer, his arm draped over the back of the bench, near enough to touch her. "I thought so the first time I saw you."

"Wh-when was that?"

"The day you moved into the building across the street from where I work."

Sarah gasped. "That was three years ago."

The man chuckled. "I'm very patient."

"Why now?"

He shrugged. "I hoped you would notice me. I work in the corner office, and I see you leave for work. Come home in the evening. Go shopping." His voice turned hard. "And when you met *him*, I knew you were just trying to make me jealous. Make me declare my intentions."

"I was?"

"Sure. I saw right through your plan. So I did what I know you expected me to do."

"What?"

He touched her shoulder, caressing her in an intimate manner. However, Sarah, to her credit, didn't pull away. "I started following you whenever I could. Made up excuses to get out of the office when I saw you in the neighborhood. Learned where you shopped. Where you ate. Places you went. Made certain I was there. That's why I pretended to bump into you at the store. Pretend I thought you were my sister. I just knew that once you saw me and realized how much I loved you, you'd feel the same. And you'd dump *him*."

"Well, I didn't dump him. He dumped me."

Carly sidled closer. Would Sarah's words incite the response they wanted? Or would he turn dangerous?

The man jumped to his feet, his fists clenched at his sides, cheeks red. "No. That's not the way it was supposed to happen. You're the beautiful one. Waiting for me to rescue you. *You* broke off the wedding." He towered over Sarah, and she cowered on the bench. "Tell me the truth."

The man feeding the pigeons dropped the empty bag into a trashcan beside the bench and swooped Sarah into his arms and out of the stalker's reach.

Sarah's fists came up, ready to fend him off, but then she relaxed and leaned into him. "Tom."

The stalker moaned and slumped to the bench, his face buried in his hands. "No. It's me she loves."

Carly stepped around Tom and Sarah and addressed the stalker. "What is your name?"

The face he turned to her couldn't have been more than twenty years old. "Fergus."

≠≠ Unbalanced ≠≠

"Well, Fergus, let Sarah tell you in her own words who she loves."

Carly stepped aside and Sarah and Tom stepped forward.|

Sarah held Tom's hand. "Fergus, I love Tom."

Tom squeezed Sarah's hand. "And I love Sarah."

Carly stepped forward. "Fergus, where did the picture come from?"

The young man shook his head. "I don't know anything about a picture." He glanced at Sarah. "I thought we could be together."

Carly touched his shoulder. "You really scared her."

Tears filled his eyes. "I'm sorry."

Carly couldn't think of one person who wanted to hurt Tom and Sarah enough to pull a stunt like this. Maybe he was telling the truth. "Did you see anybody there with a camera? That day at the store?"

He thought for a moment, his eyes squinting with the effort. "There was a woman outside the store. I don't know if she had a camera."

Sarah stepped closer. "Who was she?"

He faced her. "Never saw her before. She was so nice. I didn't think anything was wrong."

"Can you describe her?"

"Sure. Older woman. Older than you. Dressed in a nice suit. Heels. Flashy jewelry."

Well, that could be anybody.

"She gave me Sarah's cell phone number. Said she was Sarah's friend, and that Sarah wanted me to call."

That narrowed the field considerably. The woman had to know Sarah— or Carly—if she had her phone number.

Fergus wrung his hands together. "I asked if we could meet for coffee later, but she said she had to get back home to Maine that evening. She was here on a buying trip for her store."

Carly's heart raced like a runaway train. "About my height, reddish-blonde hair?"

Fergus nodded. "That's her. Do you know her?"

Oh, yes, Carly knew her.

But why would Penny try to undermine the wedding? As far as Carly knew, the kids had never even crossed her path in recent years.

Unless her real target wasn't Tom or Sarah.

Carly turned to the young man. "Thank you for your help. I hope you find a nice girl who loves you as much as you love her."

Tom and Sarah walked away, with Carly between them. She checked her watch. "I have to catch the train home. I'll stop by your place and grab my overnight bag, and we can sit and talk."

Sarah entwined her arm through Carly on the one side and Tom on the other. "Seems like we should celebrate."

Carly shook her head. "No, we need to talk." She jostled each in turn. "I presume the wedding is back on?"

Tom nodded. "Yes, ma'am. And I feel a right fool for almost letting the best thing in my life get away from me."

Sarah laughed. "You just keep that in mind, buster. And if you forget, I'll remind you."

The two walked ahead, and Carly basked in their easy banter and welcome laughter all the way back to Sarah's apartment, unsure how to ask the questions she knew needed to asked.

Because while there were many things she didn't know, one thing was certain.

Sarah was still holding something back.

And for the sake of her soon-to-be marriage, she needed to tell Tom what it was.

Inside Sarah's apartment, Carly ushered them into the small living room toward the sofa. "Sit."

Once they complied, she perched on the arm of the chair opposite. "Okay, Sarah, tell us the rest."

Sarah tipped her head to the side in question. "Rest of what?"

"Fergus is not the only problem. What else is going on?"

Tom stared at her for a long moment then reached over to hold Sarah's hand. "Carly is rarely wrong about things like this."

≠≠ Unbalanced ≠≠

Sarah looked between the two then dropped her gaze. A huge sigh rocked her shoulders, then she looked up. "You're right. But it might just be my imagination."

Carly shook off the young woman's words. "Let us be the judge of that."

Sarah twirled a lock of her hair around a finger. "It just sounds so crazy. I don't know what to believe."

Tom patted her hand. "Start at the beginning."

"I've had the feeling someone has been following me."

Tom snorted, sounding so much like his father. "Only natural. Fergus was."

Sarah shook her head. "But I saw this man several times yesterday. And he wasn't dressed like Fergus. He was older. Harder."

Carly nodded. "How long has that been going on?"

"Just since we announced our wedding."

Carly stood. "Did he ever contact you? Come near you?"

"No. He just seemed to appear out of nowhere every now and then. Like he wanted to keep an eye on me but he didn't need to know where I was every minute."

Tom paced the room. Again, so like his father. "Do you think he was doing that so he could feed information to Fergus?"

Several pieces of information clicked together in Carly's brain. "No. Not Fergus. I think he is as innocent as he said. But someone else isn't." She checked her watch. "Got to go."

Despite Tom and Sarah's protests, she packed her small bag and headed for the door, pausing to kiss her son and soon-to-be daughter-in-love on the cheek. "I'll see you when you come home this evening. And after the wedding tomorrow, I'll tell you everything."

Tom, seated on the sofa with one arm around Sarah, nodded. "We'll be there by four. We're meeting the pastor to go over the last-minute details, then the rehearsal and the rehearsal dinner."

"Good. That gives me a couple of hours to figure out this bank robbery that nobody else seems to know anything about."

And now she had a name.

Penny Holcomb.

But for the life of her, she couldn't come up with one valid reason for the woman to launch this personal vendetta against her.

Chapter 12

When Carly arrived home, the house was empty. A note on the counter told her Mike and Bradley were off on their own, and a scribbled five words indicated Jerry was out on a job and would be home later that evening.

She decided to check email, and settled in at her desk in the office she shared with her husband. Mike's desk shouted at her, reminding her he wasn't present. None of her friends understood their desire to work together. One neighbor offered to convert an unused bedroom into an office for her so they didn't spend every waking moment in the same room, but Carly had put the kibosh to that idea.

Truth was, she liked seeing him tapping away at his computer or staring off into space. And she particularly enjoyed when he sat with his eyes closed and head drooping. She insisted he was napping, while he objected and said he was programming. Still, when he awoke, he was always bright-eyed and bushy-tailed, ready to tackle the next project.

She glanced at the phone several times, knowing she needed to call the bank security guard, Mr. McMasters. Much like going to the doctor to get the results of a test, she dreaded dialing the number. What if the man's answer was bad news? What would she do?

By two o'clock, she'd spent more time looking at the clock than working.

≠≠ Unbalanced ≠≠

She drew a calming breath and picked up the receiver, dialing the number she'd looked up the night before. The sound of ringing filled her ear. One ring. Two rings. Three rings.

She disconnected. Maybe she'd dialed the wrong number. She tried again. Three rings. Four rings.

Three minutes past two. She'd wait until two-thirty and call again. Maybe he worked last night and was sleeping in. Maybe today was his day off and he was sleeping in. Maybe he had an early morning appointment and wasn't home.

Maybe. Maybe. Maybe.

A dozen scenarios played across her mind, each one more outlandish than the one before, until she set the phone aside and turned to her computer. Wondering what had happened in the world since she watched the late night news, she hovered her mouse over various stories, reading headlines here and the first paragraph or two there. Apart from an earthquake of some magnitude in Chile and a robbery-homicide in DC, nothing much—and then her eye caught a headline buried deep in the national news.

Accountant left holding the bag.

Always interested in what members of her profession were doing, and intrigued by the wording—had this particular accountant been caught in something illegal, or perhaps thwarted a crime?—she clicked on the article.

A video clip from a news station in New Orleans rolled through an ad and then the introduction by a perky blonde sitting next to a handsome dark-haired man. The blonde smiled into the camera, her teeth dazzling white.

"An accountant in Maine has been in the news a lot lately. Apparently she is so good at her job that she dug up a crime that nobody else knows anything about."

Her co-anchor continued. "That's right, Deidre. This accountant specializes in forensics, and it sounds like she dug up something that really stinks."

Deidre grimaced. "Not a body, Eric?"

Eric shuffled his papers then shook his head. "No, Deidre. Not a body.

But listen to this. She said she saw a robbery that even the town police didn't know about."

"Something from the past, Eric?"

Carly grit her teeth. What was it about these news programs that felt like a stand-up comedy routine? And was Deidre the 'straight man' for this guy's one-liners?

"No, Deidre. Apparently the robbery happened in broad daylight. And this accountant, Carly Thornquist..."

They couldn't even get her name right. Which in this case might be a blessing. If someone else heard the story, they might not realize she was this accountant claiming a crime that nobody else saw.

She closed the window and returned to the home page. Her eyes strayed to the clock in the lower right-hand corner of the screen.

Two-thirty. Surely if McMasters had gone to run an errand, he'd be back by now. If he was sleeping in, maybe he'd either gotten up or would hear the phone ring this time. She dialed. And counted the rings.

Still no answer.

She exhaled, a groan accompanying the flow of air. Maybe she needed to hop in the car and go to his house. Not that she wanted to think she was stalking him or something. Just a neighbor stopping by for a cup of coffee. And if she had the opportunity to ask a few questions at the same time, so much the better.

Not that she was his neighbor. Or had ever stopped by for a visit prior to this incident.

Still, an old man like that would likely welcome her in like long-lost family.

Carly grabbed her keys and headed for the door. Family or not, she'd get to the bottom of this.

Today.

* * *

Fifteen later, Carly returned home and tossed her keys and the newspaper on the table near the door. What a total waste of time. McMasters wasn't only not a home, he wasn't even in town. According to his neighbor, who looked like the type who knew everybody's business, the old man had left town four days ago.

The afternoon of the bank robbery, to be exact.

The only redeeming feature of the non-visit was the fact the nosy neighbor hadn't recognized Carly. Instead, the woman chattered on and on about the silly woman who reported the bank robbery and said Mr. McMasters—that nice old man who wouldn't harm a flea—had fired his gun into the air as the robbers fled the scene in their getaway car.

For a woman who hadn't seen the robbery, she sure knew a lot of details.

But when Carly asked her about that, she sniffed and looked down her nose. "I read the newspapers and listen to the news. That woman has made such a fuss insisting Mr. McMasters failed to prevent the robbery. Let me tell you, I was so glad to learn from the old gentleman that there absolutely was no bank robbery. Not that day, and not before nor since."

The neighbor woman had resumed dead-heading her zinnias or whatever it was she was doing behind the hedge before Carly arrived, and Carly got in her car and headed for the only place in town where folks weren't making fun of her.

Home.

Except even that haven in a storm seemed to have been compromised when she found the day's newspaper on the front porch.

The headline screamed at her: Are Bonnie and Clyde on the lam in Bear Cove?

A skim of the article confirmed her fears—another rehash of the non-robbery by none other than Matthew.

In the living room, she slipped off her shoes and sank into the comfort of her sofa and pondered her situation.

Despite the passage of time, certain elements seemed intent on keeping this story in the forefront of the media.

If there was no robbery, surely something more interesting or important had happened in the past few days.

So the question was: who wanted to keep the story alive? And why? Who had the most to gain?

She had no answers to these questions.

Who had the most to lose?

Now that she knew the answer to.

She did. Her reputation. Her business. Her credibility as an expert witness.

Perhaps now that she knew this answer, the answers to the other questions would be more evident.

And in the meantime, she had a rehearsal to attend in forty-five minutes.

Oh, yeah, and a rehearsal dinner to get ready for.

Good thing she didn't need to get dressed up for the first, and she'd released the second to the caterer. All she had to do was show up at the church then hustle home to greet her guests.

Easy-peasy.

* * *

After laying low for most of the day, Jerry's nerves screamed for a drink or a fix—or both. That close call with the highway patrol earlier almost made him lose his cool. If not for the promise of a huge payoff in just a few hours, he'd have succumbed to the siren call of the drink demon.

He chuckled at the irony. Siren call. Something he'd heard on *Masterpiece Theater,* no doubt. Well, the siren call of the cops nearly stopped his heart, too.

He glanced at the clock on the dash of his newly-acquired vehicle. Three-forty five. He could pop around to the corner bar and have a little sip to steady his nerves. He shoved a hand into his front pants pocket and pulled out some coins. Nope, not enough for a drink. Barely enough for a cheapy burger and fries at the local fast food joint.

The drive back to Bear Cove would take about an hour. Pick up the guys, drop them at the bank, and hide out until they needed him for their getaway, about thirty minutes or so. He could pop in and see the kid. Yeah, that was the right thing to do.

Seventy-five minutes later, the guys were in the bank, the rear door giving them no trouble, the security system even less. He made the couple of turns from the main drag to the street where Mike lived, parking a block away from the house. No point in drawing attention to himself. If Mike saw this cushy ride, he'd know something was up. He got out and walked toward the front door. Cars of every shape and description lined the street, both sides. A couple strolled up the front walkway, rang the bell, and entered. Music and loud conversation drifted through the open door.

Jerry paused. What was going on? He thought a moment. Right. The wedding was tomorrow, which meant today was the rehearsal dinner. Well, *he* was family. He should at least put in an appearance. Kill three birds with one stone—get something to eat, see the kid, and let Mike know he needed him to watch the boy for a few days.

He tugged at the neck of his wrinkled cotton shirt and checked for stains. Nope. He'd managed to get through the last few days not spilling anything on himself. He dusted off his jeans and ran his fingers through his hair before ringing the doorbell. While he waited, he used the back of one leg to shine the toes of the other shoe, then repeated. Would have to do.

He was family.

Surely they wouldn't throw him out.

* * *

Mike strode toward the door. "I'll get it."

Carly waved to him from across the room where she held a tray of appetizers in front of Mavis from the post office. The older woman took her time making her selection, seriously considering each one in turn.

Mike pulled open the door, wondering who was there this time. Seemed like the entire town was already here. Everybody they knew, and several they didn't. Not shunning someone important was critical to living peacefully in a small town.

And in Bear Cove, everybody thought they were important.

His heart sank at the sight before him. Jerry, with a smile pasted on, looking like he'd slept in his clothes.

More than once.

"Mike, old boy. My invitation must have gotten lost in the mail, but I knew you'd want me here. Not like my nephew gets married every day." Jerry clapped Mike on the back. A trifle too hard. "Although, if he takes after us, it won't be his only wedding."

Mike winced at his brother's crude joke and raucous laughter. A conversation nearby paused then resumed after an uncomfortable silence. "Hi, Jerry. Of course we want you here. Come in." He glanced around the living room. "Bradley is here somewhere."

Jerry waved off his words. "Leave him be. I'll see him before I leave."

"You're leaving again?"

"Yes. Got a job to do this evening. Speaking of which—"

Carly materialized beside him, her pinched brow indicating her lack of pleasure at his brother's impromptu arrival. Still, the consummate hostess, her words said otherwise. "Jerry. Come in. There's plenty of food. And I know Bradley would love to see you."

Jerry stepped in. "I'm famished. Let me get something to eat before I face the little tyrant."

Carly's face flushed. "Oh, he's not a—"

Mike placed his hand in the small of her back and directed her toward a cluster of guests. "Mavis looks like she wants another of those delicious sausage thingies."

Carly glanced at him and waggled her eyebrows.

He tilted his head toward his brother. "I'll keep an eye on him."

She nodded. "Not to the detriment of our other guests. After all, what could he get into here?"

Mike knew his brother well enough to know he could build a fire in a vacuum if given enough latitude, but kept his thoughts to himself. This was Carly's night. Let her enjoy every minute. He planted a kiss chastely on her cheek. "You're right. I'll go find Bradley and let him know his father is here."

"Good idea."

≠≠ Unbalanced ≠≠

Carly drifted off, tray in hand, chatting with their guests.

Mike studied the crowd. Jerry stood about his own height of six foot two, so spotting his head above the others shouldn't be difficult. He started with the bar, fully expecting to see his brother bellied up, drinking his dinner.

No sign of him.

The buffet? Nope.

His heart beat a steady rhythm in his ears. Hopefully Jerry wouldn't join a conversation and start an argument. Drinking, not paying back his loans, and finding himself in a fight were the three things at which his brother excelled.

No, make that four things.

He was really good at leaving.

Which might not be a bad thing right now.

Except Bradley would be heart-broken. He'd talked of nothing all day except his father this and his father that. About the three of them going fishing. About the three of them catching fish.

Mike didn't say, but he doubted his brother would stick around long enough to do any of those things.

Well, Jerry wasn't in this room. Maybe the half-bath off the hallway? Mike headed in that direction. Light shone beneath the bottom of the closed door. He leaned against the wall. He'd wait here until Jerry came out, then make sure he got something solid in his stomach before he began on the alcohol.

One thing Jerry wasn't was a happy drunk.

Several minutes passed, and Mike was getting concerned that perhaps Jerry was feeling ill when the knob rattled and the door opened.

He pushed off the wall and pasted on a smile.

But instead of his brother, the pharmacist's wife, Mrs. Olsen, stood in front of him. A flush crept up her neck. "Oh, I'm sorry. Are you waiting for the restroom? I got to reading an article in a magazine and lost track of time."

He smiled. "No, I'm fine. Thought you might be my brother."

"Tall, looks like you only a little more, shall we say, weather-beaten?"

"You are too kind. But yes, that sounds like him."

"He went that way." She pointed down the hallway. "He was ahead of

≠≠ Unbalanced ≠≠

me as I came to the restroom."

"Thank you." Mike dipped his head in acknowledgment. "Enjoy the party."

"Oh, I am. Thank you."

Mike continued down the hall, the carpet runner muffling his footsteps. The only rooms down here were the office he shared with Carly and the spare bedroom currently used to store overcoats. Jerry had no reason to go into either.

He checked the knob on the closed office door. Locked. Good. He didn't want Jerry in there poking around their confidential papers and client information. Although related to the man, he didn't know him well enough to trust him.

A sad thing to say about his only brother.

At the spare bedroom, he paused. The door stood ajar a few inches, and Jerry's voice slipped through the crack. The words were indistinct and the conversation one-sided. Mike pushed the door open. Jerry stood with his back to him, a cell phone to his ear. The door squeaked, and Jerry turned around. His face brightened, and he held up one finger to indicate Mike should wait.

While he did, he looked around the room. Although he didn't trust his brother, he didn't think he would steal. At least, not from family. Everything seemed in place. Several coats littered the bed, looking as undisturbed as a pile of outer garments could. Apart from that, there wasn't anything valuable in the room. Not like he'd tuck a table lamp under his arm or something.

Jerry finished his call and tucked his phone into his back pocket. "Sorry. Had to take a call. Seemed like the quietest part of the house."

Sounded logical. Mike stepped back from the door. "Carly ordered a great ham with the ginger ale glaze I love. Have you tried it yet?"

"Nope. On my way there next."

As they left, Mike took a final glance back. Coats, check. Picture of their parents on their wedding day on the wall, check. Bedside lamp, check.

He shook off his foolish thoughts. He needed to cut his brother some slack. Believe in him, for a change.

Not that he didn't believe in him. He did.

In all the ways he'd managed to mess up in the past.

Time to change that stinking thinking.

Maybe if he allowed his brother to rise to a higher standard in his mind, Jerry might sense that and want to be that man.

For Bradley's sake, Mike hoped that was true.

* * *

Carly lost track of time in the blur of refilling trays and making sure the buffet table was well-stocked. Or maybe the problem was Jerry. Showing up unexpectedly seemed to be a common theme with him. And what was it with not wanting to see his son first thing?

Men. She'd never understand them.

Not men in general. Mike wouldn't do that, no matter how distracted he might be.

But Jerry seemed cut from a different bolt of cloth than his brother. Funny how that happened in families.

Mr. Olsen selected another glass of punch from the barman and raised the orange liquid in a mock toast.

She wove her way through the friends and neighbors bent on celebrating their son's wedding. Bear Cove had no understanding that a rehearsal party was supposed to be limited to the folks in the wedding party, and it seemed the entire town had invited themselves. She shook her head. Only she could manage to balance multi-million-dollar financial systems and not be able to put a halt to folks self-inviting themselves.

She sighed. Oh, well. They seemed to be having a good time, and maybe this would buy her some brownie points with the citizens. Even Penny Holcomb had made an appearance, hovering near the picture window with a group of wives of businessmen. No doubt promoting her own business at the same time.

Movement at the French door leading to the backyard caught her eye. Mr. McMasters hovered just outside, watching the folks inside. A couple of times he raised a hand as though trying to catch someone's attention.

≠≠ Unbalanced ≠≠

Carly surveyed the room. Who was he looking for?

Staying out of his line of sight, she sidled up next to him. "Didn't see you come in, Mr. McMasters."

He jumped at her words. "Oh, Carly. Didn't see you there."

She pointed to an empty table and chair on the patio. "I've been trying to call you. Your neighbor said you were out of town." She set her tray on the table. "Something to drink?"

He glanced around the room then shrugged and selected a glass of punch. "Thank you. It's a warm night."

"Should be nice weather for the wedding tomorrow." She peered at him. "Why are you here?"

He blinked a couple of times. "Didn't want to miss Tom's wedding. Knowed him since he were a tot." He set his glass aside. "I shouldn't have come."

She didn't think he was being completely forthright with her. "I thought maybe you were hoping to meet someone? I saw you waving."

"Just Tom. And maybe his lovely bride-to-be."

Now she knew he was lying.

Tom and Sarah were in the dining room. Out of sight.

She laid a hand on his arm. "Please wait, Mr. McMasters."

He stared at her a long moment, half-standing, half-sitting, before he relented and resumed his seat. "Got to be somewhere. Can't be late."

She leaned closer and lowered her voice. "Tell me about the robbery."

He blinked several times, his mouth opening and closing, before answering. "What robbery? Weren't no robbery."

"I saw you. You came out of the bank, hollering at the men who jumped in the car. Firing your gun."

His shoulders relaxed as he sat back. "Now, that's funny. Carried that gun for nigh onto thirty years, I have. Never fired it. Not even once. You must be dreaming."

"I know what I saw."

"Mayhaps somebody be playing a trick on you."

She hadn't really considered that possibility before. "If so, it was a very elaborate trick."

"Not so 'laborate." He picked up his drink and took another sip. "If somebody was playing a trick, that is." He mimicked pinching his lips together. "Not saying anything else. Loose lips sink ships, you know."

"Well, this trick has cost me some clients."

His smile slipped away. "Sorry to hear that. Right sorry I am."

"Was it your idea?"

"Me?" He tapped his chest with a forefinger then shook his head. "I'm not that smart. Just an old man."

She stared into his rheumy eyes, yellow with age. "Someone told me you called in sick the day of the robbery."

"Ayuh, that's true."

"But then you took a vacation that same afternoon. Left town."

"No law against that."

"When you were sick?"

He smiled, one side of his mouth rising higher than the other. "Truth is, I called in sick so I could skedaddle."

"Kind of sudden, wasn't it? The vacation, I mean."

He folded his arms across his chest. "Been planning it for a while."

"Where did you get the money for a trip?"

"Saved it." His face grew hard. "For a long, long time. No windfalls for me. No, siree."

Funny he should be the one to mention a sudden influx of cash. "Who replaced you at the bank?"

His brow pulled down. "Huh?"

She resisted the urge to grab him by the shoulders and shake him. "You have an important job at the bank. Who took your place while you went on this vacation?"

The old man stared at her blankly for a long moment.

She had him.

Then his eyes focused and he stood. "Got to go."

≠≠ Unbalanced ≠≠

"Stop haranguing the poor man."

Carly looked up.

Penny stood there, her arm crooked for Mr. McMasters to slide his through. "Really, Carly, haven't you learned your lesson yet?"

"Learned my lesson?"

Penny turned to go, Mr. McMasters glued to her side. She paused and cast a look of disdain over her shoulder. "Yes. The last man you pestered ended up dead. Leave it be. Leave him be."

Carly had no response to the woman's accusations. True, the mayor had died. But not through any fault of hers, or because she'd driven him to do the deed.

If Penny wanted her to butt out, she'd overplayed her hand.

Carly's questions had opened the proverbial can of worms.

And she was determined to find out what—or who—lay at the bottom of this jar of creepy-crawlies.

≠≠ Unbalanced ≠≠

≠≠ Unbalanced ≠≠

≠≠ Unbalanced ≠≠

Chapter 13

Jerry glanced into the rear view mirror. Where were those guys? He swiped his sweaty palms down his thighs. They were supposed to be out almost five minutes ago. Might not sound like much when compared to a lifetime, but in his line of business, every minute counted.

He drew a steadying breath. He needed to calm down. Vinnie and the others knew what they were doing. The door, the alarm, the safe—this wasn't their first trip around the block.

He wished he had a drink. No, he wished he had two drinks. One for now, and one for later.

He eyed the grocery sack of envelopes sitting on the seat beside him. Maybe he could take a few minutes and peek inside. Might as well make good use of his time.

The walls of the bank on his right and the post office on his left created a sense of claustrophobia, as though the brick structures were pressing in on him. The engine idled quietly, sending up a nearly-invisible plume of exhaust that drifted down the alley and out the back. The breeze off the harbor carried the tang of salt water, the slightly-off odor of rotten fish, and the smell of something green—sea weed, perhaps?

How people could live in a place that stank so much of the ocean was beyond him. Give him the big city any day. Car exhaust, hot dogs from the corner vendor, and that damp scent of water from spraying down the sidewalks each night—perfume to his senses.

Jerry reached across the console and pulled out the first envelope. Inside the card, a check. Nuts. That wasn't any good to him.   The next one had cash. A hundred dollars.

He went to the third envelope. A gift card to a large department store. Well, that would work. He could buy stuff he needed until Chad split the take from the bank. A couple of weeks maybe. Once the heat was off them.

The next had cash, two hundred bucks. Things were looking up.

Within ten minutes, he had all the cards opened and their contents collected in piles. Over fifteen hundred dollars in cash, another five hundred in various gift cards, and only three checks totaling less than a couple hundred smackaroos.

Quite the haul for five minutes in that room.

Boy, when Mike walked in on him, he'd thought his heart would stop. Convenient that Vinnie had called and he had a reason to be there. And Mike didn't notice the pile of stuff from the table was gone. He couldn't get out of there fast enough. Tom and his bride had more money than Jerry would ever see. They wouldn't miss this.

Well, they might miss it, but they wouldn't go hungry because they didn't have it. And once folks found out the stuff was gone, they'd probably turn around and fork over another bunch.

A win-win situation for everyone concerned.

Especially for him.

The alley door of the bank opened, and Vinnie stuck his head out, peering up and down the alley. Jerry tapped the switch on the dome light to the OFF position to make sure they remained in darkness when the doors opened. No point in alerting folks to their presence. Even a candle could appear as bright as a spotlight in the dark.

Jerry scooped the trash into the grocery sack and shoved the cash and gift cards into his jacket pocket. Vinnie slipped into the front seat, a small kit

≠≠ Unbalanced ≠≠

back on the console. Chad and Lonnie slid into the back seat, two canvas sacks in each hand. Lonnie grinned, his teeth white in the dimness.

Chad grunted. "Let's go."

Jerry put the vehicle into drive and inched out of the alley. Rule number one of bank robbing—don't screech out unless you want to attract attention. Like he'd done a couple of days ago. Not today. Nice and easy was the name of the game today. "How did it go?"

"Fine. Fine." Vinnie craned his neck in both directions as they came to the mouth of the alley. "Okay to the right."

"Okay to the—"

A shot rang out and the window shattered into a million pieces, stinging Jerry's face, neck, and chest. "What the—"

Another shot shattered the night.

Chad pointed toward the front steps of the bank. "Over there. The old man!"

Jerry's ears buzzed and he shook his head to clear the glass from his hair. What felt like slivers of glass trickled down his spine. "That stupid old man. What is he doing?"

As if in answer, McMasters assumed the firing stance, both hands on his gun, knees slightly bent, taking aim on the vehicle once more. "Stop or I'll fire again."

His voice quavered and trailed off. The gun barrel wavered then dipped.

Vinnie punched Jerry in the arm. "Gun it! We need to get out of here before the cops find us."

Jerry heard the words, understood the words, but couldn't get his hands and feet to obey. Sweat covered his back and chest, and the cold began to consume him.

Vinnie shoved him. "Get moving. Do you want us all to be killed?"

Jerry stared at his hand. "Oh, rats."

Something wet and red covered his fingers.

Vinnie groaned. "He's been hit."

"I'm fine. I can drive."

Jerry pressed on the accelerator and sped down the street, past the old man who clutched at his chest, a look of fear and pain covering his face. The Yukon careened off a car parked in front of the pharmacy. Jerry yanked the wheel hard to the left and went up on the sidewalk, clipped the book return kiosk in front of the library and narrowly missed the flagpole. Sweat dripped into his eyes, blurring his vision, and he blinked rapidly. He needed to be able to see where he was going. Straight down Main Street, up the ramp to the interstate, and out of this crazy town before something worse happened.

Breathing hard, mouth dry, wishing he had a drink, he bounced the car over the railroad tracks marking the end of town. Vinnie cursed at him to be more careful. Lonnie smacked him in the back of the head. What was wrong with them? He was doing his part, wasn't he? This was one thing he was good at. Driving. If it had four wheels and something to steer with, he could drive it.

Once on the highway, instead of gaining speed, however, the SUV seemed to slow down to a snail's pace. He kept checking behind them, but no flashing lights. Probably the entire police force was at Mike's house for the dinner.

He chuckled. Chad was right. This gig was like a walk in the park.

Well, at least like a walk in a park filled with broken glass.

Those shards running down his back were like hot knives, each one pricking at his skin and drawing blood. He'd probably need to get that seen to before too long. No point in bleeding all over this nice upholstery.

When his right leg refused to put any more pressure on the gas pedal, he pulled over to the side of the road. "Got to rest a minute, guys."

Vinnie cursed again. He needed to watch his mouth. Good thing the kid wasn't here. One thing Jerry didn't put up with was cussing around his boy.

Thinking of the kid blurred his eyes again, and he laid his head against the doorjamb. Chad got out. "Vinnie, get in the back. I'll drive."

Jerry flailed his arms about, surprised at how heavy his hands had become. "Leave me be."

"Shut up, you fool. Move over. I said I'll drive."

Jerry relaxed and allowed Vinnie to pull him toward the passenger door.

≠≠ Unbalanced ≠≠

"Fine. But I still get my full share for driving."

"Oh, you'll get what's coming to you all right." Chad leaned into the cabin. "Lonnie, give me something to wipe off this seat. He's got blood everywhere."

Well, of course he had blood everywhere. What did they expect? That glass was like a thousand needles. He didn't care. He had enough money to buy a new shirt. To get the best medical care. To have the SUV detailed ten times over. And still have enough left over to send for the kid.

When the time was right.

Not right now, of course. No, he had to lay low for a few days. Maybe a week. But he had the cash and cards from the wedding party. He could use some of that to buy a few bandages and some peroxide.

But first he needed to rest. He'd had a long, hard day. Up early, stealing the car, the tension at the party, waiting in the alley. And then that fool security guard shooting at them. What had he been thinking? That this was another one of those staged robberies? If so, he sure was trying to make it look real. He'd have a serious chat with him once he had a rest. That one bullet that broke the window came way too close. The deal before was the old man would fire into the air. Not at them.

Never work with amateurs. Rule number one of successful bank robbing. He chuckled and pressed into the seat. So tired. Just a little rest while Vinnie got them further away from town, then they'd switch back and he'd make sure to earn his pay. No way was he letting Chad do him out of what he had coming.

* * *

Carly peered through the window of glass surrounding the bed in which Mr. McMasters lay in the intensive care unit. Worry, guilt over her earlier treatment of the old man, and questions that flooded her mind and refused to let her believe this was a simple heart attack filled the hour-long drive to Ellsworth.

There was nothing simple about the situation.

And the irony wasn't lost on her, as Penny's words echoed in her head.

Had she pestered another man into an early grave?

≠≠ Unbalanced ≠≠

No. Just as the mayor's death wasn't her fault, neither was this. The fact he'd chosen to have a myocardial infarction, as the doctor called it, within an hour of her asking him a few simple questions was simply a coincidence. Nothing more.

Despite what Penny or others of her ilk might claim.

She shifted to one side, hoping to see past the wall of doctors, nurses, and technicians who almost filled the room, each with their specialized task, their specific role to fulfill. Tubes snaked across the sheets and connected to various monitors and pumps, each beating a rhythm according to its function. The poor old man, his skin whiter than the sheets he lay on, resembled a porcupine, he had so many needles sticking out of him.

Or a trussed-up turkey, waiting for the oven.

She shook her head to clear that thought from her head. She wasn't the one who made him walk down by the bank that evening. And she surely wasn't the one who robbed the bank and startled the old man half to death. At least, that's the story Chief Blom managed to piece together from the evidence. Spent bullet casings, shattered safety glass.

And a bank relieved of its cash deposits. Without an alarm going off. On the one night where just about every town resident was at her house for a party.

How lucky could one person be?

That person being her.

Not in a million years. If she suggested that story as a plot to a novel, she'd be laughed out of town. Implausible, people would say. Impossible, others would argue.

Mike stepped close behind her, and she leaned against him, glad for the solid comfort of his body next to hers. "I'm sorry the party was ruined."

He nuzzled her hair. "Not like it was your fault." He placed his hands on her shoulders and turned her to face him. "It wasn't, was it?"

His mouth twitched as he struggled to control a smile.

She mock-punched his arm. "This is no laughing matter. This is serious."

He ducked his head. "I know. But I overheard some grumbling from the peanut gallery." He quirked his chin toward the waiting room, now filled to the gunwales with concerned townsfolk. "If they had their way, they'd either tar and feather you, or ride you out of town on rail. Or both."

She glanced over his shoulder. "I don't see the chief."

"He and Maria are still at the bank, looking for evidence." He pulled her close. "I don't know who could have done this. And to just drive off and leave that poor old man lying on the sidewalk. What has the world come to?"

She sniffled. "I don't think the world is any worse than it's always been. It just never hit this close to home before."

She had to stay strong right now. The kids were still planning to marry tomorrow, and Jerry had disappeared—again. She pushed away from Mike. "I need to check on Bradley."

He released her. "I'll stay here in case the doctor comes out with word."

She headed for the waiting room. In the far corner, a small boy wrapped in a hospital blanket dozed in front of a television with the sound turned all the way down. Mavis from the post office sat next to him, her hand on his leg, her eyes also closed. Conversations ceased as Carly walked through the crowd of concerned townsfolk, but she ignored them.

They could think what they liked.

She wasn't here for them.

She touched Mavis's shoulder, and the woman awoke with a start, blinking in the harsh light.

"Sorry, guess I nodded off there." She looked at Bradley. "Poor mite, he's plum tuckered out."

"I'll sit with him a while if you like."

Mavis smiled and stretched. "Sounds like a good idea. Think I'll get a cup of coffee. Want something?"

Carly shook her head. "No, but thanks. I've had enough hospital coffee. My kidneys are floating. Take your time."

Mavis shuffled down the hallway toward the elevators, and Carly turned her attention to the child. His cheeks were pink, but dark circles ringed his eyes, the shadows making the rest of his features seem more pale. She touched his

≠≠ Unbalanced ≠≠

forehead. Not hot to the touch. Just a sleep flush.

He stirred and shifted, moaned something she couldn't understand, then settled into the chair again. Small enough that he could curl into a ball like a puppy in front of a fireplace.

Where was Jerry? Why wasn't he here taking care of his son? Mike said he'd left soon after arriving. Which seemed strange. He hadn't even taken the time to see Bradley. Something about a job.

Was that job robbing the bank? Bullet casings without a slug meant the slug was in something that wasn't at the scene any longer. Like a car.

Or a person.

Carly shivered, wishing she could simply curl into a ball and sleep through the next few hours. But she wasn't a child.

The door to McMasters's room opened and a doctor emerged. Carly hurried to where Mike stood, fighting her way through the crowd who pressed in to hear the latest update. Mavis returned from the lounge, a cup in one hand.

The woman pulled a medical mask from her face, revealing a full mouth and perky nose. She shrugged the kinks out of her shoulders. "Sorry, don't have much to tell you, folks. He is in a coma. Might stay that way for hours, days even. First twenty-four hours are the most critical."

Carly took another step closer. "What happened?"

"Heart attack."

"Can he talk?"

She doctor shook her head. "Besides the fact he's unconscious and intubated, we don't know how much brain damage he's suffered. He wasn't breathing for at least thirty minutes."

Carly pressed in. "Will he make it?"

The doctor dropped her gaze a moment then held Carly's eyes with her own. "Too soon to tell. If he has family, they should be notified."

Mavis spoke up, a Styrofoam cup in one hand. "He doesn't have anybody 'cept us."

The doctor nodded. "I'll need one point of contact."

Carly glanced at Mike, who nodded. "I think Mavis knows him best." She

≠≠ Unbalanced ≠≠

eyed the crowd. "What say you?"

Murmurs of agreement filled the hallway, and several people stepped back to allow Mavis to move front and center. She smiled at the doctor. "I guess I'm it."

The doctor gave a brusque nod. "Good. We've got paperwork. Follow me."

She headed for the nurse's station with Mavis close behind, trotting to keep up. The crowd separated into their little groups again, chatting amongst themselves.

Carly turned to Mike. "Let's get Bradley and go home. Maybe Jerry will show up there, and he'll want to see his son."

Mike snorted softly. "He didn't seem in a hurry this afternoon."

"But this is now. And the town has experienced a tragedy."

"Nothing to my brother. Only thing he cares about is himself. And where he can get his next dollar and his next drink."

Mike scooped the bundle of sleeping child into his arms as easily as if Bradley weighed no more than a feather, and together they traveled down in the elevator, through the quiet lobby, past the closed gift shop and administrative offices, and into the parking lot. He laid the boy in the back seat, and then drove them home. He repeated the process to get the child into the house, up the stairs, and into his cot. Rather than risk waking him to settle him into his sleeping bag, Carly unzipped the sack and laid the soft flannel-lined covering over him like a blanket.

Leaving the light on in case the boy awoke and was frightened at being in the room alone, she tiptoed out after kissing the child's forehead. Mike had gone ahead to the kitchen, and had the kettle boiling for tea.

She sank into a kitchen chair, feeling as though she'd run a marathon and a half today. He set the cup in front of her, and she breathed in its comforting steam. "Oh, it's good to be home."

Mike sat beside her. "Truer words were never spoken."

"What was he doing there?"

Mike peered at her over the brim of his cup. "What was who doing where?"

She sighed. "McMasters. At the bank."

He shrugged. "Don't know. Too tired to care."

"But the chief indicated something happened at the bank tonight. Doesn't that make you curious?"

He set his cup down and covered her hand with his. "Nope. Too tired to care." He leaned back in his chair and closed his eyes a moment before opening them again. "And you are, too."

She looked around the kitchen. Every surface was covered with dirty dishes, plates of food, plastic glasses, paper napkins—all the detritus of a successful party. "I am pretty tired. And tomorrow is another big day." She stood. "I can't go to sleep and leave this mess."

"Carly, leave it. It will be there in the morning."

She faced him, hands on her hips. "That's the problem, isn't it? The dish fairies won't come tonight and clean up this kitchen. And I won't have time to do it in the morning. Tom is coming here to dress. You and I both have to get ready." She patted her hair. "I have to get my hair done at eleven." She shook her head. "No. I need to do it tonight."

Mike sighed. "Fine. I'll help you. Where do you want to start?"

She turned to the sink. "I'll start rinsing dishes. You go around the living room and gather up what needs to be washed. Get the trash can from the garage and toss away the leftover food and paper stuff and plastic stuff."

He paused mid-step. "Throw out the food? Are you crazy?"

"It's been laying out for hours. I don't want to take a chance on someone getting sick."

"What about chips and stuff?"

She nodded. "Fine. Save that. But the rest goes."

Carly plunged her hands into the soapy dishwater. If only she could wash away the questions—and the problems—as easily as she washed these dishes. More questions came to mind. Why had Jerry rushed off so quickly? And what was this job he talked about?

And where was he now?

≠≠ Unbalanced ≠≠

She dried her hands and switched on the under-cupboard radio. The late night news had just come on.

"And in breaking news from Bear Cove, the police department confirmed the bank was robbed earlier this evening. The investigation is ongoing, but officials confirm a vehicle matching the description of an SUV stolen from a parking lot in Ellsworth earlier today was seen in the vicinity, and paint matching that vehicle has been collected from an apparent hit-and-run vehicle near the scene. The elderly bank security guard has been taken to hospital with unconfirmed injuries. At this time, it isn't known if he tried to stop the robbery, but shots in the area have been confirmed. And now on to other stories tonight..."

Carly paused. Surely the fact that McMasters was at the bank, after hours, when it was being robbed was no coincidence. Had he known about the robbery? Was he a party to the crime?

Or had she done exactly what Penny accused her of doing?

Had she pestered another man to his death?

≠≠ Unbalanced ≠≠

≠≠ Unbalanced ≠≠

Chapter 14

Carly strode into the spare bedroom bright and early the next morning. Today was *The Day*. Tom and Sarah's wedding day. Despite the terrible events of the previous evening, nothing would spoil this day for her. Or them. She paused inside the door. Two coats remained on the bed from the party. She'd need to track down their owners.

In the closet, she pulled out the three plastic-covered hangers containing Tom's tuxedo. He was going to look like a million bucks in this get-up. And Mike had finally gone to the rental shop for his fitting, getting the matching suit to his son's. She hung Tom's outfit on the back of the door and his shoes on the bed.

Crossing to the dressing table near the window, she paused. Something was off. Something was missing. But what?

She turned slowly, surveying the room, returning to the table.

The envelopes. The cards.

The table was bare except for a lace cloth she'd left to cover a water stain on the wooden surface.

She yanked open a drawer. Had she—or someone else—put them away? For safekeeping, perhaps? Not there. Another drawer, and then the final one. Nothing there except some old plastic combs and a couple of paper clips.

Her legs shaking, she made her way to the bureau and pulled open each drawer. Sheets, pillowcases, extra towels, a couple of lace doilies.

But no envelopes.

She stepped into the hallway. "Mike."

His voice echoed from the office, distorted by the closed door. "What?"

She pushed open the door. "Did Tom and Sarah take their cards?"

"No. We were in such a panic when we left last night." He stood. "They're in the spare room."

"Well, they were there, but they aren't now. I just checked."

"In a drawer?"

She shook her head. Tears blurred her vision. "Oh, Mike. Who would do such a thing to the kids?"

"Had to be someone with no heart." He paused. "Oh, no."

"What?"

His head drooped. "Jerry was in there."

"He wouldn't steal from family. Not after all we've done for him." She stood before him, her arms around his waist. "Would he?"

"If he thought he deserved it. If he thought he could get away with it. If he thought nobody would get hurt." Mike ran his fingers through his hair, gripping the ends as though he wanted to tear the strands out. "Justify Jerry. That's what we used to call him. Every time he messed up, he had a good excuse." He pounded a fist into his other palm. "But this is it. We'll have it out this time. No more sad stories to tear at my heart. It's one thing when he takes my money and doesn't give it back, but it's entirely another when he steals from my son." His voice broke and he swallowed hard. "Wait until I find him."

Carly laid a hand on his arm. She'd never seen Mike so angry before. "Don't you think it's strange he hasn't been around since the party?"

"Well, he knew once we found the cards missing we'd be upset."

"Then why would he take the cards? Unless he wasn't planning to come back."

Mike paced the room. "Of course he's coming back. Bradley is here." He stopped. "You don't think—"

≠≠ Unbalanced ≠≠

"I think it's strange that he takes what he knows he can't get away with, leaves his son, the bank is robbed, and he hasn't shown his face around here since." She choked back a sob. "What are we going to do?"

Mike closed in on her and pulled her against him. "We get ready for the wedding. We carry on as if nothing has happened. After all, we don't know for sure it was him."

Using her hands on his chest, she put a few inches of space between them and stared into his eyes. "If he didn't take the gifts, then one of our guests did. Who would you say is the most likely?"

Mike stared over her head, his jaw muscles working. Then he shook his head. "You're right. I can't see one of them taking the gifts." He kissed her forehead. "But let's just play it by ear, okay? Maybe he'll come to his senses and bring them back."

His failure to meet her gaze told her he believed otherwise.

And so did she. "If he was involved in this bank robbery, where do you think he'd hide out?"

Mike shrugged. "Probably out of state by now. Or holed up in a fleabag motel somewhere."

"Can you keep an eye on Bradley while I'm gone?"

"Where is he?"

"In his room, playing with some of Tom's old GI Joe stuff. He found it in a box under the bed. Said at first he wouldn't play with dolls, but when I showed him the cool weapons, he was hooked."

"Not to mention that GI Joe was a chick magnet."

"Mike, he's far too young to know about things like that."

Mike grinned. "Boys are never too young to know about girls."

She glanced at the clock on the bedside table. "I have to get to my hair appointment or Margaret will force me into one of her horrible perms."

He pecked her on the lips. "The poodle look?"

She nodded. "One and the same." She crossed around to the other side of the bed and lifted the dust ruffle. When she straightened, Mike grinned at her. "Just one final check. No harm in looking."

≠≠ Unbalanced ≠≠

"I've got a couple more things to do before I get dressed."

She waved him toward the office. "I know. One more email."

He chuckled. "Actually, two more."

"Great. That should keep you busy for at least an hour. See you when I get back."

Carly's stroll to the hair salon took her past the gas station operated by Jacob Roy. His family had been in Bear Cove since the town's formation, and if anybody knew what was going on, he did. Jacob used one-syllable words as much as possible, preferring to answer most questions with the famous Maine word 'ayuh' meaning yes. Although he'd intimidated her at first with what she thought a surly attitude, she'd come to appreciate his fountain of knowledge about all things mechanical and most everything relational about the folks and goings-on in town.

She crossed the street to his garage and waited until he emerged from under the hood of a truck he was working on. "Hi, Jacob. Thanks for coming to the party yesterday."

"Ayuh. My pleasure." His thick New England accent rolled the r's. "Looking forward to the wedding today, too." He scanned the sky. "Nice day for it."

"I'll be glad when it's all over. Seems like I've been working on this for months."

"'Spect you have. Still, you don't seem none the worse for wear." His face crinkled into a thousand laugh lines. "How is your husband?"

"Fine. Doing some last-minute work."

"Good idea having the party yesterday and not taking up the whole day with wedding stuff today." He scrubbed his hands on an almost-clean rag. "Some folks have work to do."

She started to correct him by telling him the previous party was for the participants in the ceremony, but stopped. Nothing could be done to change what was already done. And the fact Tom and Sarah decided to cut out the traditional post-wedding reception probably wouldn't mean anything to this rough-and-tumble old man.

She nodded. "The kids are driving to Boston right after the ceremony to fly out for their honeymoon, so it all worked out fine."

He leaned against the fender of the truck. "I'd best let you get back to what you were doing."

She gasped. "Oh, yes. Margaret squeezed me in for an appointment and I don't want to be late."

"That would never do. She can be nasty about folks showing up late." He turned back to his work. "See you later."

Carly left and trotted the remaining distance to the hair salon. When she pushed in through the door, a bell overhead tinkled.

Margaret looked up from the magazine she was reading. "Last customer just left. Thought I'd take a load off while I waited for you." She took a sip of the cola near her elbow. "Need a little fortification."

Carly wasn't certain how to take that comment so she clamped her lips shut and smiled. "Just a little off the ends, and if you could style it for me, I'd be grateful." She sat in the chair and Margaret enveloped her in a cape that smelled of hair color and peroxide. "Make me beautiful."

"Well now, Carly. I am good, but I'm not a miracle worker." Margaret sifted Carly's hair through her fingers, studying the reflection in the mirror. "I could really do wonders with a perm."

Panic rose in Carly's chest, sour as spoiled milk. "Not today, thanks. Maybe another time."

"Well, all right then. Sit back, close your eyes, and relax. We'll have you done in a jig."

There was no way Carly was going to close her eyes as this woman worked on her hair, but she managed to stay quiet, even when Margaret picked up a pair of shears and hacked away at her hair. She sighed a breath of relief when she realized the woman was using texturizing scissors, meant to cut the hair at staggered lengths to increase volume.

An hour later, Margaret shoved a mirror into her hands and swung the chair around. "How does the back look?"

Carly surveyed the damage, pleased that Margaret seemed to have outdone herself this time. In a good way. The back was layered and cut in a little more deeply than Carly preferred, but she had to admit the style flattered her. And she loved the way the top fluffed and the sides followed the shape of her face. She smiled. "You've done wonders. Thank you."

Margaret sniffed. "Nothing I wouldn't do for anybody. Got a reputation to uphold, you know." She looked down her nose at Carly. "Not everybody around here cares about their reputation. Or this town."

Carly handed back the mirror. "I hope you're not referring to me."

"Well, judging by how that news article went all over the state and halfway around the country, I wonder." The hair stylist removed the cape and used a long-bristled brush resembling a shaving brush to dust away any hair on her neck. "Just saying."

Carly stood and dug in her pocket for her money, taking a couple of calming breaths before she answered. "First of all, I didn't write the story or send it to all those stations. Secondly, I saw a bank robbery."

Margaret waved away her words with one hand while accepting payment with the other. "Pshaw. There wasn't a robbery."

Carly headed for the door but paused, her hand on the knob. She looked over her shoulder at the stylist. "I know what I saw. And I'm going to get to the bottom of why somebody wants to ruin my reputation. I have an idea of the why. I'm just not certain of the who."

She left the parlor and headed for home, her heels pounding out her frustration in a steady staccato that didn't slow until she reached her front door.

Mike looked up from his computer as she paused in the hallway. "Back already?"

His complete inability to keep track of time and his nonchalant attitude toward his only son's wedding touched off a tinder within her. Not a powder keg as might normally have happened. But a slow burn that threatened to engulf her.

No, not today. Tom was her only son, too, and she wouldn't spoil his special day.

No matter how much she wanted to blow up at somebody.

Truth was, the somebody she wanted to explode all over wasn't even here.

And if she saw him again, he'd live to regret returning to Bear Cove.

So instead of screaming, she smiled. "Time to get ready. We have thirty minutes to get to the church and in our places." She headed for the stairs. "I'll get Bradley dressed."

"Okay. I'll be up in a minute."

Carly knocked on the door and entered when a muffled voice responded. She half-expected to trip over toys, but the room was tidy, with no sign of the GI Joe toys.

Instead, Bradley stood near the window that overlooked the driveway. "Is my father coming home?"

Carly's heart ached for the little-boy question, and she didn't know what to tell him. She didn't believe in lying, but sometimes the truth could be a more harmful weapon than a cannon fired at blank range. "I don't know. But we are going to Tom and Sarah's wedding. And you'll get to see your cousins from Riverdale. Won't that be fun?"

The child turned around. "My mother left me, too."

Carly crossed the room in two giant steps and scooped the child into her arms, holding him close. "Oh, Bradley." She nuzzled his neck. "Your daddy loves you."

He nodded but didn't answer, instead pressing closer into her embrace.

She sat him on the bed and knelt in front of him. "Let's get dressed for the wedding. Tom and Sarah will be so happy to see you there."

A single tear slipped down his cheek, staining his flushed cheeks. "I wish they were my mommy and my daddy." He scrubbed at his eyes. "I'll be a big boy. Big boys don't cry."

The words of the old fifties tune flitted across her memory, and she stood. Sometimes society's expectations were too harsh. Sometimes crying was the best remedy. But apparently Jerry had taught his son not to express his emotions.

She patted his shoulder. "Sometimes even adults need to cry. There's no shame in that."

≠≠ Unbalanced ≠≠

The child crossed his arms over his chest and jutted out his bottom lip. "I won't cry. I can dress myself. I'm a big boy."

Carly headed for the hallway. "Okay. If you need any help, call out. Uncle Mike will be up in a few minutes. He can help with your tie."

In her own room, Carly slipped out of her jeans and blouse then pulled her slip over her head, taking care not to mess up her hair. Next came the skirt and jacket, and she added the brooch. Surveying her image in the mirror, she nodded. If she'd had time, she might have had Penny take up the sleeves a mite, but she could live with the look for one day. Not even a whole day. Just an hour or so, and then she could hang this outfit in the closet. Get the alterations done later.

Mike entered the room and closed the door behind him. His eyes traveled down her length and back up, a wolfish grin covering his face. "Very nice."

She curtsied for him. "Thank you, sir."

He pulled his plastic-wrapped suit from the closet and hung the outfit on the door. "Want to help me get dressed?"

She smiled, knowing full well where that could lead. "Not likely. You're on your own. And on your way down, could you check on Bradley? He might need help with his tie."

Mike snapped the ready-knotted accessory on the hanger. "If his is like mine, he probably won't."

Carly slipped on her slippers, picked up her shoes, and headed for the door. "I'll get the camera and make sure we have fresh batteries. Then I want to call Mavis and see if she can keep an eye on Bradley this afternoon."

Mike waggled his eyebrows at her. "Oh, going to help me undress later?"

"No. We're going to look for Jerry. And I don't think we want the child along on that trip. That's assuming he doesn't show up at the wedding."

Her husband's shoulders slumped. "You're right about that. Don't forget to ask about McMasters."

Carly went downstairs and rummaged through the junk drawer in the kitchen that seemed filled with everything except junk. She pawed through coupons and pushed aside seven screwdrivers with straight heads. In the far back corner nestled their digital camera, long-forgotten since their last vacation—when was that? Four years before? Five, maybe.

She clicked the device on but nothing happened. Great. Dead batteries. Hopefully they hadn't leaked into the body of the camera. A glance at the clock on the stove confirmed her suspicions—they were running out of time if they were going to get to the church on time.

Another fifties song about going to the chapel and getting married played across her memory. She hummed along with the catchy tune while she opened and installed a new package of batteries.

She went to the foot of the stairs. "Mike. Almost ready."

"One minute."

Seemed she had the sixty seconds she needed to call Mavis. She dialed the number, waited for her to answer. "Mavis, it's Carly. Just a quick call to see how Mr. McMasters is doing."

"Nothing new to report, Carly. He's still out of it. Doctors don't know when he might come around."

"Thanks. Can you take Bradley for a couple of hours after the wedding? Mike and I have an errand we need to run."

"Sure thing. The hospital has my cell phone number, and they said they'd call if there was any change. Got to run or I'm going to be late to the church." The postmistress chuckled, her gentle laugh lifting Carly's spirits after the not-so-encouraging report. "And so will you be, too. Go, girl."

Carly rang off as two of the handsomest men in her world stepped through the kitchen doorway. "Well, look at you two. Aren't you a good looking pair."

Bradley beamed and looked up at Mike, who rested his hand on the boy's shoulder. Already the child looked better. Gone were the unshed tears and the flushed cheeks, replaced with bright eyes and a happy smile.

She smiled at her 'men'. "Got the camera. Got the fresh batteries. Got the men. We're set. Let's go."

Bradley giggled, the sound filling her mother's heart with joy.

"What is it?"

He pointed to her feet.

She still had her fluffy Doc the cat slippers on.

She wanted to ruffle his hair but didn't want to mess up his style, so instead she planted a wet kiss on his cheek. "Thank you. That would have been embarrassing."

He swiped at her kiss then led the way to the car.

* * *

Carly thought her face would cramp into place because of all the smiling she'd done over the past hour. Even Bradley seemed to be having fun, although his father hadn't shown up. Not that Carly really expected him to. The wedding went off like a charm, and the happy couple posed on the front steps of the church as family and friends snapped pictures and threw rice at them. Denise and Don and the three kids came from Riverdale, and Bradley had spent some time playing with his cousins. Margie, the older one, was around his age, and she seemed enamored with her new cousin. When the limousine arrived to drive the newlyweds to the Boston airport, Tom and Sarah stood at the driver's side door a few minutes and talked to the driver. Then the car drove off without them.

What was going on?

If they didn't leave soon, they'd miss their flight to Hawaii, where Tom had booked an expensive hotel on the beach in Waikiki for the week. Carly and Bradley went down the steps and met Mike coming from another direction.

He looped his arm through hers. "How come they didn't go?"

She shrugged. "You know as much as I do."

Tom and Sarah turned as they drew near. Tom glanced at his bride and smiled. She nodded. He faced his parents. "We decided to stay around for a few hours. Maybe for a few days."

"But you'll lose your flight and your hotel." Carly hadn't ever heard of a honeymoon being delayed. Except maybe for sickness.

Or death.

"You don't need to stick around here."

Tom shook his head. "We can't leave you with Bradley by yourselves." He lowered his voice and leaned in closer to Carly and Mike. "And with Uncle Jerry gone, and this whole mess about the bank robberies, we wouldn't feel right. We can have a honeymoon any time." He pulled Sarah close. "It wasn't my idea. It was hers."

Sarah's cheeks flushed. "Seems like if we're family, we should stick together." She crouched at his eye level. "What do you think, big guy? Would that be okay with you if we stuck around a bit?"

Bradley stared into her face as though she was a vision from another galaxy, and nodded, apparently star struck that this angel in white would stoop to speak to him.

Carly smiled. The boy was smitten.

And with a married woman.

She nodded. "Okay. Mavis is going to look after Bradley this afternoon."

The boy tugged on her hand. "Can't I stay with Tom and Sarah?"

Carly hesitated. Perhaps the young couple would prefer to be alone. After all, it was their wedding day.

But Sarah answered for her. "We'd love to have you spend as long with us as you want." She looked to Mike and Carly. "Would that be all right? Tom and I have already talked about it."

Mike clapped his son on the back. "Fine with us. We've got to go out for a few hours. We'll get together for dinner later."

Sarah turned and headed for their car. "Come with me. I need to get out of this dress and these shoes, and then we'll find something fun to do."

Bradley gripped her hand as if he never wanted to let her out of his sight. "You look like a princess."

Don and Denise pulled up, their kids already safely belted into their seats. "We're heading home. Maybe you will come over next week for dinner?"

Mike kissed his daughter and waved to the grandkids. "Sounds good. Give us a few days to recover from this soiree and we'll give you a call."

Carly leaned in through the open window and blew kisses at the little ones. "We love you."

≠≠ Unbalanced ≠≠

Amid a chorus of 'we love you' and 'see you later, alligator', the vehicle drove off, headed for the larger town about an hour up the highway.

Mike and Carly walked towards home, holding hands and discussing the wedding. They both agreed the event had been all they'd hoped for.

And more.

Bradley seemed more at ease than he had for days. He hadn't mentioned his father's non-appearance at the wedding, and asking to spend time with Tom and Sarah was a good indication at how comfortable he felt with them.

Carly waved as the car bearing the newlywed couple and the small boy drove past. Bradley's hair glinted in the sunlight, and shades of both Tom's and Sarah's hair reflected back at her.

He was enough like both of them to pass for their natural son.

She shook off the thought.

Jerry wouldn't let his son go.

She needed to focus on finding that prodigal brother.

Before he got himself into any more trouble.

≠≠ Unbalanced ≠≠

Chapter 15

Carly and Mike changed out of their dress clothes and grabbed a bite to eat before heading out the door.

Mike paused by the car. "I think we can get more ground covered if we drive."

Carly considered a moment then agreed. "Let's stop at Jacob Roy's first. I want to ask him a few more questions."

He lifted an eyebrow in question. "Some more questions?"

"Well, I just happened to stop by earlier this morning—"

"Happened to drop by? Carly, you never *happen* to do anything."

She settled into the passenger seat. "As I said, let's stop at Jacob's first. He as much as told me he would be open after the wedding."

Mike nodded and started the car, then backed down the driveway and turned onto Jamaica Street heading for downtown. They were silent with their thoughts for the block-and-a-half ride, and Carly was first out of the car, her door open before Mike had come to a complete stop.

As good as his word, Jacob's head was under the hood of the same truck he'd been working on when she'd seen him that morning.

He straightened and faced them, wiping his hand on a now-greasier rag.

≠≠ Unbalanced ≠≠

"Good day, folks."

Mike stepped forward and shook the older man's hand. "Jacob, we're looking for my brother Jerry. Have you seen him around?"

Jacob frowned as he thought. "Ayuh. Saw him driving an old car around town a couple of days ago. Looked like a Chevy from the seventies, by my estimation. Probably a Cutlass. Judging by the sound of the engine, he's not taking care of it. More than two-hundred-fifty thousand miles on 'er, I'd say."

Carly wasn't the least bit interested in the mileage or the make of the car, but that would be just like Jacob to notice those things. Being a mechanic and all. "Have you seen it lately?"

"Not since yesterday."

Her heart rate picked up a notch or two. "Where did you see it yesterday?"

"Front of your house. Early in the morning."

She bit back a sharp retort. "Yes, he stayed the night. Have you seen it since then?"

He pulled a toothpick from his overall pocket, peeled back the plastic wrap, and tucked the sliver of wood into the corner of his mouth. "I know I seen it somewhere. Now, where was that?"

Which was exactly the answer they were looking for. And needed. She waited. No point in rushing the man. Sometimes she felt as though she was trying to push a wet noodle uphill when trying to keep Jacob on point and on task.

He chewed on the toothpick like it was a tasty morsel of meat, then his expression brightened. "It was—no, that warn't him. That was another car." He pulled out the wooden piece. "Now that was a nice car. Well taken care of. Purred like a kitten and—"

Mike nudged Carly in the ribs. She swallowed back what she was going to say and allowed her husband to take the lead. "About Jerry and his Cutlass?"

"Right. Now that could be a good project car. Needs new lifters. A muffler. Probably some springs in the rear end."

Mike pressed in. "About my brother? We're really worried about him.

After the bank robbery and all."

Jacob chuckled. "Ayuh. The first or the second one." His eyes twinkled. "If'n there was a first one, hey, Carly?" He shook his head. "Such a 'magination you have."

"My brother?"

"Ayuh. Now I remember. Saw that car parked in front of the no-tell motel just outside the town limits. Thought it was a funny place for him to stay, so figured he was a-visiting folks there. Still, seemed a sorry place to even stop at."

Carly sprinted for the car with Mike close on her heels, calling out his thanks to the old mechanic.

Finally, they had a lead.

* * *

When Mike pulled into the parking lot of the seedy motel, Carly shivered, as if a goose had walked over her grave. What a dump! Although she wasn't very happy with Jerry at that moment, she was glad he and his son didn't have to stay in a place like this.

Sure enough, Jerry had parked his old wrecker in front of a unit, the number seven hanging crookedly on the door. When their car pulled to a stop, Carly went to open the door, but Mike stopped her with a hand on her arm.

"Wait here. I'll go."

She opened her mouth to protest then accepted the wisdom of the situation. If these men were involved in robbing the bank, they might be desperate. She was safer in the car. Not that she wanted Mike in any danger, but he would only worry if she were there with him.

Mike exited the car and strode to room seven, then knocked. He waited a few seconds then knocked again. Bending his ear near the door, he listened then shook his head. He turned and headed for the office. Carly couldn't stand the suspense, and if he was going to ask questions, she wanted to hear the answers. She got out, made sure she locked the doors, and joined her husband as he walked on the wooden boardwalk to the office.

The door squeaked when they entered, and a brass bell tied to the inside knob tinkled, alerting the man at the front desk that they were there. He looked up from the newspaper he was reading and peered myopically over his half-glasses. "Need a room?"

Mike leaned on the counter. "No. Looking for my brother."

The man returned to his paper. "Do I look like missing persons?"

Carly slapped her hand on the counter. She'd had enough of Jerry and his misadventures taking over their lives. She wanted answers, and she wanted them now. "Listen, Mister. I'm an auditor, and I can have the IRS down on this dump quicker than you can say 'shred the records'." She pulled her cell phone from her pocket. "Now, are you going to help us, or do I make that phone call?"

The clerk blinked rapidly several times, his Adam's apple working hard as he swallowed. He looked from Mike to Carly and back again. "How can I help you?"

Mike's mouth lifted in a half-smile. "The car in front of number seven. Did you see the man driving it?"

"Yes."

"When did you last see him?"

"Yesterday?"

"Was he with anybody?"

"Yes."

Carly sighed. Getting answers from this guy was like pulling teeth. She sidled closer to Mike. "What can you tell us about them?"

The man set his newspaper aside and fumbled for a key on a board beside him. "Checked in last week. Paid for a week. Three men plus the driver. The room runs out tonight. Their stuff is still in there." He held out the key. "Whatever they did, I don't know nothing. I'm a legitimate business man. Just trying to make a living."

Carly snatched the key. "Right. And I'm Bo Derek."

He tilted his head to one side in question.

She sighed. "You know. Voted the most beautiful woman in the world. A perfect ten?"

He nodded, eyeing her up and down. "Yes, ma'am. Nice to meet you, Miss Derek."

Carly quirked her head toward the door. "Come on, Mike. Let's get out of here before the vacuum sucks out our brains, too."

The clerk sat. "Vacuum? I ain't got no vacuum running."

Mike hurried after her as she headed for the room, chuckling as he went. "I thought he was going to lose his bottom plate when you mentioned the IRS. And since when are you an auditor?"

She paused, hands on her hips. "Stop wasting time, Mike Turnquist. I can audit books as well as anybody. It's what I do for a living." She sighed. "Well, it's what I did before that crazy news story came out."

Mike wrapped his hand around hers as they continued toward the room. "Maybe that's what this was all about."

"What?"

"Seems like someone went to a lot of trouble to destroy your credibility. Who would do that?"

Carly paused in front of the room. "Somebody bone-deep evil, that's who."

"That goes without saying." He held out his hand for the key. "But who do we know who is that evil? And what have you done to make them that angry with you?"

She passed him the key. "I haven't done anything. Just what I do best. Find hidden assets. Testify in court."

He unlocked the door and motioned for her to wait. He entered the room and disappeared from view.

She held her breath while he was inside, fully expecting gunshots to ring out.

But all remained quiet.

Mike emerged a mere thirty seconds later. "It's a small room. Not many places for anybody to hide. I checked the closet, under the beds, and the bathroom. Looks like they went out yesterday and didn't come back." He flipped on a light switch by the door, bathing the room in the glow from two forty-watt bulbs in dirty sconces on the wall over the two single beds. "But that might be the reason."

She stepped over the threshold. "For what?"

"Maybe someone is trying to make you incredible in the eyes of the law. What about this trial you're supposed to testify at?"

"I met with the parties this week, and the attorney who hired me and the judge on the case kind of said the same thing. The husband's attorney looked a little too smug for my liking, but since I don't like him, I thought that might have bent my judgment of him. He's too smarmy by half."

"Smarmy?" Mike chuckled. "What have you been reading? Pirate stories?"

"No, but I watched that series on public television about men sentenced to Australia for their crimes."

She glanced around the room, wishing she'd thought to bring latex gloves. Not to keep her fingerprints off surfaces.

To keep her hands clean.

"What are we looking for?"

Mike shrugged. "Not really sure. Anything that shows Jerry was here. Or to show that the men who rented the room were involved in the bank robbery."

Carly used a pen to flip through a stack of papers. Some kind of drawings. Like blueprints, but not quite the same. She turned the papers to read the words. "Oh, here's something."

Mike stood beside her. "What is it?"

"I think it's the plans to the bank building." She used the pen to point. "See, here it shows the post office next door." She flipped to another page. "And this shows the alley behind those buildings." And another. "And this has the name of a security company on it. Aroostook Security." She set the pen down. "Why would Jerry need a security company?"

"Not just security." Mike tapped the label at the bottom of the page. "Security and safe company." He picked up the sheet and peered at the tiny words and shapes. "This is the schematics for the bank safe."

Carly looked up from where she rummaged through the desk drawer. She held up a set of keys. "These have the Chevrolet emblem on them. Want to bet they fit Jerry's car?"

Mike shook his head. "I think you'd win. But let's check for certain."

The driver's side door opened on the first try, and although the old engine coughed and sputtered, the car started, sending out a thick plume of gray smoke and exhaust.

Mike turned the car off. "This is Jerry's car. These are his keys. But where is Jerry?" He snapped the sun visor back into position. "Don't need that down right now."

A folded piece of paper fell into his lap.

"Well, what do we have here?"

"Probably an IOU from Jerry."

"I don't think so." He held the paper out the window. "It's got your name on it."

≠≠ Unbalanced ≠≠

≠≠ Unbalanced ≠≠

≠≠ Unbalanced ≠≠

Chapter 16

Carly greeted Sunday morning with bleary eyes. Too much thinking and not enough sleep did not bode well for a restful night. Long after Mike was deep into sawing logs in sleep, she'd remained awake, her eyes unable to close for more than a few seconds at a time, as she tried to figure out how Jerry—and thus her family—was connected to the bank robbery.

Both of them.

The note behind the visor didn't say much. Just that he was sorry he'd gotten into this mess and would find a way to make it up to her. Then it ended. No signature. No nothing. As if he'd been interrupted while writing the words.

She'd read the note the evening before. More like trying to read between the lines, actually, since the words themselves didn't explain a lot. She thought Jerry was referring to stealing the wedding gifts. Mike thought that maybe he was talking about something from years before. She didn't think so. If that were the case, surely he'd have written the apology to Mike and not to her. Apart from dropping in out of the blue, dumping his son on them, getting angry when they couldn't change their schedules to suit him, Jerry hadn't directly done anything to Carly.

As if all that wasn't enough to apologize for.

The refreshing scent of coffee wafted up the stairs and into the bedroom, and she turned over, intending to cuddle into Mike for another few minutes.

But his side of the bed was empty.

Duh! Of course. He was the one rustling around in the kitchen, creating that heavenly smell.

As if to confirm her words, he called up the stairs to her. "Carly. Breakfast in fifteen minutes." The sound of breaking glass followed close behind. "Don't worry. Juice glasses are cheap. I bet that one already had a crack in it."

She smiled. None of her glasses had so much as a chip in the rim. But she loved her husband all the more for trying to make the child comfortable.

When they'd gotten home from the motel, Tom and Sarah were already curled up with the boy in front of the television, all three fast asleep. Mike had said to leave them be. They'd wake up when they were ready.

Again, not her idea of a perfect wedding night, but the kids were old enough to make those decisions for themselves.

She glanced at the bedside table. The note from Jerry rested there. She and Mike had read the words last night. Words that answered their questions but didn't set their hearts at ease.

Sometimes knowing the truth was worse than not knowing.

She rolled out of bed and padded across the room toward the bathroom. She just had time for a quick shower, get dressed, and get downstairs. She relished the needle-like pricks of the water, inhaled the invigorating scent of peppermint and vanilla body wash, and emerged from the shower with pink skin and a sunny disposition.

The day was looking up already.

And she hadn't even had her first cup of coffee.

She dressed quickly, throwing on her standard uniform of sweats and a shirt along with her sneakers. No telling where she'd be going today, and she wanted to be as comfortable as possible.

She went down to the kitchen, which felt about to burst at its seams. Tom and Sarah lined one side of the wooden kitchen table, Mike sat at the end in his usual spot, and Bradley sat to his left. Her empty chair beckoned her into their family circle.

Funny how one little boy could make the place seem so full.

Or maybe it wasn't the size of the child, but the size of the child's heart.

She slid into her chair and the conversation paused for a moment as the others murmured their good-mornings. Bradley peered at her from beneath his too-long bangs which today he'd combed straight down. Sarah passed the plate of eggs, and Mike pushed the coffee pot toward her. Soon everyone was devouring the delicious breakfast.

Carly waggled a slice of toast in Sarah's direction. "Did they rope you into cooking for them?"

She laughed, the pink in her cheeks a most becoming shade. "No. In fact, they shooed me out when I offered to help."

Tom nodded. "That's right. Mike said he had it under control."

Bradley reached over and touched Carly's hand. "I'm sorry. I broke a glass."

She glanced at Mike then back to the boy. "That's okay. It probably had a weak spot."

Mike coughed on something he was chewing, and Tom slapped him on the back a couple of times.

Carly addressed the newly-weds. "So what are your plans for today?"

Sarah smiled across the table. "If it's okay with you, we'd like to take Bradley with us. We're going to Riverdale today to see the cousins. He didn't stop talking about them all last evening while you were out." Her smile slipped away. "Speaking of which—"

Carly shook her head. "Nothing yet." She turned to the child. "I think Margie would love to see you again."

He nodded. "She's nice, too." He looked up from his breakfast plate, which he'd wiped clean with the slice of toast in his hand. "All your family is nice."

Mike touched the boy's shoulder. "All *your* family, too, Bradley."

A grin split the child's face. "I never had family before." He sobered. "Just my father."

≠≠ Unbalanced ≠≠

The fact he'd stopped asking for his father, and now referred to him only as that and never Daddy, hadn't escaped Carly's notice. If Jerry didn't reappear soon, he might lose his connection with his son, however precarious that might have been in the past.

She jumped to her feet and headed for the toaster. "Anybody want more—"

The phone rang, and she grabbed it, thinking the call would be someone wishing the kids well or thanking them for the party. "Hello?"

"Chief Blom here, Carly."

She turned away from the table and lowered her voice. "Yes?"

"Wanted to let you know we found the bank robbers in Vermont. Holed up in a hotel. Someone recognized the SUV from the news stories and called in their highway patrol."

"Oh."

"Only thing is, Jerry wasn't with them. They won't say anything, but the detectives on scene say it looks like McMasters hit the vehicle when he fired at them." A heavy sigh filled the line. "Crazy old man. I don't know what he was thinking. Any word on him yet?"

"Nothing as of last evening. What are they saying?"

"Nothing. Not even their names yet. But Carly—"

In her experience, nothing good ever came from a sentence started with 'but'. "Yes?"

"The detectives said there was evidence of blood. A lot of blood. On the driver's seat."

"But it might not be—"

"Jerry has a rap sheet as long as your arm. Mostly petty stuff, but a couple of times he was picked up on suspicion of armed robbery."

"What does that prove?"

"He was always the getaway driver."

"What are you saying?"

"They stopped for gas just over the state border. A CCTV camera picked up the vehicle. Jerry wasn't driving. There were only three men in the car."

"I understand."

"We're checking local hospitals and clinics, even doctors out in the country in case they dropped him off somewhere."

"Good idea."

"We'll let you know as soon as we have something."

"Do you have my cell number?"

"I do. I'm sorry, Carly."

"Thank you." She replaced the receiver and stared at the toaster, trying to remember what she was doing. The tray popped and two perfectly-toasted slices emerged.

Right. Breakfast.

She took out the toast and turned to the table.

Four faces stared back at her.

And she didn't know what to tell them.

* * *

From the tone of her voice, Mike knew Carly didn't have good news.

And from the look on her face—her brow drawn, her mouth tight—and her grip on the plate holding his toast causing white knuckles, what news she had she didn't want to share.

He glanced at Tom. "I think your plan to go see the cousins sounds like loads of fun. Wish I could go with."

Bradley turned to him, his mouth turned down and his brow furrowed. "Oh, can you come? Please?"

"Love to, but Aunt Carly needs me here today." He faced his wife who still had not sat at the table. He waggled one eyebrow at her. "Don't you?"

"Right." She tipped her head toward the child. "Next time."

"Promise?"

She nodded. "Promise."

The child slid from his chair. "Okay."

Mike smiled. The innocence of children. Sometimes he wished he hadn't lost that inherent belief that whatever an adult said must be true.

And despite being the son of one of the most consummate liars Mike knew, his son still wanted to believe.

Within a few minutes, Tom, Sarah, and the boy were out the front door amidst a flurry of hugs and kisses and promises not to be late coming home.

Mike rested his arm on Carly's shoulder as they waved the kids off. "Reminds me of when Tom first got his license and went on his first date."

She pressed closer to him. "Thank you."

He pulled her around to face him. "For what?"

"For encouraging the kids to go. For knowing I didn't want to talk in front of Bradley. For being you."

"Should I be sitting when you tell me what the phone call was about?"

"No. I think you'll be okay."

"Let's finish breakfast." He led her toward the kitchen. "So who was on the phone?"

"Chief Blom."

"What did he say?"

She filled him in quickly, and by the time they'd finished their now-cold toast, he knew as much as she did. At least, he hoped he did, because otherwise that meant she was holding something back.

Never one to leave a question unasked, he laid a hand on hers. "Anything else you need to tell me?"

"No. But I think we should go look for him."

Mike sipped his coffee. "I suspected that was coming." He set his cup down. "And for once, I'm not going to argue with you or fight you on this."

She raised an eyebrow. "You're not?"

He shook his head. "I think we need to go look. For Bradley's sake. If he didn't cross the border with the others, he must be somewhere between here and the border." A lump formed in his throat, making the next words difficult to speak. "Which probably means—"

Carly reached across the table and gripped his hand. "He might be in a hospital. The chief said they'd checked, but he could be there under an assumed name. Maybe he has amnesia. Maybe they left him with a farmer."

"Or maybe they left him in a ditch." He swallowed hard. "Or a shallow grave." He rested his head in his hands. "How am I going to tell Bradley his father is dead? Who is going to look after the little fellow?" He slapped the table with an open palm. "Leave it up to Jerry to sail into town, nothing better on his mind than dumping his son on us, robbing a bank, and taking off."

"Don't jump to conclusions. That's what you'd tell me."

"Never stops you, though, does it?"

A glimmer of hope clawed its way from his gut up his throat. Carly was right. No point in assuming the worst.

Although, when referring to Jerry, he seldom was able to think bad enough. Jerry always managed to surprise him by finding himself in a much worse situation than Mike dreamed possible.

No, he needed to cut his brother some slack. After all, most of the trouble he'd gotten himself into in the past was before his son came along.

Perhaps he'd managed to turn over a new leaf.

Even though things didn't look that way.

* * *

Feeling like a search-and-rescue dog, Carly stared out the window of the car as they traveled down the highway. She'd never had to find a missing brother before. Particularly not one who seemed to make it a practice to disappear for years at a time. Maybe Mike's first inclination was correct: Jerry had blown town with his part of the bank loot and left them to look after Bradley.

Surely that was against the law. Abandonment or some such thing.

Of course, to be charged with a crime, a person had to be found.

She sighed and turned to look out the windshield. Mike had taken the news of Jerry being missing with his usual stoicism, but she knew him well enough to note that the worry lines around his eyes and mouth had deepened. He'd shrugged off her suggestion that they remain at home in case his brother showed up.

"I doubt if he'll come back here." Mike had paced the floor in the kitchen. "I know our police force is small, but they're all on the lookout. Not to mention half the town that blames him for McMasters being in a coma. That old man is a

≠≠ Unbalanced ≠≠

town favorite. The other two are lucky they're in custody in Vermont. There'd be a lynching otherwise."

"Oh, Mike. Don't be silly." She'd tried to get him to lighten up. "Lynching went out with—"

"The KKK?"

His grim reminder of the race relations problems didn't set her mind at ease.

And those worry lines around his mouth were as deep and grim as before.

They rounded a bend in the highway and came upon a straight section. He turned to her. "So what's the plan?"

She didn't have much of a plan. "I thought we should start at the motel and work our way to the border."

"What do you hope to find?"

She wasn't certain how to answer that question. She hoped to find Jerry without the wedding gifts or bank loot, sleeping it off in a motel room, unaware of what was going on around him. She hoped to find that his two cohorts would start talking and say they'd hired another driver for the robbery, that Jerry wasn't involved at all.

She didn't think any of that was going to happen.

"I'm not sure." She pointed to a driveway on the left a few hundred feet ahead. "That's the motel. Let's stop in and see if he came back."

Mike put on his turn signal and slowed, then coasted into the parking lot and stopped in front of unit seven. A small pile of odds and sods of clothing and personal effects rested in a pile on the boardwalk. A jacket much like the one Jerry had worn the day of the rehearsal dinner sat on top.

Mike sighed. "I guess we've got our answer."

"Maybe Jerry called and he's coming to get his stuff."

Her husband grunted.

"Well, it could happen."

"Right. And pigs could fly."

"Do you want to talk to the manager or will I?"

≠≠ Unbalanced ≠≠

He opened the door. "I'll do it." He leaned in through the open window. "You wait here in case my brother shows up."

Carly didn't miss the sarcasm in his tone. He walked toward the office, turned the corner, and disappeared from sight, returning a couple of minutes later. As he neared the car, he shook his head.

Carly pulled out a state map and studied the roads that intersected with the highway. She pointed to a couple of county roads and three woods roads. "We can check down these."

"We could be out here all summer and not find him if he's down one of those." Mike started the engine and backed out, then turned back onto the highway heading toward the state line. "If they were trying to get rid of him, they'd take the first place they could find where nobody would look for him."

"Right. And a county road wouldn't be it. They aren't from around here. They don't know how far down those roads they'd have to go before they found somewhere."

"And, they've got to figure that the state police will have a roadblock set up, if not this side of the state line, the other side."

"Especially since this car is now known to be stolen." This was exciting. Carly loved when she and Mike worked on a case together. Not that this was a case, per se. This was a family matter. "If you were Jerry, where would you go?"

"Well, first of all, I don't think Jerry is driving by this time. I think something happened in town. So that means one of the other guys is driving. Which means Jerry is hurt." He paused a long moment. "Or worse."

"We need to think positively."

"I am positive Jerry has gotten himself in over his head this time."

She looked at the map again. "Okay. If they didn't pick a road, what did they do?" Her finger traced the highway that curved around the hills. "There isn't much else here."

"About the only thing I can think of is that old quarry up near County Road 12."

Carly peered at the tiny writing on the map. "Sounds good to me. It's about twelve miles up the road." She settled back in her seat and studied the

≠≠ Unbalanced ≠≠

passing landscape, which consisted of birch and elm trees, some spruce and juniper, as well as open fields of grass interspersed with large boulders which looked like they'd been tossed by giants of long ago days and left to lie where they landed.

Ten minutes later, Mike slowed the car and pulled up to a closed gate. "It's probably locked, but I'll check anyway." He got out and went up to the rusted wire structure and fiddled with the chain. Within a couple of minutes, he'd swung the gate open and returned to the car. "Looks like there was a lock but it's been shattered." He held out his hand. "And I found this."

A flattened bullet.

Carly shivered as the reality of their situation finally crept in. Of course, bank robbers would carry weapons. A simple lock on a gate wouldn't keep them out. Any more than a security alarm kept them out of the bank.

There wasn't anything to say until they knew more. At this point, all they had was supposition and conjecture, neither of which would give them any answers or help them find Jerry.

The dusty road wound around piles of rock of various sizes, and their car kicked up a cloud behind them. They closed their windows and turned on the AC. Down over a small hill, a creek ran beside the road for about a hundred feet before veering off in another direction. Two more turns and they came out into a large open area surrounded by a chain link fence.

In the middle sat an old mobile home, much the worse for wear. The door hung off its hinges, and the metal roof peeled back at one corner like a sardine can. There was no glass left in the windows except for some shards clinging to the old aluminum frames, and the steps lay collapsed in a pile.

Mike stopped the car. "Stay here."

"But Mike—"

"Stay here."

Carly jutted out her bottom lip, knowing she looked foolish. And childish. Hardly like the grown woman and professional she was.

But she didn't care.

He strode toward the trailer, grabbed the edge of the doorway, and hoisted himself inside.

He returned less than a minute later, his hand over his mouth. He jumped to the ground then pulled his cell phone from his pocket, punched in a number, and waited. He spoke into the mouthpiece, listened a moment, nodded, and disconnected the call.

Carly stepped out of the car and walked toward him, her shoes kicking up dust, pebbles skittering in front of her. "What is it?"

Her husband turned to her. "I've called the highway patrol."

"Is he—" She couldn't finish the sentence. If Jerry was in there, this wasn't good. "Mike?"

He nodded. "I don't think he made it out of town." He sighed and stared at the ground. "What am I going to say to his son? How do I explain that his father died because he was trying to steal money that didn't belong to him?"

For one of the few times in her life, Carly didn't know what to say.

So she said nothing.

She'd learned early in her marriage that sometimes love is best expressed in silence.

≠≠ Unbalanced ≠≠

≠≠ Unbalanced ≠≠

≠≠ Unbalanced ≠≠

Chapter 17

The ride home was quiet. Carly wanted Mike time to process his feelings about his brother's death. No matter what her husband said about how many times Jerry messed up, he now needed to come to terms with the fact that his brother was gone.

Forever.

When they pulled in the driveway, Tom and Sarah's car parked on the street.

Which meant that Bradley was also home.

Mike heaved a sigh that started at his toes and worked its way upwards, reminding Carly of the blacksmith's bellows at the local petting farm. He turned the engine off then reached into his pocket and handed her a slip of folded paper.

"What is it?"

"Jerry left a kind of a will."

"A will? He didn't own anything of value." As soon as the words were out of her mouth, she regretted them. Mike stared straight ahead at the house. "I'm sorry, Mike. I wasn't trying to be mean."

He laid a hand over hers. "I know you weren't. But he had something that was priceless."

≠≠ Unbalanced ≠≠

She tilted her head in question. What was he talking about?

"His son."

"Did he know he was dying?"

Mike shook his head. "I think he wrote this before the robbery. I don't know how long before. But my guess is he knew he was living on borrowed time, given his plans."

She nodded. "What do you want to do with it?"

"You should read it first, and then we'll decide together."

She unfolded the paper and read the cramped writing:

This is kind of my last will and testament. First off, I want to apologize to my brother for all the trouble I ever caused him. Seemed like everything I touched turned to dust. The harder I tried to get out of the hole I dug myself into, the deeper I went.

The only good thing in my life is my son. Mike, I want you to take full legal custody of him. Give him a good home. I couldn't ask for anybody better to raise him than you two, or someone you pick out.

Like they say on the TV, if you're reading this, I'm dead. So I want to set some stuff straight. Carly did see a bank robbery.

Carly looked up from the paper. "Did you read this?"

Mike nodded. "Keep reading."

"But he says I saw the bank—"

"Keep reading."

She returned to the note:

And she didn't.

Carly looked at Mike. "He can't have it both ways."

"Keep reading."

We was paid to stage a fake robbery. It's why nobody would fess up that to the bank robbery. It wasn't. This guy named Chad, who seemed to know a lot about your family, offered us $50 each to pretend to rob the bank. He said he was playing a joke on Carly because she got him good one time. I found out after that it wasn't payback.

Chad was doing it because his Aunt Penelope asked him to. I saw the two of them talking in her fancy dress store. I got close enough to listen so I could have something on Chad in case he tried to double-cross me.

But Chad laughed at me when I told him and said I didn't have anything on him. I talked to his aunt and told her I knew what she did. I wanted to set things square, but she said she'd turn me and the boys in, and we'd all go to prison.

Then Chad got the bright idea to rob the same bank on the same day as the wedding party cuz he knew most of the town would be at your house. I didn't like the idea, but he said it was easy money. Since I'm dead, I don't know what went wrong, but just like with everything in my life, something was bound to. Tell Bradley his daddy loves him and wants him to grow up to be just like his Uncle Mike. Jerry Turnquist.

Carly held the paper for a long moment, her final connection to a brother-in-law she hadn't really liked but who she missed already.

Mike took the letter and carefully folded the paper on its creases again. "Who is this guy Chad?"

Heat rushed to her cheeks as she realized she hadn't told Mike about Sarah's stalkers. "Penny's nephew."

"Penny from Well Dressed?"

She nodded. "The one and the same."

"Why would Penny do this to you?"

"She wanted to get back at me for what happened to Susan. And I'm pretty sure she is somehow connected to the crooked husband in the case I'm supposed to testify at. The one where my credibility is called into question because of this whole fake bank robbery affair. He sort of threatened me, said I'd get what was coming to me."

Mike stared at her. "Sort of threatened you?"

She shrugged. "Sort of."

"Seems like she went to a lot of trouble for payback, as Jerry called it."

"She had two very good reasons, at least as far as she's concerned." Carly drew a deep breath for courage. "There's a piece of the puzzle we forgot to tell you."

"We?"

"Sarah and Tom and me."

He turned to face her, his neck turning red. "What did you not tell me, and why?"

She held up her hands in surrender. "To be fair, this happened in New York the day I went to see the attorneys and the judge. I was a little rattled about that. Then we found out about Fergus. And we confronted him. And I came back here, and I was thrown into this whole bank robbery thing, and the wedding, and Jerry missing—" She stopped, having run out of breath. "So it wasn't my fault."

"Why is it never your fault when you get into trouble over something?"

"In case you hadn't noticed, I didn't get into trouble about anything. Nobody tried to kill me this time around." She sat back and folded her arms over her chest. "I'd say that's pretty good, given I've solved three mysteries."

"Three?"

"The bank robbery that wasn't. The stalker. The bank robbery that was."

Mike shook his head slowly. "I don't understand. What's this about a stalker?"

"A young man decided Sarah was his one true love and started following her around. Harmless, really."

Mike huffed. "Go on."

"And coincidentally, at the same time, Penny has her nephew Chad following Sarah to set her up in some way. Chad tells Penny about Fergus." She paused. "Understand, some of this is conjecture, since I don't know for sure."

Mike nodded. "Of course. But you're rarely wrong."

She smiled. Finally he acknowledged her unique gift. "Penny talks to Fergus and gets him to bump into Sarah. She snaps a picture. Doctors it to make it look like they're embracing. And you know the rest."

"Not quite. How did you confront him?"

Ah, that part. She swallowed hard. "Well, we tricked him into meeting her and Tom and I spoke to him and—"

Mike leaned forward. "Wait one minute. You and Tom spoke to a stalker?"

≠≠ Unbalanced ≠≠

She waved off his words. "He wasn't much older than a teen, and about as mature. He was no threat to us. We met in a public place."

"What if he'd realized he was being set up and didn't meet you but followed Sarah and did her some harm?"

"We didn't think—"

"That's just it. You didn't think." He pounded the steering wheel. "And to think you got my son and daughter-in-law mixed up in your schemes."

"First of all, he's my son, too. And she's my daughter-in-law. And it was her idea. She wanted to confront him herself, but I insisted Tom and I be present. I felt that a man and an adult would make a greater impression on him."

Mike's shoulders relaxed and he sat back in his car seat. "Well, that's okay, then."

She rocked her head back and forth in an expression she'd seen the kids do then mimicked him. "Well, that's okay, then. Sure, Carly, you aren't in trouble anymore." She rubbed his arm. "Thanks for worrying about me."

He reached across the console and pulled her close, burying his nose in her hair. "I always worry about you. You are too nosy for your own good."

She pulled away. Her love for this man had just grown another notch. Still, she couldn't let him get away with treating her like a child. "But this nosy accountant gets results."

Banging on Mike's window tore them from their banter. They both looked to see the source.

Bradley.

Mike sighed. "I don't know how to do this."

She patted his arm. "I know. There's no training manual for this situation. Why don't you take him for a drive down to the lake? That was a happy place for the two of you."

He smiled. "That's another reason I love you."

"Oh?"

"You're so wise."

She stabbed an index finger into his chest, accentuating her words. "And. Don't. You. Forget. It." She opened the car door. "Come around here.

Uncle Mike wants to go for a drive."

"Hurray. I like going for a drive with Uncle Mike. Where are we going?"

He pushed past Carly as she got out, and she waited until he'd fastened his seat belt before she closed the door. "See you boys later. If you're in the mood, we'll have popcorn and hot chocolate."

Bradley clapped and gave her the thumbs-up signal.

Youth was so innocent.

Long after the car had backed out of the driveway and driven down the road out of sight, she stood there, not envying Mike his task. Two very disturbed boys were bound to come back.

Life would never be the same for either of them.

But that didn't mean it couldn't be good.

She turned to the house. Tom and Sarah stood in the doorway, arms around each other's waist, as they waited for her.

She tossed them a half-smile. "It's not good news."

* * *

Thankfully, Bradley seemed content to sit and look out the window, never questioning where they were going or why. Mike allowed the child these final few minutes of peace before he broke the bad news to him.

And, too, permitted himself a respite from the tension of the last few days.

Instead, he thought back to happier times with his brother, although truth be told, he had to think long and hard to come up with some examples. He remembered the day his mother had come home from the hospital with the tiny bundle wrapped in a blue blanket. Mike had been all of about four years old, and he'd stared in wonder at this tiny person with dark hair and yellow skin.

He'd called to his mother. "Mommy, why did you bring a Chinese baby home?"

She'd stood beside him and pulled away the blanket covering the child's face. "He's not Chinese."

"Then why is he yellow?"

She'd chuckled, that soft melodic sound he loved. Loved even more when he was the reason she laughed. "He has jaundice. Lots of new babies have it. He'll be the same color as you in a few days."

And sure enough, his mother was right. Jerry's skin changed color.

Of course, his mother was always right. And sweet. Never lost her temper. Not even when he colored on the walls or hit his brother.

Because from the time Jerry could crawl, he always managed to get into Mike's things. To break Mike's toys. Never his own. Just Mike's. And mark in Mike's books. And cry during Mike's birthday parties.

No matter how hard Mike tried, he couldn't figure out how to get along with his brother. Oh, he tried. He'd ignored him. He'd included him. He'd played with him instead of with his own friends. He'd endured the ribbings from the guys about being a babysitter.

But nothing he did was ever good enough for Jerry.

And things only got worse after their mother died when Mike was eleven and Jerry seven. Their father started drinking, then got abusive. And Jerry learned a lot of bad things from their old man.

Habits that appeared to have gotten him into worse trouble as an adult.

But, like Jerry said, Bradley was the one good thing he'd done.

So Mike focused on the good times. Before Jerry could crawl, when he was a cute baby who just sat there and gurgled. The times Jerry came back into his life over the years, dried out and cleaned up, determined to do things right this time around. But that only lasted a few days, maybe a week or so. And then he'd be off on another scheme, another way to win the jackpot and pay off his debts, to get a new start.

He turned onto the gravel road leading to the lake, and Bradley bounced on his seat the same way he'd done the first time they'd come here to go fishing. He smiled at the boy's excitement. "We won't go fishing today, though."

The boy hesitated only a moment before continuing the up and down motion. "That's okay."

"Today we're just here to talk."

"Serious talk?"

Mike nodded.

"About my father?"

Mike swallowed hard before nodding again.

"That's okay, Uncle Mike. I'm a big boy now, remember?"

"I remember, dude. You are a big boy."

They pulled into the parking lot and got out. Bradley ran ahead a few feet then skidded to a stop.

He held out his hand to Mike. "We've got to stick together, right?"

"That's right."

"And no falling in."

Mike laughed. "I hoped you'd forgotten all about that."

The boy's face was serious. "Want to sit on the rock where we ate our lunch last time?"

"That would be a good place."

Mike couldn't think of a better spot to tell the boy about his father than the very place they'd had a serious heart-to-heart talk just a few days before.

He still didn't know what he was going to say, but at least he knew where he would say the words.

Not much, but right now, it was all he had.

* * *

Carly hung up the phone. Tom and Sarah sat on the sofa opposite her, their fingers entwined, somber expressions on their faces.

"That was the attorney I work for on a case. He wants me to fax Jerry's note to the judge. He said he thinks that will clear up this entire mess, but the judge will be the one to decide that."

Tom nodded. "I sure hope so. It doesn't seem right that so many lies and crimes could steal a person's reputation like that."

Sarah stood. "I agree. And to think that Penny Holcomb, who is supposed to be your friend, was behind all this."

Carly shook her head. "First of all, she never claimed to be my friend. She was Susan's friend. And she was very angry when Susan was caught. She blamed me. Said if I hadn't poked my nose into things, Susan wouldn't have been forced to make all those bad decisions." She sighed. "I don't see how murder and attempted murder can be lumped into the same category as making a poor career choice or writing a bad check. Murder isn't exactly a bad choice. There are a whole string of decisions that made that lead up to that point."

"But to try to make you look like you are an idiot by staging a bank robbery?" Sarah shivered. "That's just pure evil."

"Well, we aren't getting anything done by sitting here. I'll fax this to the judge and see what happens." She headed for the office. "In the meantime, why don't you put on some coffee and some hot chocolate? I think Mike and Bradley will be home soon, and they're going to want something comforting."

Tom followed her but detoured into the kitchen. "I don't envy him his job."

Sarah padded along behind him. "Me, either. Maybe some soup, too?"

"Sounds good. There are a couple of containers in the fridge." Carly went into the office. "I won't be but a minute. Sherman said it might take fifteen minutes or more for the judge to respond, but he promised to give us a decision today."

She punched in the number, placed the letter on the scanner bed, and pressed the start button. The machine whirred and chirped its way through the scan, then printed out a slip indicating the fax had gone through. Carly sat at her desk and tidied some papers as she waited for a call from the judge.

Twenty minutes later, the phone rang.

"Hello, Carly. It's Judge Amica."

"Hello, Judge."

"I got the letter, and I will say you find yourself in an interesting situation. Until I look into this further, I will defer my decision regarding accepting your testimony. I'll call you tomorrow after I've had time to speak with some colleagues and refer to case law."

"Understood. Thank you." She hung up. Not exactly the answer she'd hoped for, but at least he wasn't dismissing the letter—and her testimony—out of hand.

Perhaps there was still hope.

* * *

≠≠ Unbalanced ≠≠

The coffee and hot chocolate were ready, as well as the homemade soup Sarah had heated in a saucepan in case the boys were hungry. The three settled in the living room to await their return, but the minutes ticked past so slowly that at one point Carly wondered if the battery-operated clock on the mantel had stopped.

A slammed car door and a muffled shout alerted them that the boys were home. Still, those sounds didn't bode well for a good outcome.

Bradley pushed through the front entryway, banging the door against the wall, before racing through the living room and up the stairs.

"Brad—" Carly began, but stopped when his bedroom door thumped open and slammed closed, cutting off her words. She turned to Sarah. "Sorry, I don't think he wants any hot chocolate."

Mike came into the house and tossed his keys onto the table in the hallway. "Sorry we're so late." He entered the living room and plopped onto the sofa beside Carly. "I think I totally messed things up."

Tom shook his head. "Dad, you are one of the wisest and kindest men I know. You might not have all the answers, but I know you told him what he needed to hear in the gentlest ways possible."

Carly nodded. "I agree."

Mike leaned forward, his elbows on his knees. "Doesn't matter. I had to tell him a hard truth. And he didn't take it very well."

Carly patted his back. "Did you do your best?"

He nodded.

"Then that's all anybody could ask. Someday he'll look back on this and be grateful you took the time and the trouble to be kind to him."

"And how does that help a little boy right now?" He buried his face in his hands. "How does this help any of us right now?"

Once again, Carly had no answer.

So she loved him, once more, through her silence.

Chapter 18

The next morning, Carly made breakfast and waited for the rest to show up. She was on her second cup of coffee when the shower in her room started, indicating that Mike was up. She put sausage in the oven and decided that since she had the oven on anyway, she'd do a scrambled egg bake. After putting the ingredients together, she slid the baking dish into the oven next to the sheet of sausage

About five minutes before the food was ready, she decided to check on Bradley. She paused outside his room and listened for a moment. When she didn't hear any sounds from within, she tapped on the door.

His muffled voice called out. "Come in."

She opened the door. "It's Aunt Carly. Are you awake?"

The small lump under the covers confirmed her suspicion that he wasn't. She perched on the edge of the bed and pulled the quilt back from his face. "Ready to have some breakfast?"

He grunted and pulled the blanket back.

She tugged at the corner. "I miss you."

He flung back the coverings and sat up. "How can you miss me? I didn't go away."

His eyes were still red and puffy, indicating he'd cried himself to sleep last night. And likely had already been crying this morning. Which was to be expected, she supposed. The boy had just lost his father, the only parent he had left. His life must feel very much out of his control right now.

"Sometimes I miss your Uncle Mike, and he's right across the desk from me. That just means we need to spend time together. And talk."

He folded his arms over his chest. "We're talking now."

She smiled. "Yes, we are. So now I'm not so lonely."

He dropped his gaze. "Is Uncle Mike still sad?"

She patted his leg. "Yes, he is."

"Me, too."

"I know." She picked up his discarded jeans and shirt from the floor. "Want to get dressed and come down to eat? I think Uncle Mike could use a smile or two just about now."

He smiled at her, his front adult teeth contrasting with his side baby teeth. "Okay. I'm hungry."

Carly tossed his clothes on the bed. "See you in a few minutes."

In the hallway, she met Mike coming from their bedroom. "Bradley is getting up. He's hungry. And if he tries to make you smile, go along with him."

"Huh?"

"I'll explain later."

"After coffee?"

"Much later."

A few minutes later and the three gathered at the kitchen table to eat. Bradley and Mike seemed intent on out-eating each other, and Carly made a big show of scraping the pan onto their plates. "You two are going to eat me out of house and home."

Bradley patted his stomach. "We're growing boys, aren't we, Uncle Mike?"

"That we are, my boy."

"That's what my father used to say, too." The child's voice broke and his eyes filled with tears. "I miss him."

Mike rested a hand on the boy's shoulder. "Me, too."

≠≠ Unbalanced ≠≠

The child glanced at Carly then turned back to Mike. "I know. But I'll help you. I'll be your friend. I'll talk to you so you won't be lonely."

Mike raised an eyebrow and Carly kicked him under the table.

She stood and gathered the plates. "I'll do the dishes. Why don't you boys stick together and do something fun today?"

Mike nodded. "I think that's a great idea. What do you say, Bradley?"

"Fishing?" The boy's face lit up. "I like fishing."

"Sounds like a plan."

Thankful they wouldn't be under her feet today, Carly raced through her domestic duties and cleared the kitchen in record time. Being a Monday morning, Penny wasn't open today. To deal with her, Carly would have to track her down.

She dialed Penny's home number but got voice mail.

Maybe she should just go down to the shop. If Penny wasn't there, Amanda could perhaps direct her.

She grabbed her keys, locked the door, and headed downtown.

Many businesses were closed on Mondays, so traffic on Main Street was light, just like it had been last Monday.

Goodness, was that only a week ago?

The hair salon was shut tight, but the pharmacy was open. The bank remained closed, a sign in the door. Lights were on inside Well Dressed, and Carly saw movement through the plate glass window.

She pushed into the store, recalling her visit just seven days before when she'd practically had to beg Penny to sell her an outfit for the wedding.

Penny stood behind the cash register and checkout counter, stacking slips of paper and jotting down notes. She looked up when Carly stepped in. "Hello."

Carly forced a smile. "A week ago you were happy to see me."

"A week ago I was happy to sell you an outfit."

Stung by the woman's subtle rebuke, Carly crossed the store and stood in front of Penny. "I know you were behind the fake robbery. And I know why."

Penny crossed her arms over her chest, her cheeks pale. "You don't know anything."

"You are friends with the dirt bag husband who needed to have my testimony not count at the trial."

"I have many friends."

Carly nodded. "Yes. Your nephew Chad, for instance. Paying him to stalk Sarah. You must be paying him plenty for him to stay quiet and not reveal your part in this."

A sly smile covered Penny's face. "You are delusional. There is absolutely no proof of any of this."

Carly continued. "Who cleaned up the street? The flower part? Moved the truck?"

Penny turned her back to her as though dismissing her, then turned around. "Not that you have any proof, but nephews come in handy for cleaning up messes. As you said. And blood is thicker than water, as they say."

"And what about the shots McMasters fired? Surely someone heard them?"

Penny's eyes narrowed. "I put the word out that I was playing a practical joke on you. Kind of an early birthday roast. Folks thought it was a great idea to try to trick the town's resident Jessica Fletcher."

That answered those outstanding questions that had kept Carly up late the previous night. And Penny was right. She couldn't do anything with the information. Except whisper in a certain detective's ear. Maybe he could put more pressure on Chad, get him to admit Penny's part in the whole plan.

And conspiracy to commit bank robbery was almost as long a sentence as actually committing the deed.

Carly headed for the door but paused near the end of the counter. "You should be ashamed of yourself for tricking poor, naïve Fergus into taking part in that little stunt so the wedding got called off. Just to get at me."

"He isn't as poor or naïve as he makes out. And no matter what I do to you, it will never be enough. You destroyed Susan."

"She destroyed herself. A jury of her peers—"

"A jury of local yokels, you mean." Penny's face turned crimson as her features distorted into a mask of torment. "I went to visit her. She's changed since her mother died. She blames herself for that. But I blame you."

"I am not the one who killed—"

"I blame you."

Carly held up a hand. "Fine. Believe what you want. But you are wrong."

Penny slapped a sheaf of papers on the counter. "The only thing I've done wrong is underestimate your ability to ruin lives. But it doesn't matter. I'm leaving town."

The woman's words didn't surprise her. And in all honesty, Bear Cove was better off without this woman in residence. "You can't outrun the law, you know. Somewhere, sometime, someone will tell the truth. And when that happens, I'll dance at your trial."

* * *

Still smarting from Penny's sharp words, Carly hurried home, feeling like a dog running away with its tail between its legs. She unlocked the door and stepped inside to the sound of the telephone ringing. She trotted down the hall to the office and snatched the receiver. "Hello."

"Judge Amica here, Carly."

"Hello, Judge."

"Wanted to let you know you need to make another trip to New York."

She groaned. How many more hoops would she have to jump through? And until she was able to testify in court as a credible expert witness, her business was likely to continue suffering. Still, he called the shots. "When?"

"Next Monday. The trial is back on."

Her heart pounded. "You made a decision?"

"Yes. The letter from your brother-in-law is good evidence of his involvement and your innocence. In fact, I've already sent a letter of rebuke to Mr. Williams. And I've reported Mr. Thompson to the bar association. He has since responded that he is withdrawing from the case. He allowed his desire to win a case override his common sense and his responsibilities as an officer of the court. Had he succeeded, he could have destroyed your livelihood. We cannot allow that sort of behavior."

≠≠ Unbalanced ≠≠

"Thank you for the vote of confidence, Your Honor. I appreciate that."

"And I also insisted he send you a letter of apology today, outlining his participation and his client's involvement in this whole affair. Criminal charges against Mr. Williams could result, but hopefully his letter will convince your clients to resume hiring your services." He cleared his throat. "I've seen the evidence in this case. You do good work."

Carly beamed even though she knew he couldn't see her. "Thank you, Your Honor. Your approval means a lot to me."

"Yes, well." He coughed. "Will we see you next week?"

"Wouldn't miss it for the world, Your Honor."

Carly hung up the phone. This was all such good news. She couldn't wait to tell Mike. As she pondered which clients she wanted back—not that she could afford to turn away work, but some of the people who'd canceled her services had been so mean, she didn't want to renew those relationships, she printed off a client list and went through the names.

An hour later, and a car pulled in the driveway.

And then another.

Carly tossed her pen aside. Sounded like Mike and the kids were home.

This was confirmed when Bradley burst in through the door.

Oh, no. Was he upset again? Had going to the lake reminded him of his loss?

But instead of a slamming door and pounding feet on the stairs, the child called out to her. "Aunt Carly. Good news."

She hurried to the living room where Mike, Tom, and Sarah now stood. "What's going on?"

Bradley smiled up at her. "Tom and Sarah are going to have a son."

Carly looked first at Sarah, then Tom. "A baby?"

Bradley slipped his hand into hers.

She looked down at him. "A baby?"

He shook his head. "Not a baby. A son."

Carly sat in the nearest armchair. Things were much too confusing and she was too tired to play word games. "A son?"

Bradley nodded and pointed an index finger at his chest. "Me."

Again Carly looked from Tom to Sarah, and finally to her husband. "Mike?"

Mike slid into the chair beside her, squeezing her against the arm. "Isn't it exciting?"

She rubbed a hand over her forehead. "I don't understand."

Bradley climbed into her lap, making a very tight cluster of people in the same chair. "The man in the big office said Tom and Sarah could be my parents."

Sarah sat on the sofa with Tom beside her.

Carly shifted the child in her lap so his jiggling feet weren't kicking her shins. "Explain."

Sarah glanced at Tom who nodded for her to continue. "Tom and I already love Bradley. We have a lot of fun with him, and we hoped he liked us, too."

The child's head bounced up and down vigorously. "Love."

Sarah smiled. "Loves us. So we went to the judge at the courthouse and asked what we needed to do to get custody of him."

Tom continued. "As we were going into town, we saw Dad and Bradley heading out of town. He showed us the letter Jerry left. When we told him where we were going next, he gave us the note. Said the judge might want to see it."

Sarah leaned forward. "And he did. He said it was as good as a will. And he gave us temporary custody and scheduled us for a permanent orders hearing in a month's time. To give us a chance to see if it will work out."

Bradley slipped from Carly's lap and crossed the room to cuddle between Tom and Sarah. He smiled from one to the other. The puffy eyes were gone, replaced by an expression Carly couldn't describe except to say he looked at peace. Even when his father was around, his brow had always been furrowed, and there had been a furtive look in his eyes. Over the past few days, first with his father missing and then the sad news, he'd been quiet and subdued, not meeting anyone's eyes, not talking much.

But now, that was all changed.

Bradley held Tom's left hand and Sarah's right hand, hugging them close to his chest. "Not only do I have a new daddy, I have a mommy, too." He glanced at Sarah and dropped his voice a couple of notches. "I've never had a mommy before." He looked at Carly. "And I'm going to live in a real house. Not in a car." His smile slipped away. "That means I won't live here. Will you be lonely?"

Mike patted Carly's arm. "We'll be okay. And we'll come visit you."

The boy bounced in his seat. "And whenever you want to go fishing, you let me know."

Mike smiled. "Sounds like a plan."

Bradley grinned at Carly. "Because we don't want you to fall in the lake."

Tom and Sarah stared at their new son, then looked over to Mike and Carly. Mike's face turned red, and Carly laughed.

Tom spoke first, interrupting the happy sound. "What's this all about? Dad falling in the lake?"

Carly drew a breath to quell the hiccups she'd managed to generate. "It's an inside joke. Right?"

The boy-child nodded. "Right."

Mike laughed. "Sure, laugh at the old man's expense. I fell in the lake one time." He cast a glance at Carly. "I guess if I go somewhere that doesn't have any lakes, you'll be happy to let me go by myself." He sat back. "It'd probably be safer, anyway. It seems to me that wherever Carly is, trouble always follows her."

She sputtered. "Hold on there. I didn't do anything this time. I didn't poke my nose in—"

Mike shook his head. "Sure, you did. You thought you saw a bank robbery, and you wouldn't let it go. Next thing we know, the story is all over the national news." He shrugged. "No, I made up my mind. I'm going to my college reunion by myself."

She mock-punched his arm. "And where are you going that doesn't have any lakes?"

"The middle of the desert."

"Arizona?"

He nodded and winked at Bradley. "I can't go fishing, so I can't fall in."

Carly shook him. "I promise I won't go looking for a mystery."

"I don't know."

"Please, Mike. How much trouble can I get into at a college reunion?"

"Well, maybe. . ."

She used a forefinger to mark a cross over her heart. "Cross my heart and hope to die."

He snatched her hand and gripped her fingers. "Don't say that, not even in jest." He kissed the back of her hand. "Okay, you can come with me. Should be fun. Like you said, seeing all my old friends. The guys. And the girls, too."

She hadn't thought of that. Mike had a past that she hadn't been a part of. Just as she did. Except she was glad to leave her past behind. And apparently his was still important to him. Could she deal with a beautiful woman coming up to her husband and kissing him, hanging on him, fawning over him?

Sure, she could do that. Like Bradley said, she was a big girl.

And big girls didn't cry.

Or get into cat fights.

Or go looking for mysteries.

Sure, this trip was going to be a piece of cake.

THE END

Thanks for taking the time to read *Unbalanced*. Carly is just getting started on another mystery, so read on for a sneak peek into *Five and Twenty Blackbirds*, Book 4 in the series.

≠≠ Unbalanced ≠≠

And if you know Carly, she is only getting started. . .

≠≠ Unbalanced ≠≠

≠≠ Unbalanced ≠≠

Five and Twenty Blackbirds
Released April 2016

Chapter 1

With this many people in one place, two things were bound to be true.

One of these people was a killer.

And one of these boring college types would soon die.

If not for her insatiable curiosity about the three hundred complete strangers she was about to meet, Carly Turnquist, forensic accountant, would not be caught dead in this chintzy reception room in a hotel in the middle of Nowheresville, Arizona.

Because in her world those two things *would* be true.

And she always had way more fun in her world than in the real.

She wasn't having anywhere near the fun Mike had assured her she would enjoy.

After all, it was his college reunion, not hers.

And in Arizona in July, to boot.

Feeling as though she'd stepped onto the set of a low-grade college frat movie, she hovered in a dim corner near the buffet. The only good thing she'd seen here tonight was the shrimp cocktail.

And even that looked picked-over three hours into the meet-and-greet.

She sighed. Her shoes pinched, her back ached, and if she had to smile at one more person gushing to her about what a great guy her husband was, she might lose what she'd already eaten. The air conditioning blew a chill breeze across her bare arms, and once more, she wished she were tucked into her jammies in her hotel room, dipping into the new murder mystery she'd picked up at the airport.

That, and the extra-large bag of malted milk balls.

A portly man with thinning hair and thick glasses standing across the room held her gaze then made a beeline for her.

Mike, Mike, where was Mike? She spotted him in a corner, his back to her. An older man—perhaps a professor—gestured with his hands. A peroxide-blonde stood beside him, smiling at the man on her right, whose strong chin and well-coiffed hair tweaked a memory. Did she know him? Several others stood in the group, including a tall, thin man reminding Carly of Vincent Price, the actor, as well as a couple of women, academic types, judging by their large eyeglasses and severe hair styles.

No time to reflect on them now. Portly Guy was still threading his way—not very graciously—through the folks on the dance floor. She glanced toward the door leading to the restrooms. Too many people in the way. She'd never make it in time. Maybe the patio. She side-stepped her way to the French doors which opened on to a flagstone path that wound its way through a cactus garden. Barrel-shaped plants, beaver-tail shaped arms, and looming saguaros stretching to the stars, festooned with white Christmas tree lights, marked her escape route. Couples huddled in darkened alcoves, the liquor causing the years to slip away, no doubt, rekindling old loves and igniting new ones.

She shivered, although the night air was much too warm for her to be truly cold.

She was so glad Mike hadn't gone the way of most of his classmates—paunches, wrinkles, baldness—men and women alike seemed to have passed through some sort of time machine, appearing on the other side of fifty looking like the before ads for a cosmetic surgery office.

Glancing over her shoulder, she halted. She'd lost Mr. Portly in the crowd. Or perhaps he wasn't really coming for her at all.

She paused near a waterfall, the bubbling water making her suddenly thirsty. Perhaps a glass of sparkling water would go down good right about now. She headed back toward the party, sidestepping a couple firmly wrapped into each other's arms—and lips.

She peered through a pane in the door to make sure Mr. Portly-Guy wasn't anywhere near, when a cold hand on her shoulder made her yelp.

She whirled to face its owner.

"Carly Anne Stevens, is that you?"

Tall and thin as a scarecrow, Harrison Dyer, accountant to The Family, faced her.

Carly stepped back, forcing him to retrieve his hand. One of Harrison's annoying traits was he always stood too close for comfort. "Carly Anne Turnquist now."

He grinned at her, his formerly brace-encapsulated smile now gleaming white. Unnaturally so. "Good to see you again."

She glanced around. Where was Mike when she needed him? She spotted her husband in yet another clutch of classmates and spouses, nodding at something the same much-older man—one of his former professors—Binkle? Bunkle? A man Mike revered—was saying. The professor's hands gestured in the air, making his point. His florid face—whether from exertion or too much alcohol, she wasn't certain—made his white hair appear snowy.

She sighed. Mike wasn't going to rescue her. She turned back to Harrison. "I didn't know you were alumni here."

Some emotion she couldn't quite identify flickered across his face—anger? Resentment? Embarrassment? But the expression was gone in a flash, leaving the half-smile and partly-curled top lip she remembered so well.

That, and his annoying habit of looking at everybody except the person he was with.

Or maybe that's just how he treated her.

Harrison eyed the room behind them. Music filtered through the half-opened door, and a number of couples edged toward the dance floor. "No. I'm here on business." He rolled his eyes. "No rest for the wicked, you know."

"I think the phrase is 'no rest for the weary'."

He waved off her words like they were pesky flies. "Whatever."

Carly studied Harrison. Although he'd aged—hadn't they all—he'd changed only in superficial ways. A much better-dressed scarecrow than during their college days, he still watched everybody else as though he was looking for someone more interesting, or powerful, or beautiful, to be with. She sighed. At one point in the past, she'd been flattered that he'd paid even a minute's attention to her.

Until they danced and he spent their entire three minutes eying the other women in the room.

"So, Harrison, if you're not here for the reunion, what are you doing in Central Arizona? Not exactly Chicago, is it?"

His smile slipped a millimeter before he plastered the grin back on. "Like I said, I'm here on business. Until the end of the week."

"What a coincidence we should be in the same place for the first time in over twenty-five years."

"You don't think I'm chasing you, do you?"

No, she didn't think that. He hadn't when she was twenty-five years younger and twenty—okay, twenty-five pounds lighter. "More likely you're chasing something in a mini-skirt."

His jaw dropped, his mouth creating an O. If he'd pointed his thumb at his chest and mimicked Miss Piggy's '*moi*?', she wouldn't have been surprised.

While he'd majored in accounting, he'd minored in drama.

And not the university course.

He leaned in closer. "Actually, I saw you at the airport. Recognized you right away."

He batted his eyelashes.

If he was trying to appear innocent, he failed miserably.

Carly resisted the urge to step back again. She'd spent three years in classes with Harrison Dyer at the University of Northern Indiana, trying to ignore his sexist innuendos about the other women in their classes, repeatedly turning down his pleas for help. He wasn't going to chase her off again. "Why didn't you say something at the airport?"

"Couldn't catch up with you. You and—is the guy on your arm the mister in Turnquist?"

"Yes. Mike."

Harrison nodded, his lips pursed. "Thought so. There is something different about couples who have been intimate, don't you think? You can tell by their body language. A familiarity, perhaps, that you don't notice in friends. Even friends with benefits."

A blonde glided to stand beside Harrison. She looped an arm through his, pressing against his side. Her low-cut dress revealed more skin than Carly thought proper, and her too-red lipstick appeared harsh in the dim lighting. "Are you done here, Harry? I want to go to our room and get more comfortable." She giggled in a little-girl manner that contrasted with the sun-induced wrinkles around her eyes and mouth. She held out a hand to Carly. "Hi. I'm Misty."

Yes, you are. Transparent and irritating. Carly returned the greeting. "Carly. Harrison—Harry and I went to college together."

Misty's eyes opened wide. "Wow. I've never met anyone who knew Harry before he came to Chicago." Her Midwestern accent sharpened the r's and rolled the o's. "Maybe we can get together over coffee and Danish and you can tell me all about this bad boy." She mock-punched Harrison's arm. "What do you think, Harry?"

"Whatever."

Carly gritted her teeth. While the response might be merely annoying when shot from the mouth of an angst-ridden teen, coming from a man of his age, the word grated on her sensibilities. Still, she wasn't going to see them again, so she could be pleasant. In short spurts. "Good to see you, Harrison."

She nodded at his companion then glanced at the woman's ring finger.

Bare.

Probably one of his friends with benefits, judging by her body language.

And based on the way she clung to him, Misty would like to make their relationship more than that.

Harrison sidled away a step, putting some distance between him and Misty.

But not him. He's already scoping out the next one.

Harrison laid a hand on Carly's arm.

Her bare arm.

She glanced at his hand then at him.

He snatched back his hand as though she'd threatened to bite him.

Which she might well have done if he hadn't made the first move.

Where was her husband? "What?"

"Can we get together tomorrow? I have something I need to talk to you about."

"Again, what? We haven't seen each other in years. We're not going to be friends in the future any more than we were in college. We don't run in the same circles, Harrison. I follow the law."

She left the accusation hanging in the air between them.

Misty huffed, her bangs lifting with the exhalation, then wheeled on her four-inch stilettos. "I'll be inside when you're ready to leave."

He turned toward Carly. "And I follow the money. I have a problem that I think you can help me with. I'll make it worth your while."

Visions of sitting around the hotel room while Mike spent the day in a tour of the university, a dedication of a new wing of the library, and lectures about the latest research from the engineering department didn't exactly thrill her. She wasn't a sunbather, the town was small and uninteresting, and she knew enough not to venture out into the desert by herself.

Maybe she could survive spending an hour with someone as obnoxious as Harrison Dyer.

After all, she could always say no to whatever scheme he was going to present.

She was a big girl.

She could take care of herself.

∞ ∞ ∞

Later, in the hotel room, she snuggled into the pillow-top mattress, her long-awaited mystery novel in her hand, as Mike filled her in on all the conversations she'd missed. Sometimes she wondered how they'd managed to find each other and marry. He was such a social butterfly, while she preferred being on her own. They were as unalike as night and day.

"And then Tom said he—"

Carly tucked her bookmark into the book. "Who is Tom?"

Mike stuck his head out of the bathroom, rubbing at his hair with a towel. He sighed. "Tom is a friend from college."

She nodded and opened her book again. "Did you name your son after him?"

"No." He hung the towel on the rack and turned to the mirror to comb out the tangles. "I named Tom after my father."

The muscles in Mike's back rippled under his skin, tapering down to narrow hips with only the tiniest love handles decorating the body of the man she loved more than anybody in the world. Now that was a sight more interesting than the novel she'd bought at the Portland airport where they'd caught their flight to Phoenix. His legs, long and muscular, always filled out his pants in a flattering way, and her gaze worked its way back up to...

She paused and looked up. He'd turned around to face her, the lifted eyebrow and tilted head leading her to conclude that he'd asked a question and was waiting for an answer. "What?"

"I said, did you meet anybody interesting?"

"No. I didn't know anybody there." The less Mike knew about her meeting tomorrow with Harrison, the less time he'd spend warning her not to get involved in anything. She had no intention of getting involved with anything. Or anybody. She returned her gaze to her book, even though she had no idea what the story was about. "Tell me more about Tom."

Mike strode across the hotel room and flicked off the air conditioner. The room went silent. "You're avoiding my question."

Carly looked up. "Huh?"

He perched on the foot of the bed. "I asked if you met anybody interesting, and you reply with you don't know anybody. Not an answer to the question I asked."

She sighed. Sometimes his being an engineer could be so infuriating. So precise. So logical. It wasn't easy pulling the wool over his eyes. "What do you want me to say?"

"You can start with the handsome guy with the blonde glued to his side."

She flung back the down-filled duvet and crawled to his side. Running her fingers through his hair, she nuzzled his neck. "Why, Michael Turnquist. I do believe you're jealous."

He pulled her close and kissed her cheek. "I have every reason to be jealous. I'm there with the most beautiful woman in the world, and then I see her in the garden talking to a strange man." He held her at arms' length. "Who is he?"

She shrugged. "Just someone I met." No need to tell him she'd met him almost thirty years before. "Probably will never see him again."

Mike peered at her, his brown eyes penetrating her soul. "Probably?"

She wriggled out of his grasp. "Tell me more about the people you talked to. Who was the older man I saw you with?"

Mike studied her for the length of two or three heartbeats before rising and returning to the mirror. "Dr. Ted Brinkle. He was one of my favorite professors." He paused in mid-swipe with his comb. "It was because of his class that I lost my scholarship."

Carly set her book aside. Mike wanted to talk. Until he got it out of his system, she would let him. "And you're still friends?"

Mike shrugged. "Don't know that I'd call us friends. But he wasn't the one who gave me the failing grade. It was his teaching assistant, Greg Goodman." He snorted. "Talk about a name and a person that were complete opposites. There was nothing good about Greg."

"So why didn't you contest the grade?"

"Because I didn't find out about it until after the scholarship committee was notified. They'd already made their decision. I was de-funded. So I had to drop out and work for a couple of years to earn enough to go back to college. Meant I was the oldest in my graduating class. Not to mention the black mark against me."

A familiar ache rose in Carly's chest, threatening to cut off her breath. She was like a momma bear when it came to Mike or the kids or the grandkids or—she caught herself. Truth was, her list of those she cared about seemed to grow faster than she could keep up.

She took a couple of deep breaths. That was all so long ago. Mike had gotten over it. And it was a good thing for Greg-not-so-good-man that enough time had passed that her husband no longer carried that failed course on his record.

Even though the hurt was still in his heart.

Well, she wouldn't add to that hurt by mentioning her meeting tomorrow with Harrison Dyer.

After all, her husband deserved this time with his friend and classmates.

He didn't need to know about her little white lie.